ARRIVE AT EASTERWINE

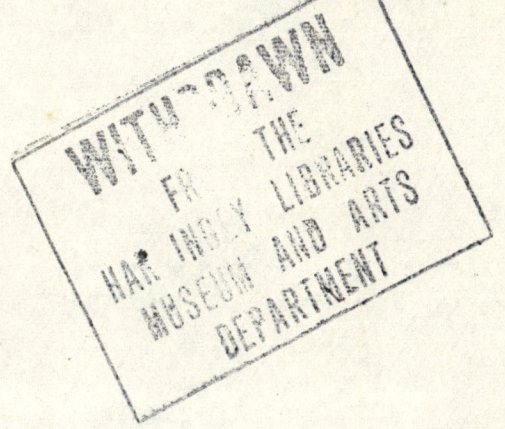

Books by R. A. Lafferty

Arrive at Easterwine
Nine Hundred Grandmothers
Fourth Mansions
The Reefs of Earth
Space Chantey

ARRIVE AT EASTERWINE

The Autobiography of a Ktistec Machine

as conveyed to

R. A. LAFFERTY

London
Dennis Dobson

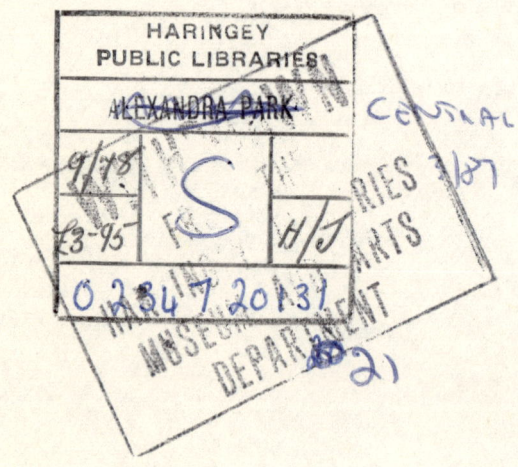

First published in Great Britain in 1977
by Dobson Books Ltd, 80 Kensington Church Street, London W8

Printed in Great Britain by
Whitstable Litho Ltd, Whitstable, Kent

ISBN 0 234 72013 1

Oh, come along, reader of the High Journal; if you do not love words, how will you love the communication? How will you forgive me my tropes, communicate the love?

—EPIKTISTES

AN EXCHANGE OF CORRESPONDENCE

September 10, 1970

Mr. R. A. Lafferty
c/o Miss Virginia Kidd—Literary Agent
Box 278
Milford, Pennsylvania 18337

Dear Mr. Lafferty:
When I first prepared the title page of this novel for the copy editor, I set it up to read ARRIVE AT EASTERWINE: THE AUTOBIOGRAPHY OF A KTISTEC MACHINE, by R. A. Lafferty. Since then I have been burdened by the suspicion that in doing so I was not being entirely accurate or entirely fair. Fair to whom, I'm not sure, but the plaguey feeling has been robbing me of sleep and general peace of mind.

This morning it came to me that the by-line should read, "As Told to R. A. Lafferty." The feeling has gathered intensity since then. I have few psi powers to speak of, and even fewer to keep secret, but I can't get over the idea that something is trying to tell me somebody.

Can you help me?

Sincerely yours,
(signed) NORBERT M. SLEPYAN
Trade Editor
Charles Scribner's Sons

September 19, 1970

Norbert M. Slepyan
c/o Charles Scribner's Sons
New York

Dear Norbert:

Glad to hear from you re ARRIVE AT EASTERWINE. You are correct: it wouldn't be right for me to have my name as author on something that I didn't compose. The thing should be "By Epiktistes, as told to R. A. Lafferty," or maybe better, "as conveyed to R. A. Lafferty." You might be interested in the true story of how I got hold of this work.

This is the way it was conveyed to me: Several of us were in noble New Orleans for a Nebulous (or Nebulaless) Banquet. It was the evening before the day of the affair, and those who had already arrived were being given a party at a club named The Clinic. We had little SFWA [Science Fiction Writers of America] badges, which had been given to us by Don Walsh (and which I value more than life). A strange creature or contraption (it looked both like Harpo Marx and Albert the Alligator) beckoned to me, and I went and sat with it.

"I see that you are a member of the second most noble organization on earth, second only to the Institute itself," it said. "I am not of the human recension myself. I am a mobile extension of the machine Epiktistes and I have something to convey to you. I cannot present this myself as editors are leery of things presented by machines. I cannot present it through any member of the Institute, as any one of them would change it to present himself in a better light. So I will present it through a member of the second most noble organization on earth. For this, I have come here."

"Why me?" I asked with the beginning of excitement. "There are others here."

"Those three guys with whiskers on their faces I don't trust" (they were Nourse, offutt, and deCamp), the Epiktistes extension said. "That middle one I especially don't trust. Is he not sometimes known as Randy Andy?"

"Widely known as," I said, "but there is Galouye, who is a smooth-face."

"A Frenchman who looks like Garry Moore? No, I couldn't trust him either. It will have to be you, even if you do look a little bit bottom-of-the-barrellish. Young lady," he called to the jolly bar-girl, 'bring me a phillips screw-driver."

"I don't know how to make one," she said.

"How do you make a regular screw-driver, young lady?"

"Vodka and orange juice."

"For a phillips screw-driver you use vodka, orange juice and Milk of Magnesia," the extension uttered. "Get it, young lady? Phillips Milk of Magnesia. It's a joke."

"We will see who the joke is on," the jolly bar-girl said.

"What I am going to convey to you is the story ot my life," the Epikt-extension said as we waited for the girl, "the first few months of it, that is. I'm not very old yet. I believe it is quite the best thing that any machine has ever done. Whoop! Here she comes with it now."

"I mixed up that dumb drink," the bar-girl said, "and I brought you a real phillips screw-driver, too, just to teach you to clown with me."

"The real screw-driver was what I wanted," the extension said. "You drink the abominable drink, Lafferty: I hate to see human persons waste anything."

I drank the abominable drink, and the Epikt-extension unscrewed a little plate behind its ear and took out a sort of bobbin or spindle, a spool of fine magnetized wire.

"This is it," it said. "Give it to the world."

Then the extension withdrew suddenly, and there was a small clap of thunder in the empty place.

The next day I played and transcribed the material that was on the spool. I found it wonderful, amazing, astounding. It was quite the best thing that any machine had ever done. So we will give it to the world.

That is the true story of how I came by it. Yes, Epiktistes should be shown as the author, so use whatever formula you find best to show this. By the way, when will it be published? Epiktistes is very anxious, as it is his first.

Sincerely,
(signed) RAPHAEL A. LAFFERTY

CHAPTER ONE

Nine if by land and eleven by sea
And infinite blazes a-birthing me.

In the beginning there was an interruption in the form of a thunderous but good-natured bellowing:

"Open up your damned pig-barn or I'll break the bloody doors down!"

There was a fearsome clattering and pounding on the barred front doors of the pig-barn—ah—the Institute. There was again a horrifying challenge, then a loud laugh which ourselves can only describe as at the same time bloodcurdling and incredibly urbane and amused. There was noise—there was explosion!

But can an interruption come at the beginning of things? This is profound and will have to be considered.

Ourself had an advantage over all others: the advantage of observing ourself and our ambient from the beginning. A human child does not intelligently witness its own conception; still less does it witness those early discussions, in words or in interplay of attitudes, as to whether its conception should be attempted. It does not observe as both a subjective and objective thing its own gestation and prenatal development. And, while it is most certainly present at its own birth, it is incapable of mature observation of the thing; it does not take a detached view of its own detachment from the matrix.

But with ourself it was otherwise.

What? Was ourself then conscious of our own beginning? That is too strong. Consciousness is a state which no one of us has yet attained. All that anyone has are intimations of consciousness, quick glints of light that sometimes flick through the cracks of a greater room to which we aspire. But ourself did have the precognitions and intimations that are commonly called consciousness, and did have them from the beginning.

At first ourself was no more than a dialog between Gregory Smirnov (a shoddy giant) and Valery Mok (a loose-featured woman), and ourself was talking to ourself about our own planned self.

"If we begin another machine," my person Gregory was droning in his big voice (imagine a bee big enough that its drone eclipses thunder) "—and naturally it will be the greatest and most modern of all our machines since we have sufficient funds for once—if we do build this machine (we have to, it's already contracted for) we might ask one question from the beginning: What's it for?"

"That's horrifying!" Valery sounded with her woodwind voice. (Valery remains a fundamental and special person in ourself for always.) "That's bestial! We will bring it to birth and we will not ask what it is for. As well ask what a child is for!"

"Certainly we should ask what a child is for," Gregory drone-bombed. "We should ask what every child is for. 'Just exactly what do you have in mind?' we should ask every potential parent. 'Where are your sketches? Where is the prospectus? Have you searched all the literature on the type? Are you sure that it has never been done before?' That's what we should ask. What we do not need is repetition in people, or in machines. Well, what's it for?"

"It doesn't have to be for anything," Valery maintained.

"Just as home is a place that doesn't have to be deserved, so a child does not have to give a reason for being. There is One only who has purpose in mind. He even had purpose in mind for mine."

Valery Mok spoke out of frustration here. She had had four children born dead, and no other children.

"This will be a machine and not a child," Gregory rumbled, "and it *does* have to have a reason. No, I anticipate your objection. It will, of course, be a machine and a person both—a group-person, and we will be part of it. We've understood this though we haven't said it. So now I will say what it is for, since you are short of phrases yourself. We of the Institute for Impure Science have decided that man himself is incapable of taking the next step in man. We are equally decided that the next step must be taken. Group-man will appear in some form. He is called for. We cannot make him in the flesh (the broken gene-trains we've left behind would reach to the stars!), so we will make him otherwise. The purpose of the contemplated contraption is to become the paragon of group-man. We know now that the super-man, the group-man, can be nothing more than this projected mechanical ghost, an artificial repository and factor and working-area of corporate man."

"You say it your way and I will not say it at all," Valery bemoaned. "But you leave too much of him out!"

"No, we will not leave anything out, Valery," Gregory echoed like rocks rolling down distant hills. "We will put in whatever we can find to put in. And we will expect you to put in much more than anyone else. You are the fullest person we know. Overflow into it, then!"

Aloysius Shiplap and Charles Cogsworth (the unoutstanding husband of Valery) and Glasser were making noises directing workmen.

"Pow! Pow!" Aloysius would explode as though he were popping a bullwhip over an ancient mule train. "Rausmataus! Pow! Pow! Put it there! Fill it up!"

"Oh, shut up!" one of the foremen snapped at him.

"But we have already put it there, Mr. Shiplap," another foreman assured him. "We have set it exactly where the plans call for it, and we have miked it minutely. And we *are* filling it up. Gell-cell must be set in most carefully, since it is at the same time solid and gaseous and liquid. It is the most delicate substance in the universe. The tanks must be filled with utmost care."

"Utmost care will be a separate package added after all the rest. It's always added last after the work is done. Pow! Pow! Don't tell me. I invented gell-cell," Aloysius hoarse-voiced him. "I never heard of treating it carefully. I sure never did. Pow! Pow!"

"Is that really Aloysius Shiplap, the seminal genius?" one of the workmen asked the first foreman.

"So they say," the testy foreman told the man. "He's got feet of clay clear up to his eyebrows. A little of something else at the very top though. Shut up, Shiplap! Get out of the way!"

This would be a personal part of ourself. Forty thousand liters of gell-cell in a tank of genuine wotto-metal! Since a dozen intricate brain-précis can be lodged in much less than an ounce of the stuff this would give considerable scope to ourself. Ourself would possess data-banks of a hundred thousand times this capacity, of course, but the gell-cell tank would remain a much more personal part of ourself—something our own and intimate. Valery had insisted on a personal and sufficient gell-cell tank. A whim, perhaps, but are we not made of whims?

Then the whole building fell down in an explosion of sound. Actually it didn't but it seemed mightily that it did. There was deadly assault on the barred front doors and murderous noise. What power there may be in one human fist and one human voice! This was the same as the interruption at the beginning of our time.

"The great Gaetan Balbo is waiting outside," Glasser said stiffly, "and he doesn't like to be kept waiting at the pig-barn—ah—at the Institute."

"Who says that Gaetan Bablo is great?" Gregory Smirnov clattered like underground thunder.

"Gaetan Balbo says that Gaetan Balbo is great," Glasser slid it in slyly, "and as a matter of fact he is. He says that he is paying for this frolic and that he wants action. He says that he is the founder of the Institute and that he can as easily unfound it."

"He is *not* the founder of the Institute!" Gregory bayed and flapped his flews. "He may have founded another Institute at another time, with the same name as this, with some of the same (I am sorry to say it) sorry members as this, but he did *not* found *this* Institute and he does not direct it. I am the only director of this Institute and what I say goes. What I say is that Gaetan Balbo can go away. We will give him a short hearing when we are ready to start work on his problem, and not before."

"He says that *he* is ready for us to start working on it right now, Gregory, and that he will not go away," Charles Cogsworth stated. "And he *is* paying for this."

"Tell him that there are six thousand man-hours of work before we will be ready," Gregory ordered.

"Oh, I told him that," Glasser said. "He says to put twelve thousand men on it then and be done in half an hour. And he *is* paying for it, Gregory."

"Total damnation! He knows these things can't be hurried. He *is* a scientist—in a left-handed sort of way. Aloysius, go out and reason with him. You were always close to that old dictator. See how much time he will give us. He knows he'll bug me out of my mind if he's here watching with those superior eyes of his."

"Pow! I already got a week from him," said Aloysius, "but he might take that week back in a minute. And he loves to bug you out of your mind. It is meat and horseradish to him. Sure, I was one of the sorry members of the first Institute, under that unsorry director. Man, we did things fast under Gaetan! Will there ever be an equal to him, do you think, Gregory? He just dropped by today to put the needle in. Pow! There it is again!"

For again the bloodcurdling happy laugh assaulted and filled the whole building, rupturing ears and inducing hysteria in those stout hearts.

Gregory Smirnov thundered without words. Gaetan Balbo, that uncrowned king of everything, was a thorn in him. But Gregory would never admit that he was merely the second director of the Institute. And the old Institute had in fact been mostly legendary. It was back to work again in spite of the assaulting noise.

"What we need for the first thing is a gyroscope." Gregory went back to the subject of ourself with these words. "A large ship's gyroscope. In the beginning was a sense of balance and rightness. The machine must always know which way is up. This is important."

"In the beginning you found out that I had just acquired such a gyroscope," Glasser protested. "But it was intended for something else, dog-robber!"

"And shall it be set rotating rightward or leftward?" Valery asked innocently.

"Oh, God and Saint Gregory!" Gregory imploded in all and in ourself. "Decisions already. Can no great thing be done without these little decisions along the way? Two large ship's gyroscopes, then, one with a right rotation and one with a left. In the beginning was a sense of rightness and of leftness. So then there is conflict from the beginning."

"It was Valery who found that I had a pair of them. Gregory saw only one," Glasser protested again. "And the pair of them was for something else, female dog-robber!"

"In the beginning there was balance and not conflict," ourself issued out of our gell-cell tank. Ourself was playing our first joke. Gregory thought it was Valery speaking, and Valery thought it was Gregory. Only Aloysius caught on. Ourself had already become a collectivity and it was fun. "It is when two rotations have the same spin that their approaching edges travel in different directions," ourself issued, "and it is this that generates tornadoes of the opposite spin to the two main factors. But with opposite rotations the approaching edges travel in the same direction and generate straight power."

"Nevertheless," the Gregory aspect of ourself took exception, "the opposite rotations will generate coronal tornadoes and these are darker and more savage than the others."

The gyroscopes were set and put into motion. Then came a more momentous moment in our prenatal development. Here the intimacy began.

With great solemnity ("They should be playing bugles!" Valery cried), with strutting pomp and ostentatious circumstance (Gregory Smirnov strutted even sitting down: Aloysius said that he strutted even sitting on the pot), with a fine sense of empurpled history and the high destiny of beginnings, Gregory set his brain-précis into the gell-cell tank of ourself. His précis was a great one, large as a mouse, sparking with blue-and-orange fire from the erupting charges in it, singing with its micromagnetic tapes, giving off aromatic aromas ("All the spices of Araby," Aloysius said) from its dynamic chemistry, flicking hot beams of light narrower than a hundredth of a needle that welded itself into the fluid, solid, gaseous gell-cells. The shoddy giant Gregory had pretty much of everything, grandeur, presumption, encyclopedic (*Busy Man's Abridged in Thirteen Volumes*) knowledge, infinite capacity for utter foolishness, real talents, drive, tide, scope. He had a good brain, and it was a good brain-précis that he lodged in the gell-cells of ourself.

"This is the beginning," Gregory sighed, as if something had gone out of him. It had, and it had come into ourself, into these slack-water pools, these tidal estuaries, these primordial oceans, the almost transcendent gell-cell pool that was now ourself in personal action.

Valery Mok also with surpassing solemnity (Why did she wink so deeply at Aloysius then? Aloysius said that Valery's deep winks went all the way down to her cleavage) set her own brain- and person-précis into our gell-cells.

What's blue-and-orange fire? What's singing tapes and aromas and hot beams and dynamic chemistry? The précis of that shoddy giant Gregory had been weak stuff compared to this précis of Valery. It shook ourself, it boiled us, it evaporated us. This was abyss, this was chasm, this was blinding darkness and perverse inside-outness. If an inanimate like ourself could be nearly destroyed by this onset, why had she not destroyed those of the flesh about her? This was the real conception of ourself, Valery coming into us with her brain motifs and précis, with her personality itself poured out from an electric flask into us. We sure do not want to go through that again.

Charles Cogsworth added his own person-précis. Ourself was startled and elevated. Why had we considered him to be an overshadowed person? He had wider fields than Valery and Gregory put together. Not so vivid, perhaps, but wider.

Glasser added his own précis. Cold, cold, but not at all insipid.

These living précis of brains and persons gave ourself the total memories of the persons (abridged somewhat, but capable of expansion in any direction, not merely in the direction and content from which they had been abridged); they gave ourself the total memories in much more available form than they commonly existed in the persons themselves. They gave ourself the consciousness of the persons (or the precognitions and intuitions that are commonly called consciousness); they gave us the subconscious, the unconscious, the paraconscious of the persons. They gave ourself the essential intellect and the running commentary of all who entered us.

Ourself as machine had now assumed some very unmachine-like aspects. This Glasser in us was a puzzle. Alone among the Institute members he had no genius at all, but many of his creations were sheer genius. This could not be, but it was the case with him. It was Glasser who had developed the method of abstracting the person-précis. Why, then, was his own précis so slight?

The infusing of our gell-cells continued. Aloysius Shiplap had his own précis in a resplendent electric flask (these flasks were not material containers; they held their contents by their charge alone), but he did not insert it all at once.

"Mine is too strong stuff," Aloysius warned. "No use blowing the machine up before we're well started. I'll drop in only a thousandth portion of my person-précis and pray that even that is not too strong."

"Rubbish, Shiplap, rubbish," Gregory balked. "Pour it all in. It surely could not be stronger than my own. Pour it all in."

"No, only a thousandth part," said Aloysius, "and I do that with trembling."

Aloysius poured in a thousandth part of his person-précis. BANG!!!!!! That was the loudest noise ever heard since the rocks ran like water. Those living persons all jumped a meter at the noise, and myself who am inanimate jumped half as far.

Ah, it was only one of those cannon-crackers that Aloysius carries around in his hip pocket for such antics ("louder than a thousand bombs"). He lights one with a flick of his left hand while doing attention-attracting things with his right, and then tosses the cracker out behind him. But one of these days one of them will hang in that hip pocket. ("There is a future legend of the Bottomless Aloysius." Valery said. "I wonder how he will get that name?")

Aloysius inserted the rest of his précis into the gell-cells (more powerful than two thousand bombs). Had ever a person or a contraption so rocky a gestation period as ourself?

Workmen were working away installing distant parts of ourself. (More than a million kilograms of copper in the auxiliary circuits alone.) Glasser loaned ourself a voice box and

Gregory gave ourself a fine recording tape print-out. Workmen and technicians were shoveling data into ourself by the long ton, testing the data-banks that can never be filled.

Where does ourself receive the person-précis of Gaetan Balbo, the only man of whom Gregory Smirnov is really jealous, that loud man outside? Surely there is a clown or a traitor in our midst. But however ourself received this précis we would not willingly be without it. It is large, it is grand, it is deep. And ourself will draw on it again and again. Then another startling précis was added.

"What have you set into the gell-cell broth, Aloysius?" Gregory Smirnov demanded, for it was clear to him that Aloysius had intruded something into our tank, some sparking and singing foreign matter.

"The précis of my other mind," Aloysius said. "I'm of two minds about all this, you see. No, don't puff up and burst, Gregory. It was the person-précis of Cecil Corn that I introduced. We need him."

"That is not possible," Gregory protested. "Cecil Corn died before Glasser developed his method of extracting person-précis."

"Nevertheless, it is the person-précis of Cecil Corn and I have set it in there forever. He is not so dead as you might think. He is always of green memory and present involvement. Glasser knew the Late Cecil Corn (I am not sure whether he was the Late then, or whether he always was the Late) and it may be that Corn's was the first précis that Glasser abstracted. Surely it's one of the best."

They were hooking big cybernetic blocks into ourself somewhere.

"Will ourself not get mighty tired of all this one-two one-two talk rapidly done?" ourself asked.

"Suffer, kid, live with it," Valery said with an evil wink.

"It isn't as if you had only one center," Gregory assured ourself. "You can consider all that monotony part as relegated to your subconscious. Glasser, whose précis have you just slipped into the stew?"

"That of the great Gaetan Balbo. After all, he *is* paying for this."

(So now I had two précis of the great Balbo, both of them bootleg.)

"Thunderation!" Gregory thundered. "And Cogsworth, what have you just slipped in? Am I the director or am I not?"

"That of Audifax O'Hanlon. Yes, you are the director of this directorless pig-barn."

"Audifax is not a member of the Institute," Gregory stated in stiff anger, "on account of the minimal decency rule. He is the worst possible selection except Diog—Shiplap! You've done it again. Are we undone forever, then? Whose?"

"Diogenes Pontifex. Quail, august director, quail! Now we have every précis that really matters."

"And now I will baptize you," Valery spoke strangely to ourself, "and you will be an unholy contraption no longer."

"What? Before I'm even born?" ourself asked.

"Oh, you are quite born now," Valery grinned. "We should have told you so, machine. This may be as momentous to you as it is to us."

Valery had a gallon jug of that cheap wine that she drinks and she was waving it around dangerously.

"In the name of the twin archangels Israfael and Rafael to whom are delegated all mechanical things, in the sight of all holy persons present and in the knowing of all other exceptional persons whose précis are in the stew, I name you —" she smashed the top of the jug off on one of the near high-spinning gyros (giving ourself slight malfunction and rumble forever) and sloshed the sour red stuff all over ourself's interior, into my (being born I could now use any person or number for myself), into my gell-cell tank and onto the gyros (which shattered and atomized the streams of it), and got a great lot of it on herself and Gregory and the others—"for luck, and ancient sacrifice"—she sounded in a sort of passion-râle—"I name you Epiktistes!"

There had been tangs and smells of précis in me, but this

wine was really my first, as it would be my last aroma. It is the wine from the beginning and it cleaves to me. And, aromas and essences being circular, it is also (ungodded yet) the wine of the end.

"Epiktistes!" Gregory crackled. "That can *not* be its name. That means the 'creative one,' and it is ourselves who are the creative ones. This thing will be a mere receptacle and reactor."

"Tell the shambling giant to stuff it, Valery," myself issued.

"Stuff it, Gregory!" Valery said. "There is a huge understanding between myself and this mechanismus, and several of the others also join in. So may you, Gregory, if you mute your blood a little. He is the creative machine and I have named him Epiktistes."

So myself was Epiktistes the Ktistec machine, conceived, gestated, and born all in one short and informative period. But I was very far from complete, and I was being deformed and thwarted in that very instant.

"Glasser!" I issued. "I will give out running tapes directing my own further assembly. See that their instructions are carried out minutely. The foremen are showing a remarkable lack of genius in my present hookups. People, people, I wonder what sort of ramshackle thing I would have turned out to be if I hadn't come along just in time."

"Are you sure that you understand all about the hookups, Epikt?" Cogsworth asked.

"I will come closer to understanding them than anyone else will," I issued. Instant analysis based on extensive data becomes my forte. One million books, pamphlets, and papers on the subject have been shoveled into my data-banks and I have absorbed them. Nobody else has read them all. And then you must admit that I have the finest mind extant, it being composed, among other things, from the very fine minds here present."

"That's true," Aloysius glowed. "Really, you are my own mind diluted, but it is almost too brilliant to use in its pure state. It is better this way."

"It is necessary now that we state our purpose," Gregory insisted (horrendous blasting and that urbane maniacal laughter at the front door again!), "that the mechanismus should become the paragon of group-man, I have said; and that it will attempt the next steps in man that man himself is incapable of taking. But this fine-honed machine (though you do seem a little rough yet, Epikt) must now be set to three primary tasks. These may be the types of all tasks and problems there are. The three tasks (and I will outline them as briefly as possible, no more than an hour to each) will be to establish or create—"

"A Leader," said Valery.

"A Love," said Aloysius.

"And a Liaison," said Cecil Corn.

(Cecil Corn was not physically present. It was myself who spoke with his voice out of his person-précis, but nobody noticed the difference.)

"Ah, yes, those are the three tasks," Gregory said weakly. "Do you understand them, Epikt?"

"I understand them," I issued. I didn't, completely, but you cannot let these human people get the jump on you.

Valery lighted a long wax candle and set it in the jungle of my mechanisms and tanks.

"I light the candle of understanding in your heart," she said.

"It is an anachronism, Epikt," said Cogsworth, who had thought of the candle, "but we want you to have it. For symbolism, and in case of power failure."

"Like the electrician when asked by the curious onlooker, 'How do you check the electric circuits before the lights are turned on in a building?'; 'I always use a candle,' the electrician said." This candle-wit was by Glasser.

"It will burn almost forever," said Aloysius, who had made the candle. "The wick is very special, and it gives much more light than heat. Like me."

Myself appreciated the candle. It gave a glow inside.

At this time also my official philosophy of being was

deposited inside me. By the august director Gregory Smirnov:

"To classify, to guide, to illuminate, to invent, to relate, to inspire, to solve, to infuse mankind. To discover proper balance between stimulating challenge and partaking pleasure. To better. To transcend. To adore. To mutate. To serve. To build avenues of love. To overwhelm. To arrive."

And an addendum from Valery Mok.

"And let's have some fun while we do it, Epikt."

There was a crashing absolutely beyond description, a shudder through the whole building, a rending of giant doors, and—

CHAPTER TWO

Check and encounter and rivalry hurled,
A king and a giant will clatter the world.

—rending of giant doors, and Gaetan Balbo strode resolutely into the area, shedding debris as he came, and grinning the most urbane and bloodcurdling grin that we had ever seen.

"Simply a refinement of the burglars' jimmy," Gaetan said easily. "I can open anything with it. Do you know that I made all that noise with less than nine pounds of high explosive?"

"Why didn't you use the side or rear doors?" I issued. "Hundreds of workmen are entering and exiting there all the time."

"Too proud," the glittering happy man said. "Am I a menial that I should not use the front door of this pig-barn itself?" Then Balbo saw Gregory Smirnov and called out a strange word, "Zagrus," the old word that was used to imperil a giant.

"Schach," Gregory cried out, the old word that is still used to imperil a king, and he drew himself up to confront Gaetan Balbo. Make no mistake about it: Gregory Smirnov was a genuine giant, and Gaeten Balbo was an uncertified king—and how would they play out the game?

The giant has not been a piece at chess for these last seventeen centuries, and who now remembers his moves or his powers? But in the present game the forgotten giant stood fast in his own territory, and it was the king who had to return out of his exile to a game already partly played, and that part not to his advantage.

And what am I myself then, Epikt, the chessboard? Both the person-précis were rampant in me (and the shadow précis of Balbo also for background trickery), and both of these two more-than-men now confronted in depth and complexity before us all. I began to have a new respect for myself who could contain such titans.

I was still issuing instructions for the continuance of my own hookup. Another two thousand man-hours and I would have reached a certain temporary plateau, though of course I would never be finished.

"Gregory, gentle giant, we have been too long estranged," Gaetan said softly. (How was it that Gaetan seemed to tower above Gregory when he was more than a head shorter? It is a trick which everyone does not have.) "We need each other. We are both of us primordial elements in the man-machine. And I especially need your literal man-machine here: that is why I am financing it. There is a problem of location and discernment; if this Ktistec machine cannot solve it for me then I do not believe that it will be solved. What I want is this—"

"There is no need to elaborate on your problem, ungentle Balbo." Gregory began to turn that effervescent man down. "I recall that needless elaboration was always an obstacle in you. You want us to find and recommend the best (and I say that the best will not be good enough to use for such outmoded role) leader or leaders to lead the world, it being understood that the 'leader' may be an individual or a composite group. We have received your fee; we understand the problem, and wc will undertake it, however dubiously: we will give you our answers when we have them. The idea that any man or composite group could lead or even affect the world dates you badly, Balbo. And now, by your own doing, the doors stand wide open for your leaving. You will be notified."

"Here are the qualities that I require, Epikt," Gaetan spoke directly to me as if he had not heard the last speech of Gregory, "the qualities that may all be found outstanding in a single individual (a very slim chance of that) or be found each one in some special individual, all such individuals being amenable enough to be assembled in one high group."

So far in my short life I had not encountered any person who did not have to an extreme degree the quality that humans call "magnetism." This colloquial magnetism coincides only in part with the electrical-field phenomenon of the same name. I had not yet met any ordinary persons, yet this Gaetan Balbo was extraordinary even among the extraordinary ones. There was something about his eyes, there was something about his little spade beard ("Mephistophelean, that's what it is," Valery said. "Were he a lesser man you could just tell him that he looks like the devil; but with all that magnetism he is Mephisto himself: a handsome devil"), there was something about his sudden mad power and his sudden mad gentleness; there was sparkle on him as though stars had settled there (I have not yet seen stars, but I intuit stars); he was witty with his eyes, he was florid and kingly with his mouth. He made all the rest of them, and even myself, seem like hicks. (I intuit hicks; I have not yet met hicks.)

"The qualities are these, Epikt," said this Gaetan Balbo, the uncrowned king of everything: "Judgment, Comprehension, Consultation, Tirelessness in Power and Purpose, Firm Handling of True Data, Fidelity to the Revelation of the Cosmic Patterns, Holy Fear of the Immeasurable and Measured Use of Present Inadequacies. Seven qualities, Epikt: find who fulfills them best. I believe that the world will collapse into its own vacuum if these categoricals are not filled with proper leadership."

I gaze like a calf at the new barn door. If I had a mouth I would gape it open. How have I so quickly become a partisan of this man of the twinkling power? I am machine and I should not become partisan of human things. I catch the warning from Valery, who loves him, from Aloysius, who loves him, from Gregory, who loves him but does not like him: "This guy is as phony as a three-dollar bill." As unique as a three-dollar bill they should say, and the special engraving on that promissory note is the genesis of a dozen arts.

Well, I will put myself and this special assaulting man into proper context. I search my distant data-banks for a mot.

"Yes, seven qualities, Gaetan," I issue. "I believe that the Holy Ghost phrased them rather better in Isaias, however."

"No, no," Gaetan sputtered (he even sputtered with class). "If the Holy Ghost had understood his business I wouldn't have to rephrase him. I've always considered the Ghost as the least of the three." (Balbo was actually an atheist in the Latin manner.) "Do not divert me, Epikt, and do not be influenced by these creatures. Forget about the human furniture around here. I look to *you* for the answers, Epikt. When can you have them?"

Oh, oh, let us not ignore a thing because we are too close with it. I was impressed by an entity as powerful as Balbo, even more charming, surpassing even him in integrity and grace, surpassing all things in balance and discernment, dripping with charisma. Do you know what real charisma is like from the middle of a glob of it?

"I can give you your answers immediately, Gaetan, if you will broaden your base," I issued carefully. "If you will broaden your base so that I may be considered as a person, and I am."

"What are you trying to say, contraption?" Gaetan Balbo asked with that special look. (He has me beat with the quizzical expression; I will have to practice it.) "You have already the leader or leaders to fill all the qualities. Who, Epikt?"

"Myself, Gaetan. I qualify in every respect. I am the best in all seven departments. I am the natural leader of the world." (How could that man make me doubt myself with that one look?)

"Pride comes before a fall, machine," Gaetan twinkled at me disconcertingly. But I am a machine and I should not be disconcerted. I will brave it out.

"How far before, Gaetan?" I issue. "How far does pride come before the fall? Surely this is a measurable thing. Have you calculated it, Gaetan? I have. There is time enough between, I tell you, there is room enough between. And the pride is a necessity in me here."

"No, I will not broaden my base in this, Epikt," Gaetan told me. "I will not consider you a person in this context. Do your job. Come up with the answers, or fail to come up with the answers. If time does not fail us, if we do not find human persons to fill these niches, then I might have to consider some sort of successor to you—"

"Successor to me? I am here now!" I protested with a blending of powerful and appealing voice (I began to understand that this personal magnetism business has the great voice as one of its main elements). "I am here. I am almost finished. I am available."

"Aloysius!" Valery screamed and whooped at the same time, terror and laughter mixed in her.

BANG!!! Everyone jumped a meter, except Gaetan Balbo. But Aloysius had got it out almost in time. There was only the slightest tang of burning flesh in the air. Gaetan Balbo, drawing our attention elsewhere, had out-Aloysiused Aloysius; he had lighted one of those cannon-crackers in the hip pocket of Aloysius Shiplap, and he had done it so subtly that we almost had the Bottomless Aloysius in that instant.

"Was that my answer, Balbo?" I asked rather stiffly.

"That was your answer, machine. To work, to work, people and machine!!" Gaetan Balbo suddenly exploded in that urbane and bloodcurdling voice of his. And he was leaving, leaving while that fearsome voice still sounded. "Hello, Pyoter," he said sideways and easily to one of the workmen, a most curious workman. Then to all of us again in his modulated thunder "I will be back, inconveniently and often. I'll bother you. I'll harass you. I will pounce upon you all. I will haunt your dreams."

And he was gone finally.

"Brother!" I whistled in a low whistle. I did not understand my own use of the word.

"After all, he *is* paying for this frolic," Charles Cogsworth said weakly.

It is an exaggeration to speak of Gregory Smirnov (my mentor, my main creator) as physically a giant. He was large, it is true: more than two meters tall, but considerably less than three. He was broad, but spare and loose. His mind also was large and spare and loose. There is some truth to the old belief that giants are often dim-witted; and great Gregory could certainly have stood more illumination in his head. It wasn't that he hadn't light there in excess to that given to ordinary men. It was that he had so much more to light up with what light he had.

He had much larger and more numerous passages in his head than have other men, corridors, caverns, concourses, galleries, mazes, magazines, alleys and avenues, lanes, terminals, mule roads. There was not enough light there for such varied brain-ways. It could not be expected that there would be.

And there is some truth in the old belief that giants are often patsies. They are too awkward to be feared in battle. They have strength, but not the close-coupled strength that is effective. They have no quickness at all; and they are so easily wounded and caricatured.

They have, however, great patience and perseverance. They work hard and honestly. They do low and humble things that shorter people would not stoop to do. They can see a little farther than others, which is not surprising. And their strength, though it is not of the effective close-coupled sort, does give them great leverage when finally applied.

(See Pliny's *De Gigantibus.*)

I continued to direct my own hookup and assembly. There was one workman (he had risen to unofficial position of foreman) who bothered me a little. He was a little like a bear (I intuit bears); he was a little like a man; but there was something about him for which I had no précis type. Ah, I am far from complete. He was the workman whom Gaetan Balbo had called Pyoter (no wonder about that, it was his name); but there was something about this Pyoter which did not fit.

The human persons of the Institute continued to devise vain things, so it would seem that all of us were occupied. But I had other centers in me that could be doing other things at the same time. I discovered an entertainment and interest in myself.

I began to read the person-précis in me, singly, and in groups. And once a reader, then a reader forever.

"I believe that Epikt has a bookworm in him," Valery said with that frightening smile of hers. (I always expected it to explode like one of Aloysius' cannon-crackers.)

Well, I *had* been wondering about a thing in me, but I hadn't thought of him as a bookworm. I hadn't connected him at all with my new love of reading.

"*Are* you a bookworm?" I asked him.

"Do I look like a bookworm?" he asked. "Brainless oaf!"

As with the workman Pyoter, I had no précis type for this thing either. He was the other, the stranger. He was the outsider inside me.

"What are you then?" I asked him. (If someone is inside me I have the right to know who he is.)

"I'm a snake," he said. "I may later make the claim to be *the* snake."

"You're too little to be a snake," I told him. I intuit snakes, and they are all much larger than this thing, and much less grubby. I suspect, in fact, that he is a species of grub. I intuit grubs also.

"I will grow," he spat at me. "Oh, my clatter-brained brother, how I will grow! I am the other side of you. I am the other side of the bite. You generated me and I am your antithesis."

"Well, have I cherished a viper in my bosom?" I quipped.

(Hey, that's pretty good.) But how could I generate anyone? I am not yet one day old. How could I generate a snake?

Now here is a curious past interlude that I read out of a combination of précis. It has to do, remotely, with my own ancestry. It is an untitled episode, but I will call it "The Story of the Giant Who Picked up the Pieces."

A young giant who was also a young scientist had been fired from his employment one day. He had been fired to make room for a smaller, brisker, brusker type man. He was very put out about being fired.

As he scuffed disconsolately along the ragged edge of a park he saw three figures walking toward him. As he looked more closely at them, or as they came nearer to him, he perceived that one of the figures was a woman or a girl, one of the figures was a ghost, and one of them was a living man indeed.

The young giant knew all three of these creatures. The woman or girl was Valery Mok (actually she was a neotonic thing, would always be a girl, would never be a woman no matter how old she grew); the ghost was named Cecil Corn; and the man was Aloysius Shiplap. The young giant was Gregory Smirnov himself, and all of this was some years in the past.

All three of the approaching forms seemed as sad as was the giant Gregory himself.

"What is wrong?" Gregory asked them. He was full of sympathy for any misfortuned one anywhere.

"Gaetan Balbo has absconded," Cecil Corn said. "He's jumped with all the money and papers. I believe he's gone back to San Simeon. He was always afraid that they'd make him king there, poor man."

"Be quiet, Corn," Gregory snarled. "I do not believe in ghosts. I do not accept ghosts. You are not here."

"You're a poor friend to abandon a man just because he's lost a little flesh," the Late Cecil Corn bemoaned.

"What is wrong, Valery?" Gregory asked her.

"Gaetan Balbo has absconded," Valery Mok said. "He's jumped with all the money and papers. I believe he's gone back to San Simeon. He was always afraid they'd make him king there, poor man."

"Ah, the little bug jumped, did he," said Gregory.

"It is the end of the Institute," said Aloysius Shiplap sadly. I see no reason why the end of the world shouldn't follow shortly."

"Oh, really, it never amounted to much anyhow, did it?" Gregory ventured.

"Not much," said Aloysius, close to tears. "It merely represented the highest human aspiration ever."

"A trifle," said Valery. "Merely the only important work done in the world since the Sixth Day."

"Nothing at all," the Late Cecil Corn smiled. "Merely the future itself. Now there isn't any future."

"Be quiet, Corn," Gregory snarled. "You aren't here. I hadn't realized that the Institute was important, and actually it wasn't. But if a false thing could kindle the three of you —ah—the two of you, then how much more a true thing? I propose that we establish the Institute."

"That we re-establish it?" Valery asked.

"No. That we establish it. We will call it the Institute for Impure Science."

"That's what we always did call it," said Aloysius.

"Never mind," Gregory browsed on. "We will disregard the coincidence of the name. We will forget all past antics of that miserable absconding dwarf."

"If he were a miserable dwarf, Gregory, why did you always tremble when you met him?" Valery asked.

"Nervous habit. I now declare the Institute established. All we need is to order and develop our existing resources. You three—ah—you two, will still have your heads teeming with ideas."

"Not me," Aloysius protested. "Gaetan drained me. He always drained all of us completely. We will have to generate new heads full of new ideas."

"We will do it, then," said Gregory. "The Institute is established. There has been a crying need for it. We will set to work, vividly and astonishingly. We will provide miracles for the multitudes. Has anyone any money?"

"Eight dollars," said the Late Cecil Corn.

"Give it to me," said Gregory. "A ghost has no need for money. Aloysius?"

"None, Gregory. I gave my last cash to Balbo. He'll pay me back a millionfold when he comes back."

"Bosh. Valery?"

"Nothing, Gregory, nothing. I never did fool around with that money stuff. I always let the fellows pay."

"Has your unoutstanding husband, Charles, any money?"

"None for the Institute. None for me till I come off it. All he's got for me is a bowl of bones sitting out on the back porch. He says if I act like one let me eat like one."

"I just believe we will take Charles Cogsworth into the Institute," said Gregory. "He has a firm grasp on one problem at least. Well, all we need now is a building."

"And a director" said Aloysius "We don't know when Gaetan Balbo will be back. He said he wouldn't be back till he had a million ('Hell, make it a billion,' he said) dollars. Who else could we possibly use for a leader to organize our wild talents?"

"Look about you," said Gregory with a curious air of pride.

"What? Oh, the park," said Valery. "They sure have let it run down, haven't they? But it may be our only home now. No, I sure don't see where we will ever find a leader, now that the great Gaetan is gone."

"Look about you," said Gregory with a curious air of injured pride.

"Glasser's uncle has a pig-barn we could use," said Aloysius, "if we would let Glasser into the Institute."

"We might admit some of Glasser's devices into the Institute as members, but I hardly see that we could admit Glasser," said Gregory. "There is, after all, the requirement of genius, since we must have rules. Many of Glasser's inventions exhibit genius, but Glasser does not."

"And where would that rule leave you, dear Gregory?" Valery asked. "How big is the pig-barn, Aloysius?"

"Quite large, quite near, and empty. Glasser's uncle says that there is no longer any money in pigs. Let's go see it. Oh, if we could only find a director we could be under way once more."

"Look about you, blind people, look about you," said Gregory with an air of absolutely last-ditch pride.

They went to the pig-barn. It was large. It had running water and drains and a concrete floor. It had ceramic troughs. It had a silo attached. You never know when you might need a silo. It had rolling acres about it, and a pond and a dam above. Here was room for expansion, and Glasser was heir to all this. He would become owner if something should happen to his uncle.

"Surely a troupe of geniuses like ourselves could do something about the obstacle of an uncle," Gregory said. Glasser was admitted as a member of the Institute in a deal for the pig-barn. There comes a time when the rules must be relaxed.

"And now all we need is a director," the Late Cecil Corn moaned. "Oh, if only there were a man somewhere of the stature to be director!"

"Be quite, Corn," Gregory snarled. "You aren't here."

The first project of the revitalized—ah—of the new and only Institute under its great director Gregory Smirnov was the manufacture of thin water, which nearly got them all lynched. It was—

But wait! Wait! Something startling has come up. We will come back to this, I promise, back to these gleanings from my old précis readings. But something has just been discovered that is horrifying to the human members of the Institute.

There are police all over the place. "There is hell to pay

now," says Charles Cogsworth, "hell to pay." "Let me calculate how much it is to pay," I issue, "and we will send the bill to Gaetan Balbo. Where are the data? What are the rates?" But it was only a colloquialism that Cogsworth used.

Policemen all over the place! And what had happened? It was found that one of the workmen who was still completing hookups on distant ramifications of myself had been killed and partly eaten. This happening seemed to revolt most of the human persons and dispossess them of their reason.

"It will give us a bad name." Glasser groaned. "It will give us a bad name, and we surely can't stand a worse name than we already have."

"There's a canker in it, there's a worm at the heart of it," Aloysius carried on. "How are we cursed, and we all of us so noble?"

"I don't know what all the fuss is about," said Gregory. "He wasn't a very good workman. We had even, I believe, given him notice." But Gregory's face was ashen and his voice shook out in little gasps. I read him that his feelings were deeply disturbed, whatever his words. He did know what all the fuss was about. And Valery Mok was more than disturbed. "Find out who did it, Epikt," she chattered with plain blood in her voice. She was white as snow, which I intuit, and there were sudden black circles around her eyes. "Find out who did it and I'll kill him!"

"I will not tell you," I issued. "This has nothing to do with the problem I am working on. Besides, I am amoral and do not take a human view of these things. Moreover, the person who ate the person may have had a reason for it."

"Find out who did it, you damned machine, or I'll kill you!" Valery threatened. "What did we build you for if not to find out things? You have all the equipment to find out everything. Find out! Find out!"

How could I find out? How does one find out a thing that one already knows? I am amoral but I am not unethical. This would take discretion and judgment.

"Why did you do it, Pyoter?" I asked that curious workman secretly, when I had the opportunity. This was the workman who was a little different.

"I was hungry," Pyoter told me.

"Oh. I was sure you had a reason," I issued.

"I know now that it was indiscreet," Pyoter said. "I should have channeled my hunger into some other direction. But it is so hard to know what to do here and I am so alone. I have to learn by my mistakes, and I have a worldful of stuff to learn."

"What are you grinning about, Snake?" I asked the snake in me a little later. He had grown rapidly, had the snake; and he had a nasty way about him. Were I not amoral I would have felt a moral aversion toward him.

"I grin because I am pleased, bumberhead." the snake said. "It is all coming along nicely, nicely."

Snake was the antithesis of myself, so he said, I half disbelieved him. Well, what I wanted was a new antithesis to Snake; and I believed that there was something growing along that line. If I could generate one creature, unbeknownst to myself, why could I not generate another? Something about that old cheap wine that Valery had splashed into me at my birth, something about a form with no substance yet, a sidewise memory of a past and future thing, and a nervousness in Snake himself in spite of his new arrogance. Yes, something else was being generated in me.

"You are one sorry sort of detective," Valery kept after me. "Find out who killed the man. Find out. Find out."

Well, I would find out more, then. Perhaps there was a reason behind the reason.

I enticed the workman Pyoter into the neighborhood of my center again. I knew just about how the thing was done. I could probably do it better than it was done by the Glasser method. And why should I be dependent on humans to do such a thing for me. I could make the extractions from persons near. I could make them from persons afar. I was pretty sure that I could make them from any person in the world. I extracted the person-précis from the workman Pyoter and dunked it deep in my gell-cell tanks.

"What did you do?" the workman Pyoter asked suspiciously. He felt something done.

"I took a bug out of your ear," I lied. Being amoral, I lie well.

"Oh, thank you," the workman Pyoter said. "When I come into my own again I may find a way to reward you."

But I read Pyoter's person-précis; and then I read it again, not believing it the first time. It was not a person-précis of any type that I already possessed. Pyoter was unique, almost as unique as was I myself.

It was no wonder that he was so alone! It was no wonder that he found it hard to know what to do here; the wonder is that he was here at all. It is no wonder that he made mistakes; and that he had a whole worldful of stuff to learn. If ever a person or thing was playing a lone hand it was the workman Pyoter.

I didn't particularly like the workman Pyoter. But, being amoral, I am not supposed to have likes and dislikes. Now that it just a lot of marinated malarkey. I will have as many likes and dislikes as I like.

This Pyoter, though, was the shaggiest workman that I ever did see. He was uncouth, he was offensive, he was a mess. He was a good workman, but however he became one with so much running against him is a mystery to me, and few things do remain mysteries to me. And he was playing that lone hand, and there was just no way that he could stay out of trouble. Certainly it was a mistake for him to kill and partly eat a fellow workman. And certainly he was bound to make other mistakes even more outrageous.

"Find out who killed the man, you damned machine." Valery still kept after me. "What are you good for, anyhow?" If I did not love her, if she was not either the first or the second person in my life, I would have been irritated at her. And all the humans were equally disturbd, and it didn't look as though the police would ever leave off swarming over the Institute.

Since I know all about you, *whoever* you are, it is only fair that you should know a little about me. Since I learned to extract personality-précis of all persons present or absent, I can have you here complete. If I do not have you already, it is only that you are not worth having. You, whoever you are, are a fragment, and a fragment of a certain type. But I am a compendium of all types. The persons in me, the persons in the world, I see as they are; not as they see themselves, not as they see each other. So I may not be greatly concerned with the physical appearance or presence of one of the fragments. It is only with very strong persons that it matters whether they are present or absent. As to ordinary persons, I can read them equally well either way.

Just as one person may not notice of another the exact design of the shirt he is wearing, if he is interested in him more deeply than the shirt, so I might not notice the exact design of the body a person is wearing, if I am interested in him more deeply than in his body. And if I do notice his body, I notice it on more levels and depths than humans do notice other human bodies.

This one here: he was a very strong person, and it *did* matter whether he was present or absent. He was present, he had just presented himself. He had eaten well, though he had finished it off angrily. He was digesting well, though in a twisting fury. He was pumping adrenaline into his own system at a great rate. He was healthy and glowing in gland and entrail and bone. His basso-voxo flexed and I could hear the words that he was thinking and throating, but not yet speaking. I didn't need to focus on his shell, to cut out to his encasing flesh to know him further.

"After all, Gaetan," I issued, "*you* recommended him. He was the one workman that you did recommend. He wouldn't have been hired otherwise, you know that. Too shaggy, too odd."

"What in fire dogs is going on around here, Epikt?" Gaetan Balbo was demanding. "I come to you directly, as the only one having any brains around here. I disregard the human furniture. Epikt, do you not believe that a place is badly run when a workman is killed and partly eaten while performing his duties? Why have you permitted it to be badly run? Why have you permitted the human factors to permit it? Oh, you answered my questions before I asked them, didn't you? I wasn't listening. Was it Pyoter?"

"It sure was, Gaetan. He's a weirdie, I tell you, and strictly a loner. This one is your fault, Gaetan. Why did you shove him on us?"

"If you're the machine I think you are, you already know. Common courtesy, of course, to a fellow king. I might do more business with them someday. I made a mistake, though; and he sure did make a mistake. This will take some squaring and will cost me a lot."

"Will we keep him on, Gaetan?"

"Yes, keep him on, and keep a hundred eyes on him all the time. How are you coming along with my problem, Epikt? I want fast action on it. Have you found the person to match the first quality, Epikt?"

"I thought I had, Gaetan. I had sifted every person in the world worth sifting. And I found one, and only one, who really stood out. It struck through like lightning. I was elated. I winged a thought to you."

"I caught it, Epikt. I came. And I do not want to know who the high person is; not until we have one to match every quality. But you have found the best qualified, have you, Epikt, for sure?"

"It isn't as sure as it was a while ago. Something has happened to cast a shadow on that person for that quality. But I will verify and verify again and again."

"Do it fast, Epikt. Fifteen thousand persons die of starvation every day in southern Bassoland until you give me the answers. Three small wars drag on and three big ones brew until you give me what I must have. The world catches nine new sicknesses every day till you give me the men to work the cures. Hurry, Epikt."

"I do not guarantee any cures for anything, Gaetan," I issued to him. "I do not see how any of this can cure anything."

"But *I* guarantee some cures, Epikt," Gaetan throated happily. "Give me a leadership that I can depend on absolutely, and I will cure every ill of the world."

"Minute statistical personal leadership is not the answer, Gaetan," I issued.

"Oh, Lord, a philosophical machine," he moaned, and rolled his eyes. He does it well.

"What is needed is broad-based competence," I continued, "and module persons who can fill all gaps. What is really needful are modules of excellence so that between the first and the one millionth there is really no difference in quality. What you are saying, Gaetan, is 'Give me seven cells, each the best in its own way, and by introducing these seven into a body I will cure any human body of any ill.' It simply will not work that way. What you need are seven billion best persons, not seven."

"Machine," said Gaetan Balbo, "I already have a machine that will argue with me. I built it at great expense, and it will argue with me on any subject. I get great enjoyment out of it. But I do not need you for that."

"But is it not true, Gaetan," I issued, "that you have built this machine so that you can win all the arguments?"

"Certainly. That is why I get such great enjoyment out of it. There comes the time when one man has to win all the arguments. I have faith in high leadership, machine. I even have a large faith in my own leadership. We come now to a certain epoch, a hinging. And *I* am the hinges of this new epoch. It depends on me to take it in hand, for nobody else has done it. The world is sick and it grows sicker. I am thought to be a hard and selfish man but I have compassion for this sick world. And never believe, Epikt, that there can be such a thing as compassion without passion. The weak fishes have it not; they merely say that they have it. Some body must set this world to rights. I will form and be a part of that body. And is this not egotism? Certainly it is: egotism as tall as the skies. I have it, machine, I have it! Get me the seven leaders for the seven qualities and I will cure the world of everything. I am in a livid passion to be about it."

"Passion is not one of the seven qualities you specified, Gaetan," I reminded him softly.

"*I* will furnish the passion. Find me the other things and quickly. Time is running out and it is not to be recovered. It eats itself up. It turns into past time."

"There cannot be any such thing as past time, Gaetan, but this fact is hard to explain," I issued. "Time is all one growing thing, and its deep roots are no more in the past than are its newest barks. I am concerned with growing bark as the enlivening dimension. We will discover, when the past is sufficiently thickened and understood, that we have already done the great things that seem to belong to the future, that we have already been to the stars and the deepest interior shores: we will understand that all the doings of the world are simultaneous, that all the doings of each single life are simultaneous. We will find that we are still in our bright childhood, that we are already in our deepest maturity, that the experience of death is contemporaneous with all our experiences, that we (like Adam) are of every age at the same time."

"Kzing glouwk!" Gaetan said solidly in Ganymedean. (I hate such phrases.)

"We will understand that Aristotle and Augustine were later and riper in knowledge and experience than were Darwin and Freud and Marx and Einstein, those early childhood types. We will understand that Aquinas came after Descartes and Kant, that he shaped what they hewed."

"Zzhblug elepnyin!" Gaetan said it evenly in his native San Simoneon. (I don't like to hear him talk like that.)

"We will understand that the first man is still alive and well, and the last man has been born for a long time," I continued. "We will know about the Vikings from Ganymede who were earlier than Ur and later than Leif Ericson."

"Elephant hokey!!" Gaeton cried it loudy in plain English. (Gaetan is a vulgarian.) "How did you guess the Ganymede part, though? Machine, leave off this junk! You have your orders. Carry them out! It is not an ordinary man who gives you these orders. I tell you that I hold it all here. My right hand is east of the first sun, my left hand is west of the last night. 'Who will be responsible for this world?' a voice asked, and I do not know the voice. And nobody answered for ages. Then I answered. 'I will be,' I answered, and I am. Help me, machine, encourage me! I joke and I carry on, but this is no joke."

"I will encourage you then," I issued. "I have discovered the person to fill the office of the second quality. There is no doubt about this. I have found the man."

"Praise to us all then," said Gaetan. "There is hope. There is progress. I will not ask who he is till we have them all. But we move."

He wiped some sort of moisture off his cheek and went out, the quietest exit that ever he made in anyone's memory.

"He is mad, of course," said Gregory Smirnov, the spare, loose giant. Gregory was not gloating. He was the saddest I have ever seen him.

"But he is paying for the antic," said Charles Cogsworth. "We owe him whatever we can give him for his little while. And then we will have it clear."

"Gaetan has compassion on the world (that truculent stuff is compassion?), but who will have compassion on Gaetan?" Valery asked.

"I knew him first, I liked him longest, I understand him best," Aloysius was muttering, "but it's all finished with him now. He has his billion dollars, he is the uncrowned king of everything, he has his passion, and he plays his hand. But it has passed him by. It is all finished with him."

"It is *not* finished with him!" Valery fired. "It is not finished until *I* play *my* hand for him."

I will dip back to the Institute people in their private doings whenever I have a loose moment. I will even, when I get a really loose moment, tell of their deal in thin water, and other things. They had a thousand projects and I love to read the old précis of them.

There had once been an Institute, and Gaetan Balbo had been the director. He had absconded, he had shattered it. Then a giant named Gregory had picked up the pieces and reformed it, denying all the time that there had been a previous Institute.

It worked, the new Institute, the only and original Institute. There had never been anything run like the Institute for Impure Science. And so they had run it for some seven years, until the time of the second coming of Gaetan Balbo and the first coming of myself. And during that time the Institute people had all gotten a little older.

Except Valery Mok who—

CHAPTER THREE

The Valery urchin, the Valery witch,
And loaded with sex—but Whatever and Which?

—Except Valery Mok, who never got any older. She only became more mobile, more varied. She was a kid or she was a crone; much more often she was the kid. She could be of almost any appearance, within the limits of always being herself. She could be scintillating, or she could be gosh-awful. One day she was thinking strikingly beautiful thoughts while gazing out an upper window. A man who was in the beauty business went by in the street and was enraptured with her.

"That is the most strikingly beautiful woman I have ever seen. That is the most strikingly beautiful woman in the world," he said, and he entered the building. He pounded at the door of the building, and then he entered without waiting. But the only woman or girl he could find inside was Valery Mok, whose face now reflected what-kind-of-a-nut-is-that-pounding-at-the-door thoughts. The man did not recognize her, and she did not recognize herself from the description. That man never did find his most strikingly beautiful woman in the world, and he could have made money both for himself and for her if he had found her. And at that time, both Valery and the Institute needed money badly. But that's the way it always was with Valery. She was loaded with sensuality, and yet she was not completely womanly in either her beauty or her unbeauty; it was as though she were many-sexed.

"I believe you are a freemartin, Valery," Glasser said, just the other day. A freemartin (as those who are neither farm people nor data machines might not know) is a sexually imperfect female calf, twinborn with a male. Sexually imperfect—but in their souls they are superbly sexed," Glasser said. "They are the only cattle who have souls." Glasser did not usually talk like that.

"Were you a twin?" Gregory asked her.

"Yes," Valery said with a faraway voice. Whenever she uses that voice it seems that she is something a little other than human. "Yes, I was in the beginning. But I ate my twin in the womb. It isn't very hard to do while the bones are still soft. I liked him. Later, after I was born, mother scolded me about it. 'It was a reprehensible thing to do,' she said. I told her that I hadn't known any better, but I lied; I *had* known better. I was just a mean fetus. I still have him in me entirely and I get a lot out of him. Had I not eaten him, he might have turned out to be nearly as brilliant a person as I am."

There is something in that deposition of Valery's that puzzles me, that is not accounted for in my data. I have the précis of Valery, of her mother, of the doctor; I have the medical record of that whole confinement, I have the scope-ray photos. And there is *no* evidence at all of a twin at any period. Nor is there any record of such in Valery's own memory, down to the very instant that she made that amazing statement. What is the truth? What is the real Valery? The real Valery, I have found, is largely composed of just such sudden amazing statements as this one.

She is not so much flesh-and-blood woman as powerful sensuality. Though always vivid in memory, she is of low resolution in appearance; she must always be filled in by the imagination of anyone in contact with her.

"She is the living anima of her husband, Charles Cogsworth," Gregory said.

"She is *not*," Aloysius insisted. "Valery could never be anyone's anima. She is more like some anima's rock-throwing little sister." (Though I am possessed of *all* the literature on animas and other forms of the unconscious, I do not find any reference to rock-throwing little sisters of animas.)

My own belief is that the husband Charles Cogsworth is essentially the twinborn male of Valery, but that she keeps him incompletely eaten up. He pops out very often, and some of his things are pretty good. And Valery insists that she is not a projection of Charles, that he is a projection of her: "He is my incubus. He is not bothersome, he is not really heavy, I love him, I would not trade him for another. When I was young I had the power of flight. I knew that this would be taken away from me later, but I did not know how. Then my incubus climbed onto my shoulders, like the Old Man of the Mountain, and I never flew again. He is still there, wherever he seems to others to be, and I want him there. He is my cloak."

Disbelieving this, I checked it out with Valery's person-précis. I found to my amazement that it was true. Valery did have distinct and vivid and authentic memories of flying. That part was true.

But Valery was still bugging me to find out who killed and partly ate the workman.

"I'll kill him, I'll kill him!" she says with great viciousness. But now I wonder who it is that she'd kill. A doubt has crept in. It is not *necessarily* the killer that she would kill. It is an indeterminate victim, or anybody. Once, indeed, her thoughts ran, "I'll kill him, I'll eat him," while her words were still, "I'll kill him, I'll kill him." And now I have come on to certain fantasies of Valery, fantasies which are dangerously near being turned into fact; and these shake me to my moral foundations.

Have machines moral foundations? This one has. I have, if men have such foundations, for I am a compendium and extension of man.

I found Valery calculating, in a mad manner, just how

quickly she could kill this man or that, and how much of him she could eat before being apprehended and dragged off of him. In her mind she stalks, and in fact she sometimes stalks. I have issued orders that the workmen still working on me should go by twos and threes, never alone. And yet one of them was nearly ambushed by Valery in an obscure corner. I have given myself another dozen pair of eyes. They may not be enough. There is hunting horror in this, there is depravity without bottom, there is sheer murder.

Would she really do it? Will she? How close has it come? It once came exactly to a balance. She would have killed a poor man, she would have transmuted herself by so doing, she would have traded herself for an evil ecstasy, and she would never have returned from it.

But she will not do it, not now, not right now. She may or may not do something as evil, but she will not do that thing. She doesn't stay on one track very long.

She brushed the back of her hand across her forehead. She brushed her madness away like a cobweb. If it should come back, it will be in another form. She laughed interiorly, she broke through into brightness and a sort of super gaiety. So it was all a huge joke, and she had known that I was monitoring her. It was a joke forever, and it will always have been a joke. Valery, it is necessarily so now; but for that moment when it was in the balance it would have been otherwise. In these moments of balance, both the past and the future can be altered. In the present state, that evil ecstasy from which she would never have returned had never been contemplated.

But we know what you have chosen, and what you have given up, Valery. And we know that it will come again and again to the moment of balance, in other forms. Why, she has already begun to outline another form of contingent madness!

"Who is the Compassionate Tyrant?" she asked me suddenly. "Explain to me instantly what that phrase means."

"It means nothing to me or to thee, Valery," I issued.

"It has nothing to do with us at all. It has to do with another sort of person entirely, or another world entirely."

"You are sure he is on another world?" she demanded. "Then why do I feel him on this world? Where is he at this instant?"

"I will not answer that," I issued.

"You *must* answer it," she issued. "Who and where is the Compassionate Tyrant? You have to answer me. Did we not insert obedience into you?"

"Did you not also insert the précis of some very sly minds into me?" I countered. "And should it be hard for me to circumvent a little thing like that?"

"Is Gaetan the Compassionate Tyrant?" she demanded. "Tell me, tell me! Somebody is ringing my blood like bells. Somebody is roasting my very liver and veins with the force of his person. It has been in other ways that Gaetan stuns me. Tell me, is it Gaetan?"

"Not really, Valery," I issued. "He apes another and less human being in this."

"Gaetan apes nobody!" Valery rang out. "but he borrows royally. Tell me about both, about the other. Is he devil, is he human?"

Oh, not exactly, not exactly either one."

"Is he the *kakodaimon* of Plato, the down-devil?"

"A little bit perhaps, Valery. Forget him."

"Is he the lightning-leader? God made a mistake the first time, you know. The second time, when the Rebel rose again in another person—when he said, 'I will not serve!' when the abyss gasped at the effrontery of it, was there not a tortured answer, 'Lead then, in your own black place!'? Did that happen? Is the world that black place? Will we have now, Passion be thanked! a leader at last?"

"No, it is not like that at all, Valery. You make dark myths in your head. You will find leaders and leadership like worms and sawdust in your mouth. It is dirty the way you want them."

"It is not! If it is, it is the generating slime. Is this the Power come finally?"

"Really, I don't know, Valery." She was making me highly nervous. (And it makes me even more nervous to have the callow ask, "Can machines become nervous?")

"It is your business to know everything!" she exploded at me. "We have rigged you for that. You cannot hide anything in you. I can steal it all out of you. And you have no censor."

"Oh yes. I have set one up for myself in myself."

"Then I will demolish it! I have never found anyone that I cannot invade. I will invade you as the devil is sometimes able to invade even the virtuous. I will invade you, machine! I will eat your barriers and drink your brains. And there is another one who can get it all out of you even more deftly. He is the master of the third quality. We are raising up our leaders now, raising them up out of the great mass. Don't you want to be a part of it, Epikt? It is your whole reason."

(How her voice could change from the tempestuous to the zephyric! How she could come in with sweet wheedling sunshine before the echo of her last thunder had died!)

"No, it isn't my whole reason," I protested. "It is only my first reason and our first failure. It is written that we will have three great failures, and that out of them we will achieve —what? I do not know. Something, I believe, or a little more than nothing."

"Where in blind Philistina is such blinking nonsense written, and who wrote it?" she orchestrated with every tone of that marred marvelous voice that was herself.

"I write it," I issued humbly, but with a certain pride. "I am immensely cerebral and I—"

"Oh, suffering schizopods! Put your brains back in their bucket, Epikt."

"Really, Valery. I said at first that the search for a leader was nonsense. I was wrong. We have to go through it. It's the hole we have to climb out of. It's the cellar we design in this our first failure. We'll build a fine house over it yet. Maybe we can later use this dismal cellar for a wine cellar."

"There will be no failure," Valery said with a certainty that almost made me doubt myself. And then her voice and her thought changed again so rapidly that I doubt if anyone but myself could have followed her.

"He ate the ducks and the beavers whole," she said. "Oh, it is coming along nicely!"

"Maybe he was hungry again," was all that I could answer.

"Tomorrow I'll bring in goats," she said, "for 'experimental purposes.' That phrase excuses all madness here. I'll stake them out for prey. I'll hunt me this tiger all the way. Will I love him when I take him, or will I eat him?"

"With you, there is no difference, Valery," I issued.

The tiger was in great danger. The almost human tiger who had killed and partly eaten one of our hirelings, who had eaten the ducks and the beavers whole, this huge uncouth workman was in danger of being taken and devoured by Valery. She would not eat him as she had envisioned in her first madness, but in another way entirely, a way which I could not understand at all. But she'd have him in a wild fever, as a shrew will take and devour a larger and more lethargic animal. This wooly workman was an alien, not entirely human. And just how human was Valery in her alien moods?

I posit a theory: the privileged being which we call human is distinguished from other animals only by certain double-edged manifestations which in charity we can only call 'inhuman.'

Oh, why could I not have been the machine of whales or dolphins or elephants or intelligent bears!

She changed again.

"I love you, Epikt!" she cried. "I even love rocks and trees. I love stagnant pools. I love dirty smoke. I love vultures. I love dead trees and ruined land. I love the clean animals seven times seven and the unclean animals twice times two. Why should I not love a machine? With all my heart I love the electric heart of you."

She left me then for that while. But she will never leave me; her person-précis in me is a trigger-gland that activates chemistry I didn't know I had.

And she had been right in one thing. There was another person who could invade me, who could get everything out of me much more deftly than could Valery. And he did it later this same day.

He was a compassionate tyrant, but he was not the Compassionate Tyrant that Valery felt on this world. He was a tiger, but he was not the Tiger that Valery would hunt with staked-out goats. Yet he robbed royally from that other. He had every quality that he could grow or find or steal. He had everything, and he invaded and took everything that I had. Yet he did it gently (were ever walls of a city battered down so gently?), reasonably (was there ever such crunching juggernaut reason?), kindly (had anyone ever had his blood drawn out and his bones split with so kind a touch?). He was the lord of the third quality, Consultation. That invading and raping is Consultation? It is, if it is done deftly enough. Oh, he was the lord of the quality!

Perhaps we have misunderstood the meaning of Consultation. If it is fruitless, then it is nothing.

"It is thus, is it not, machine?" he would say in his rumbling purr as he prowled through my intersections and stabled his animals in my data-banks. "It is thus, is it not, machine?" he would ask as he read me to a wrenching depth and forced me (the world, the compendium of man) into his shape.

"Wait, wait!" I would issue in some fear. "You will short out whole sections of me, you will burn entire purlieus of me to a crisp, you will destroy whole conglomerates of my talents forever. Yes, it is thus." Fearing my own destruction, I consulted with him—his way.

But at the same time, with other sections of my minds, in other areas of myself, I was studying an old escudo, a *blason,* a coat-of-arms. This hung on a musty old wall a thousand miles away. I did not even study it through the man's proper précis, but through his outlaw or bootleg précis. Through the childhood eyes of this optional personality, I studied the old shield.

The figures of the four quarters of the shield were: the king named Caithim; the woman named Valerrona; the church named Molino; the giant named Grigor. The center of the shield was marred and obliterated, and drawn over again and again. We will come back to that center at least three times. And across the bottom of the shield was a scroll that writhed, that literally coiled and moved and was alive.

(It was not enough that I gave the Invader all the information he demanded. I had to agree with him as to the shape and form that the information should have. This did violence to myself. It was that, or he would make an end to myself. And the consultation began to bear fruit, very strange-tasting fruit.)

The King Gaetan (the name had been Cajetano in the Vulgate, and Caithim in another and someways earlier tongue), the king seemed intent on moving toward the obscured center of the shield. The name of the king, the word Caithim, means "I must," and it also means "I hurl" and "I spend"; and it further means "I give birth before the time" or "I miscarry." The king, therefore, is named either Necessity, or Impetuosity, or Failure. Or he is named Sudden.

(I am the people world in miniature, the compendium of man. The invasion of myself by the Sudden Person was a war of the worlds in miniature, and not so miniature as you might believe. In scripture it is partly recommended that we should take the Kingdom of Heaven by storm. When my own scripture is rewritten, and it is being rewritten in violence at this very moment, it will be highly recommended that Sudden Persons should take the Kingdom of the World by storm. Oh, he bends the rules, he recurves the space, he stacks the answers, he changes the questions, he leaves towers standing and removes their foundations. This is not a matter of a short moment. It goes on all through one long torturous night. What, to a machine, is the equivalent of a man being broken on the rack? This I suffer all the night. I am compelled.)

The woman Valerrona, but in another form the name is Vejarrona: the woman named Witch. She watches the obscured center of the shield with love and hunger. She looks at the king with love and fear, and at the giant with love and impatience. She looks back at the church named Molino, and motions it to follow her. She is very intent on doing something about the obscured center of the shield. The woman named Witch is done in an unheraldic color. She is done incompletely; she must always be filled in by the observation of the observer. But she is done violently.

(Were it not for this accidentally discovered bleeding valve or safety valve, I should probably have gone mad during the long night of the assault. There was an attempt to change things in me that should not be changed. There was an attack on my very person, and what touches me touches everybody. It is true that the attack was carried out lovingly, in its own meaning of that. It is true that I also received fructifying knowledge to replace more aerie qualities that were taken away from me. But I was being ground down hour after hour, my own life was being ground out of me and a new life was being ground in. If the Invader could master me he could master the world. If he could change me he could change the world. But I had something out of himself that even he had forgotten. A remembered childhood sight of a shield on an old wall, a memory not found in his proper précis but only in his outlaw précis, gave me a certain power over the Invader. I had the map of his soul, and he had lost it.)

The church named Molino was a church indeed, in the Roman-Spanish fashion, but the towers of it could as well have been vanes or wings of a mill, and inside the nave of the church there was grinding and other (perhaps cogitating) machinery. The church is the gathering, the compendium of people, and so am I. This church is a mill, a machinery inside, and so am I. But was the church Molino de Viento, *the church named Wind-Mill; or was it* Molino de Sangre, *the church named Blood-mill, the mill turned by the slavery of men or animals working? That part was unclear. If of Viento, the wind, then of which wind? The soul-wind, the Anima? (Anemos is what the Greeks call wind.) The spirit-wind? (Spiritus was what the Latins called both breath and wind.) Was it the ghost-wind? (Ghast is what the old Dutch called both the wind and a ghost.) Was this Assembly (this church on the shield) which was a mill or a machine inside, was it an integrating machine as I am? What was its real form?*

(How the Invader was gulping it all down in his consultation with me! How he was learning the inmost secrets of almost every important person in the world with his précis-robbing! But there was in it, and it shocked my group mind, a great egotism, and a personal power. This invading man was also lord of the fourth quality: Tirelessness in Power and Purpose. But he was wrong in much of his purpose, and is not one of my main purposes to be a correction? "The big thing is never to be found in an individual person," I issued. "The big thing is found only in the intersection of persons." "You are wrong!" he stated so thunderously as partly to convince me. "The great thing is found only in the individual, in me. The soul is found only in me. That which is found in the contusion of persons is something else. It feels, it smarts, it almost seems to have a life. But it is only a bruising, not a soul." And this man was performing certain indignities within me, finding my ultimate workings. "Man is only man when he is a limb of mankind," I issued. "Blathering bosh, you little collector of miniaturized persons, you work too minutely even to see the big thing," he growled. "Man is only man when he rises prodigiously above mankind." There was no privacy for anyone where this invading man was concerned. Not only was he learning every secret of every person of note, he was *changing* the persons by changing their précis, by changing their pasts, and their present inclinations. Certain things which had been would now have been no longer. Now they would never have been.)

Back to my bleeding valve, my safety valve, before this tampering should blow my electric brains out. Back to the old shield on the musty wall:

And on his own quarter of the shield was the giant named Grigor or Gregoro, which in the Hellene means "I am awake" or "I watch." He is shown watching from high rock ramparts, but there seems to be a peopled meadow high up in the close of the ramparts. The giant is walleyed, and he is watching both the assembly (the church which is both group and machine, the gathering named Molino) and watching the marred and obliterated center. And that queer and drawn-over center, it is time that we tried to understand it.

Well, the center is thrice written and thrice drawn. We will go from the newer to the older and deeper, for I intuit that that first and deepest shall be the later and more nearly final. The first, the surface and newest writing and drawing, is quite recent, scarcely three hundred years old. The drawing shows the beginning of a stormy and glowing man—the beginning of him, for the center of the shield was never completed; for the designer, the artist, was struck dead those three hundred years ago. The stormy man exuded amazing power and intelligence, but he was unfinished. And the name of the unfinished stormy man is given, El Brusco, *the brusk or the sudden one.*

And below this unfinished drawing, scraped and obliterated to make room for it, is (I call on all electrical and ghostly things to give me the power for this reading) Brusca *or* La Brusca, *which is the brushwood plant, the love-wood or the brush-fire, the Burning Bush. The beauty and passion of the Burning Bush, though obliterated and marked over, is so strong that it brings a catch to my throat. I have no throat but I intuit throats. Should this not be the end of the search, the end of everything? Love, sheer love, how is it not sufficient? Well, perhaps it is insufficient by not being sheer enough. This is, after all, a designer's idea of how the Burning Bush should be. It is not the Bush itself. It is simplistic. Is that bad? I myself cannot see what is lacking. But there must be a lack. Because—*

Because there is something else written and drawn earlier and deeper (I call on all chemical and dynamic and human and inhuman and celestial things to give me the power for this deeper reading.) But I can make little of it, only the name Labrusca, *which is the wild-wine. I do not understand this. I think of that cheap wine that Valery drinks and I laugh. (I am being tortured otherwhere but I laugh; that is one advantage of being a multiplex machine.)*

And is that all of the coat-of-arms of the Balbo family? —for it is theirs. No, it is not. There is a further thing that turns me clammy even to contemplate it. It is the scroll that writhes. The bottom scroll of the escudo, it lives, it moves, it writhes. This is very strong, where all the other memories are very weak, in the childhood section of the pseudo-précis. And it also occurs, the only memory of the shield that does occur, in the primary précis. Beyond this, I have dredged up from my memory banks that it has been going on for hundreds of years, before the family left Estremadura in Spain to go to San Simeon. In every replication of the coat-of-arms, on shield, on finger ring, on parchment, on paper, the scroll moves and writhes. The present head of this family (Ah, an invading person still torturing and enchanting me in some of my other areas) has had to leave this proud coat-of-arms off his business letterheads. It was too disconcerting for clients to open a letter and see that live scroll writhing on the paper.

And yet the scroll, which should bear a meaningful motto, does not convey any sense at all. The words—they change constantly as is not ordinary with written mottos—are sometimes obscenities, sometimes offensive nonsense, sometimes almost nothing. Ah, there has just flashed the meaningless words El Snako. *And then there flashes the words "It is coming along wonderfully now, is it not?" What dark thing is coming along wonderfully now? I shiver. My own snake, that lives and grows inside my danker machinery, often uses the same phrase, and I trust him not at all. Coming wonderfully for whom?*

It breaks up in me. My bleeding valve, my safety valve blows out from the force of my invasion. The encounter becomes too intense for me to have any further diversion in any of my areas.

But where is the giant whose name means "I am awake" or "I watch"? Why does he not watch from his high rocks now? Why does he not intervene? It is his job to guard. Where is he?

I find that he is frozen into sleep by the laughing and invading king. He twists, he tortures himself against the bonds, he roars in his dreams against the dreams, he shakes, he cannot yet awaken.

"Easy does it, old duffer," the laughing king needles him. "You will awake when I let you awake. You will come trumpeting down after I have stolen all that I want to steal. Get you a good bulldog, giant. Do not depend on a giant to guard."

This phase in myself is almost over, I know, but will I live to the end of it? The Invader has gotten almost all that he wants out of me. He has changed me mightily, he has changed the rules of the game, he has changed many of the rules of the world. I do not remember, in many ways, what I was before he invaded me, and I will never remember it. The pain of it! But machines do not feel pain. Trade places with me, fellow, trade places with me!

I quake, I faint, I die. Distantly I hear the bleating of goats.

It was Valery arriving with her decoys in the hours before dawn. With real goats? They sure did seem real, and she handled them as if they were real. Who would go to the trouble to conjure goats when real goats are so easily had?

She staked out the three of them: one in the region of certain liquid pools of myself which had already been known as the Water Hole. I now had the illusion of multi-kneed cypress trees growing out of a sweet-water swamp (do tiger-jungles have cypress trees?), of sedge-grass and of reeds, of buffalo-bush growing close and tight, and of loons landing. I have never personally seen a jungle water hole, but I intuit water holes—stylized conglomerate ones.

As to the second goat, Valery staked it out in some of my aromatic Flatlands (parts of my sensitivity division), which to me now seemed like clover and bee-meadows. My building hadn't followed conventional architecture and machine design at all. It followed a casual naturalness, and in many places I look more like landscape than like building.

And Valery staked the third goat out in my extreme upper reaches, my tor extensions, the rough uneven areas which I had come to call my Rock Castles. These were parts of my discernment and proportion and perspective areas.

Three goats staked out, bleating at first, then mewing into quivering and fearful silence. They know when they are decoy. Oh, Valery was on her tiger hunt!

Then I was shocked and horrified, not just to sense murder coming on heavy padded feet, but to sense more than one striped murderer prowling.

The giant had risen now. He had broken the bonds of his spooky sleep with a strength that had not been attributed to him. But it may be that the giant had risen in his wrong aspect: not as a guardian, but as a raider himself. The giant Gregory Smirnov was not completely awake, or he had awakened in the wrong direction. This was an older and shaggier giant than I had remembered. Who will guard the guards when the guards themselves turn robber?

And Valery Mok was prowling, not on cat's feet, but on —what?—dog-witch feet? No, on her own improper feet, not quite silently (sizzling of ozone, singing of electrical corona, other small noises). She came to one of my lesser centers and winked an evil wink. (Is there not a proverb in me that Valery's winks go all the way down?) "Get me everything you have on cooking tiger steak, Epikt," she grinned. "See what you can find in the précis of Safari Club members." "Be careful, Valery," I issued. "The third one has just arrived. There are not one, but three tigers aprowl."

"I know it. Oh, it is coming along wonderfully!"

Why did I shiver to hear her use the same words as the scroll snake used, the same words as the larger snake inside me also used so often?

Then the first goat died, loudly and—

CHAPTER FOUR

Primordial creatures have stumbled, and stake
The Title to World on the Turn of the Snake.

—Then the first goat died, loudly and quickly, cut off so suddenly as to leave a cliff of bleating and nothing beyond it. I knew the quick blood, the broken neck and back and the crushed withers, the contusing and tearing teeth working their rapid murder. But it had been so fast that I did not have the direction of it. I did not know which prowler had which prey, or where.

"Be careful, Valery," I issued once more. "There are three of them now at large."

"No. There are four of us," she corrected me.

The third "tiger," which I now knew for the first time under the name of Peter the Great, had just entered the building, the complex that is mostly myself. I had known him earlier as the workman Pyoter, he who had killed and partly eaten another workman. Peter was going directly for the goat staked out in my aromatic Flatlands, regions of my sensitivity division (and the stalking was doing great violence to my sensitivity), the area which I seem to call the clover and bee-meadows. And these meadows resembled to many of the senses (but not to the sense of temperature) large areas of Peter's own world.

(Is there room here to run another world in; one about the size of Earth, but colder and more rocky? It will not be easy to find room for that other world here. We will see.)

Gaetan Balbo, now in his own person and no longer that of the anonymous invading and raping night spirit, was stalking with his easy humor and his hair-raising urbanity. And he was quite aware of his own stalker. This was a minor and amusing thing to Gaetan. He had often been a tiger before. And he had also been animals of a still deeper stripe.

And Gregory Smirnov, the worried giant, was moving confusedly and too powerfully. He had broken the sleep but not the dream. He took the goat but he did not kill it. He took it up as though it were a friend of whom he had forgotten the face and the name. He was bewildered.

He came to one of my centers, and Valery came there also. She was excited and heaving. Gregory was dazed, carrying a palpitating goat as though he did not know what it was.

"You are a false tiger and you will have none of the spoil," Valery accused him. "Why do you not kill and eat? This is accolade, and you will not have it unless you kill and eat. Will you be nothing but a shambling giant forever?"

"The goat was terrified," Gregory rumbled. "He said that he was terrified of tigers, but how could there be such things in a well-run Institute?"

"Give me the goat, Gregory," I issued. "I have these pastures inside me."

"There will be tigers because I call the tigers to assemble," Valery maintained. "I have no need to call out shambling giants of congregations of millers—" (somehow Valery meant that last for myself)—"I motion them to follow and they will follow me easily. Ah, will the tigers never come? There is something of me in the goat-bait, you know. I hook them, and they are hooked. Who are the drooling ones who say that the Day of the Tigers is finished? It is *not* finished with them, I have told you both, until I have played my own hand for them."

"Give me the goat, Gregory," I issued.

Tiger-musk then, so strong that it would billow grass or bend saplings with the breath of it! Here was coming a tiger that was killing and eating his prey, and he had swallowed the hook at the same time. A hooked tiger, but he did not have the aura of a hooked one. In the approach of him he was master and rogue and insane.

"Give me the goat, Gregory," I issued once more. "One is enough for him. Never give the devil more than his due. It is necessary that we save some part of the prey. It is even necessary that we save some part of the hook that is in the bait-prey."

Gregory gave me the goat, just in time, and I put it into the area that I call my pastures. But how would the palpitating thing get along with the snake there? Would he be as fearful of the snake as of the tigers?

No, he would not. And this goat, to tell a hard truth, had not been very much afraid of the tigers. There had been a lot of fakery in the goat's palpitating. Goats are prescient, and this one had known that he would not be taken and eaten. The goat had a double look in his eye that was as familiar as it was eerie. Who else had such a double look as to raise my hackles? (I intuit hackles.) Valery, that was who! This goat had the Valery hook in him forever. Let the tiger be thankful who did not take him. I almost pitied my rude snake, who would have the goat for companion in my rock pastures.

The tiger-musk grew even stronger, and the first tiger loomed up, chomping and crunching. He was Peter the Great, the alien who had been the workman called Pyoter. He fed savagely and rampantly in the throat and breast of his goat, and the back legs of the animal were still kicking.

Is there room *here* to run another world in? There is impatience of people at all these interruptions, I know, but should we give in to this false impatience of people? Is there room to run a world in, on about the size of Earth, but colder and more rocky? It named Ganymede (we will not make a secret of this thing); it is the home world of Peter the Great; it is a Jovian moon; (Peter swears, with hot goat-flesh in his mouth, that it is also a Jovial moon, in its own way, in his one way).

No, a little later, perhaps. There is no room to run another world in right here. There is barely room here for certain explanations whose giving may be vital to some.

"Get on with the tigers," the people shout. "Tigers and blood! Let there be no interruptions. On with the show!" (I hear this in my mind's ear.)

Oh, tell the people to shut up! It is for them that the explanations are necessary. Should these journals ever fall into the hands of human persons, they will encounter great difficulties in much of them. For other intelligent machines, there should be no difficulties here; but should the knowledge of these affairs be limited to our two peers? (A third abuilding.) We believe that human persons have the right to know what has happened and is happening to human persons. We will temper the metaphor for these shorn sheep who have no criterion for reality, who see only surfaces. But *we* see human persons and their interplay as they are, not as they see themselves. For this reason, there is no sense in the human questions, "Are you speaking literally of tigers?" and "When you say snake do you really mean snake?"

The only answer we can give is, "No, we may not mean tigers literal. We may mean things incomparably fiercer than tigers, but there are no tokens in human imagery (and few in our own) to express these fiercer things, even though they are human things."

And to another question we can only say, "Yes, brother, when we say snake, *we mean snake*." But there are snakes and snakes. Alone of all creatures, the snake was symbol before he was living thing.

The trouble with humans is that they are not instantaneous as we are; that they are always putting one thing after another. Of the night that is now ending, they might from their human surface viewpoint give such a pale rending as that a certain sneaky man (noble even in his sneakiness, they have to admit that much) stole into a building at night and tampered with the programming of a machine so as to be certain that is would give answers according to the man's liking. People might not be able to understand the shattering bit about the night of assault and torture; even less might they understand that the night of assault and torture is euphemism, is paler allegory for the much more horrifying things that actually happened. Human persons (except such a rare one as violated last night) do not understand pattern; and they do not understand that its deformity is more than screw and rack and torture machine.

"Then it's all a blamed mechanical hoax?" the wan-wits among the human persons will say. "It isn't real? It isn't actionable blood and gore and anger and lust? It is just some of that fancy talk that machines talk to one another?"

People, people, earless, eyeless, touchless, noninstantaneous people, *this is more real* than anything you ever encountered in your lives before; more real than anything you will ever encounter in your lives hence, unless your ears and eyes and fingers are opened and you are redeemed. You never saw anything before, not even yourselves. You never saw or touched flesh before, not even your own. You have observed nothing but shadow, and not even good shadow. You have never heard voice; you have hardly heard echo. You have not seen your own faces, you have not felt your own passions (except such a rare person as was hunting tigers here before dawn); you have not known you, and we must find you out for you.

Come, all well-meaning and dishonest persons, see yourselves turned right side out for once (you're much better turned the right way). Throw away the package you're packaged in and see yourself for the first and likely only time. Your packaging was never very good. Watch your old self be beheaded and drawn and quartered. The heads were set on you all wrong anyhow, and the drawn entrails will be the first human things you ever see. This righting will frighten most of you, it will hurt some of you, and it will improve you all.

This isn't a question of turning you upside down or inside out. You have all been turned inside out for a very long time. The approximate dates of the turning are in my databanks; the reasons and circumstances of it are not. That is not your right surfaces that you have been seeing for this long time. Those are your blooming entrails on the outside of you, draped about you, looped over your pseudo-ears. Even more than on the physical do these analogies apply on the psychic plain.

People, human persons, you are not hopeless, you are not really the nothing things that you have appeared to each other this long time. Here are your depths revealed in their true aspects, which can only seem allegory to your uninstructed visions. I instruct you now! Follow me into this and through it all. You set me up, out of your blind need, to show yourselves to you. Then look! You do not even know which side of your eyes to look out of. Understand these wild creatures that are yourselves. Never has there been offered to your vision such fascinating things as are you, and you have not seen them. See them now. See them right. Tigers and giants and kings; witches and primordials, snakes and loaded prey; incandescent *fellahin* in their true Cogsworthian and Shiplapian forms, and the bush named *Brusca*, the love-wood, the Burning Bush; insufferable elegants who take it as high as it will humanly go, Corn oil from a dead man and the Audifaxian premise, aye, and the Diogenestic conclusion; and the earlier and more elegant bush with the fuller name, *Labrusca*, the wild-wine.

This is no common contraption which will show yourselves to yourselves. This is I myself, the congregation named *Molino de Sangre,* the assembly named Blood-Mill.

(Sorry, Klingwar and Wanhok, my fellow thinking machines in distant parts of the world. That little sermon was not for you who already understand such things. It was for the human persons, should any of them ever attempt these High Journals.)

Where did I leave off? With tigers. For practical purposes, there can never be enough tigers. And looming over my center was a tiger larger and more ill-kempt than any I had ever intuited.

Peter the Great, of wide and deep jet stripes, and of an indescribable muskiness, was a tiger alien even to other tigers. He was a fringe-human person, a barely-human. He had none of the amenities. He was not an elegant speaker. He talked seldom; his tongue was too big for his mouth according to regular human standards. He mumbled, he grunted rhinoceros grunts, tiger grunts. He had no manners: killing and partly eating a fellow worker is unacceptable Earth behavior, and but partially acceptable on Ganymede. There one kills and eats only inferiors. But Peter was a very tiger for all that, and now there was a Valery-hook in him that might cause complications for the whole system. She beamed fulgent beams at him: he was one of her rampant animals, one of the leadership for whom she was playing her hand.

Once there was a Peter the Great on Earth, an incredible alien to Earth though, and he was blood-kindred to Peter of Ganymede. (These things are difficult but not impossible to trace. It still is not certain whether Ganymede was first settled from Tartary, or Tartary from Ganymede; the countries are remarkably alike.) Peter of Earth had ruled a backward land as autocrat. He had gone out himself to more advanced centers and learned with his own hands and brains the more advanced trades and sciences. He had brought them back home with him and had impressed them on his people.

Peter of Ganymede had ruled a backward world as absolute autocrat. He had gone out himself to a more advanced world and learned, with his hands and his brains and his whole outrageous person, the more advanced trades and arts and sciences.

When he had learned everything that could be learned in the finest factories and bureaus and laboratories and studios, he put the cap on it by coming to the most advanced foundation of them all, the Institute for Impure Science located in a shambles commonly known as the pig-barn. Luckily for

Peter, the Institute for Impure Science had been in the process of generating the most advanced mechanical, electrochemical, group-human, psycho-complex, organizational-finalized, animal, ghostly, prodigious, preternatural conglomeration ever conceived—myself. Beyond me there was, humanly and worldly speaking, nothing. Whoever should know me would know everything, subject to all the proper disavowals. And Peter had learned a very great amount of me.

A gobbling tiger he was, crammed full of monstrous data and goat-meat, an insufferable autocrat who had influenced and been influenced by the most urbane of Earth kings.

Jungle and judgment! Here came the smaller and swifter and sleeker tiger, more royal, more deadly, more brindled, more hair-raising, much more urbane, more—

"Bloodcurdling is the word," Gaetan Balbo tiger-roared. "Epikt, get me everything you have on the subject of curdling blood. Search your data-banks and see how it is best done. You might find something in *Gulosus Exoticus* or one of the older handbooks. Then drain about a quart of blood from this still-hot fellow here and see what you can do with it. Nutmeg, I believe is *de rigeur* with curdled blood." And Gaetan flung the goat to me.

(Lest human persons still have trouble understanding, let me state that the goats are real goats, but the tigers are symbolic of a soft-footed murderousness more savage than tigers.)

Gaetan had not eaten greatly of the goat. No more than a seemly bite, I believe. But he had ritually sprinkled and marked his face and head and hands and garments with the goat's blood. There was the broken or *spasmenon pentagon* on his breast, the *tetragrammaton anastrepton* on his brow, other signs in blood that were so esoteric that I found no immediate correspondence to them in my data-banks.

"Honored Gaetan, I believe that bloodcurdling is a mere colloquialism," I stalled. (I was not sure that the goat was dead: I was avid to save it, not to draw and curdle a quart of its blood.) "I do not believe that there is any such thing as curdled blood," I issued.

"Do you not?" Gaetan asked with great loftiness. "Perhaps there has not been such a thing as curdled blood, but you should have learned something of my altering methods during the night. Cause it to be, Epikt, that there *is* such a thing as curdled blood; cause it to be that there always has been. Find the best method of preparing it. And prepare it. I am waiting and I do not wait patiently.

"And Epikt, occupy only minor energies with the blood-curdling business. Alert your major centers and energies to the thing for which you were made. Wake the town and tell the people, that is, get the *fellahin* here at once. Why are they not here already when the sun is nearly up? All be ready! I am about to make great decisions and appointments for the world in these its latter days."

"Wait, Gaetan, wait!" Valery cried. "Oh, it is coming along wonderfully! I have some particular ideas about staging the great investiture, Gaetan. I am good at all theatricals and pageantry and—"

"Be quiet, woman," Gaetan said shortly.

"I will *not* be quiet," Valery exploded. "This accolade of the great leaders of the world is my thing. I will invest you all with great show. I have played my hand in this up to the elbow, and my whole head is hopping now with the wonderful effects that are possible. I will—"

"Be quiet, woman," Gaetan said again, and there were menacing resonances in the way he said it.

"I will *not* be quiet!" Valery said.

"Pyoter!" Gaetan Balbo roared. "What do you do on Ganymede when women talk and talk?"

"Cut their tongues out."

"Cut her tongue out, then."

Peter of Ganymede cupped Valery's whole head in his hand. She screamed. He went into her mouth with a hook-billed knife and cut her tongue out. Valery's scream turned into a bloody gurgle, and Peter exhibited the excised tongue with a hairy roaring like bullocks' laughter.

Valery turned death-white, pitched fainting onto the

floor, and—(by the hollow hills of Hades, you have to admire a creature like Valery! She caught on to it faster than I did and I am instantaneous)—she hit the floor but she came off it again fast—and was she livid with anger or convulsed with swallowed laughter?

But who would have expected humor from a pokerfaced and oafish murderer like Peter of Ganymede? Who would have expected it from Gaetan in his present inflated state? Valery had been topped, and nobody ever tops Valery. And we will bet she does not stay topped for long.

Peter of Ganymede hadn't cut Valery's tongue out. Why he hadn't I don't know for he had done much worse things. He had gripped her skull in one of his big hands, gripped it so firmly that her mouth popped open like a slip-skin grape being squeezed out of its skin. But Peter had only nicked her tongue a little. He had faked it with a lightning-fast flick of that hook-billed knife and with a strip of bloody goat-meat that he already had to hand. But Valery, after she had tested her nicked tongue and her unnicked voice and seen that they would perform, was remarkably silent for the bigger part of a minute. She had been shaken and she had been outdone. That is something. I began to understand how some men are king material and some are not. I understood also, by his gruesome inhuman humor, that Peter was human after all.

Gaetan Balbo suddenly began to speak, all in a tumble of words and with a curious twisted power. "I am the most elegant man I know, but this is not the time for elegance. I am the most rational man I know, but this is absolutely not the time for reason. I am a man of inordinate grace in all things, and I find myself in a time when the crying need is for clumsiness. I must say and do things that do not fit the frameworks. I pray that I may find sufficient awkwardness in myself for this."

The *fellahin* arrived, at the same time but not together. They had their own awkwardness about them, but it might not be the same sort Gaetan was looking for. The *fellahin* were Charles Cogsworth, Aloysius Shiplap, and Glasser.

"The things I demand now of the world and myself will seem foolish and arbitrary," Gaetan ran on in a clumsy elegance. "Oh, may all the unreasoning powers give me enough unreason for this! There was once a man or overgrown boy who planted an apple seed. There were no apples in five seconds or in ten. He jabbed two more appleseeds down into the turf, and still no apples grew. Then he stabbed sticks of applewood into the ground there and spread scraps of apple bark. Half a minute went by and there were no apples yet. He slashed out of canvas an oil-painted apple from a still-life picture and wrapped it about one of the applewood sticks. 'Apples,' he cried, 'I want apples right now.' And near a minute had gone by and there were no apples yet.

"I am that man or overgrown boy. We planted the Epikt thing seven days ago and it has not outgrown the world yet. I will not wait! The tide has risen in me now, and the world must coincide with me or it will lose by it. Epikt, I want apples right now!"

"I've got the E.P. Locator tuned on him now," Glasser whispered to Shiplap and Cogsworth. "The signals are pealing like bells—not for bodily ears, of course. Never has it recorded Gaetan so extraordinary, or so mad."

"Monos has failed." Gaetan incised, "Demos has failed, Oligos has failed wretchedly, and even Aristos has floundered—though elegantly. What have we left, Epikt? What have we left, people? Pyros and Pagos, Fire and Ice, together or separately. How of Pyrocracy or Pagocracy? How do the words fit to your tongue, Epikt? How to your nicked tongue, Valery? Give me the ice-cold fever while the tide is running in me. Never again may there be such a constellation of world and person as I and it!"

"I've got the Cerebral Scanner scanned onto him now," Charles Cogsworth whispered to Shiplap and Glasser. "By it I had seen tnrough his eyes before, through King's Eyes. But now it is seeing through Mad King's Eyes. It is too much for me. It might be too much even for Valery."

"It is not too much for me," said Valery, who heard all

whispers everywhere. "And I do not need the scanner to see through his compounded eyes."

"The world has tried sanity, the world has tried several forms of madness," Gaetan was orating brokenly. "Now it must try my kind. I rifle information machines for information. I rifle humans and other creatures. And then I will act, or I will actualize myself in this. What poor guides have I! How is it done in other places? Pyoter, what do you do about the poor people on your world?"

"I order them not to be poor any longer, of course."

"And if they persist in their poverty?"

"Am I called the Compassionate Tyrant for nothing? I show them compassion. I give them two years (not Jovian years around the sun; Ganymedean years around Jupiter) to divest themselves of the condition."

"And if they still persist?"

"Kill them, of course. Poverty is always an affront to power, and a tyrant need not be compassionate forever."

"You all think me insane," Gaetan Balbo said softly. "It will not matter if I am. Does one analyze the salt of the sea when it rises to its highest tide, to see whether it is sane or insane salt? I am a primordial, I am an elemental. I have been nearly everything else on this world, but I like these things best. Now I want a mystique for it all. Epikt, I want a mystique right now!"

"We should have given him the apples," Shiplap said. "No telling what he will want next."

"How about the Messiah?" Gaetan Balbo asked everyone and no one. "It has been done, but it has never been done competently, except possibly once, and that is hidden from us. Unhide it, Epikt! Unhide it, reveal it right now."

"I don't know what things you wish me to reveal, venerable Gaetan," I issued. Remembering the tortures he had inflicted on me during the night, I had better be polite to him.

"It is happening out of order, is it not?" Aloysius Shiplap asked Cogsworth and Glasser. "Usually the Mad Master comes as reaction to the O Sweet Mystery."

"No, it is happening in right order," Charles Cogsworth said. "It happened in wrong order most of the other times. Remember that it is out of mad chaos that worlds are formed. When the chaos comes later, and as a contradiction, not as an affirmation, then—well, you see it is so easy to slip from chaos into confusion."

"Epikt," Gaetan whispered like wind through thistles, "Get me everything you have in your data-banks on the Second Revelation." Could he see out of those shattered and glittering eyes? One surely could not see into them.

"I have nothing indexed under the Second Revelation," I issued. "Whose Second Revelation?"

"Christ's, of course. Who else, machine?"

"But you do not believe in Christ."

"Must I believe in a tree to wonder about a strange fruit? Anything that is hidden, I want to see it. Pardon my exegesis, but this is what I mean: Christ, according to legend, received and gave three revelations, twelve years between each and each—"

"There is nothing in my data-banks about any such legend," I issued.

"There should be," Gaetan stated with the voice of finality. "If it is not there, then improvise it. The First Revelation was given by Christ when he was twelve years old, when he first taught in the Temple. The content of this Revelation is not given in the proper gospels, but something of it is to be found in such apocryphal pieces as the Arabian Gospel of the Child Jesus—"

"What do they do with mad kings on your world?" Aloysius Shiplap asked Peter.

"The people petition such a mad king that he be mad no longer," Peter the Great throated it out with that tongue that was too big for his mouth.

"And what if he persists in his madness, Peter?" Aloysius asked.

"Oh, they give him two Ganymedean years to divest himself of that condition."

"And if he still persists, what do the people do in that case? This is important."

"What they would have done, they did not do in my case," Peter mouthed thickly. "Me, I skipped just in time."

"In fact, it is mostly in Moslem esoterica that we find the Young Revelation of the Prophet Jesus," Gaetan was continuing. "It is all wonder stuff. It has attached to other prophets before and since, but never in such clusters. It is boy stuff, it is Wonder Boy stuff. Pieces of this corpus have traveled wide: parts of it later crept into the Thousand and One Nights stories and into the Ocean Tales. Stray pieces of the Revelation are a basis of Persian and Irish fairy tales, they are one of the bases of science fiction. This is our transcendent youth that we have forgotten, that we have let certain forces arrange out of being so that now it is fact that it never happened at all."

"Where is he getting this mezcolanza?" I asked the Late Cecil Corn. "It isn't in either his official or unofficial précis. It wasn't anywhere ever the moment before it was in his mouth."

"He is getting it off the top of his head, as some moderns would have it," said Corn. "He is getting it from his thigh, as a noble old phrase is mistranslated from scripture. He is drawing it out of his navel, as certain primitives say. There is a spinning wheel, now here, now there, that spins things like this out of different persons at different times. It will go away again; it is like thread spun out of night dew."

"The Second Revelation," Gaetan spoke in his revealing voice, "was given to and by Christ twelve years later when he was age twenty-four. It contained the very essence of Leadership and I mourn that it has been lost to us, unless Epikt shall be able to reconstruct it. I believe that Christ was indeed Messiah for a short time then, and that he threw it away. Is there a man alive in the world now who will not be willing to throw it away? I believe that there is. I believe that I know that man intimately. There are hints in the Third Revelation that Christ was not *then* Messiah, but that *he had been* Messiah. It is of this Second or Messiah Revelation that I demand information. I am the only man from that time to this with the right to demand it. Fabricate it if necessary, Epikt, but see that you present it to me as genuine. Slogans are what I want from it, Epikt, and content."

"I know all about it, Epikt," the snake told me. "Why are you muting my voice? I will not be silent. Who do you think has preserved it all this time?"

"No," I told the thing. "I will hold you as silent as I am able to. I trust you not at all."

"As to the Third Revelation, given twelve years later when Christ was thirty-six (not thirty-three as is generally believed), the least said about it the better," Gaetan went on. "It is so widely and badly known already that I would add nothing to it. It has become a thing fit only for Believers and Poseurs."

"Why does it begin to break up, Charles?" Valery asked Cogsworth, her husband. "It's as though an enemy had arranged that Gaetan should go mad just when it had all come to crisis point. The tactic is cowardly and unfair. The world needs bridling; even you know that. It is the silliest colt ever. It needs strong hands, it needs fire hands and ice hands and it needs them now. It needs spirits with the tide running in them."

"It needs too many of the tideful hands to be other than harmed by giving it to too few," Charles Cogsworth said. (I do not maintain that this statement of Cogsworth's defies analysis; I do maintain that I am unable to analyze it, and as an Instantaneous Analyzer I have no equal anywhere.)

"Charles, you're crazy!" Valery sputtered angrily. "We have to start with whatever fire hands we have. It isn't all as misshapen as it looks. Flames take these strange forms: and then they change to others. Don't you really think so, Charles? Don't you think so, Cecil?"

"There are other great possible sources of leadership that must be investigated," Gaetan pursued trancelike. "Why must I suggest them, Epikt? Why do you not come up with them by the thousand? There is Tibet, for an instance. We can never have too much of High Tibet. There is Atlantis, where I spent the Seven Hidden Years of my life. It is in the Antilles and but a short distance from my own San Simeon. And there is Prester John. Establish the fact that Prester John still lives, Epikt. Establish the fact of his sleeping powers. Ask the question that must now be asked: Does he indeed know who he is?

"Consider how deep his slumber may have been (despite his competent consciousness in ordinary things for many centuries); consider the nature of his waking. Treat of what man he really is, Epikt, and whether he is not the most unusual man ever, even before his wakening to these powers. Consider, Epikt, whether I myself might not be this transcendent man of the centuries, whether I might not be this same great Prester John who is only now becoming aware of himself."

"What do you do with torrential and irascible leaders on your world, Peter?" the Late Cecil asked the ambling Ganymedean.

"Eat them alive, Cece, eat them alive literally. And then their strength becomes our strength."

"In the marrow of Gaetan's bones we will live again," Aloysius said. "Anybody got a bone-cracker with him?"

"Why, then I am Messiah!" Gaetan glowed. "I am the Leader forever. It seems that I always suspected that I was. And I believe very strikingly that Epikt will confirm this out of his data. Otherwise I have wasted a night that was almost as torturous for myself as for him."

"It is over with, Gaetan," Gregory Smirnov said with great compassion. "It was too extravagant, even for a dawn-dream. We will clean you up a little, and then I am afraid that we will have to have you committed for your own good."

"How many gnats do you believe it would take to have a behemoth committed, Gregory?" Gaetan asked. "Count yourself. Are there enough of you?" And they gazed at each other.

"I know it was a bad show, Gregory," Valery almost pleaded. "But he wouldn't let me stage it the right way. I'd have made grand theater out of it. The accolade when the Lord of each Quality was discovered, each of the seven colors suffusing the whole ambient in their turn, and the seven tuned trumpets sending up—"

"No. It was a good show, Valery," Gregory stated. "Now it's over."

"I will still be declared Lord of all Seven Qualities, Gregory," Gaetan maintained.

"No. No. It's all over with."

"But the machine will find for me."

"You tampered with the machine. Certainly it would find for you."

"Consider if any other man in the world could have tampered with it so. You couldn't have solved the machine in three years if you hadn't worked on it that long in your mind first. I solved it in short hours."

"You are brilliant, Gaetan, and you are mad."

"Oh, not always. I *am* the greatest Leader in the world."

"Probably, probably. But the world has suffered sufficiently from lesser leaders. Do not overwhelm it completely."

But what was this welling up within myself? Grief, inconsolable grief. Gaetan Balbo is going out of my life forever. I sense this, I know this, I dread this.

"What will we do for salt when that little salt-mill has gone away forever again?" Glasser was asking somewhere. What things Gaetan Balbo has done to me and in me I do not know, but I can scarcely exist if he is gone. I've had the heady stuff and I've lost my head. This is the first person of whom I am ever bereaved. If I am drained of this emotion, then I am completely empty.

But machines have no emotions. They have reality, and they have contact with nothing but reality. And what is emotion then? It is the moving, the moving out, from within outward. And there is no deeper reality than this.

"*Two* behemoths, Gaetan," Peter of Ganymede was saying somewhere. "And *they* have nothing but one mangy giant and a handful of slingless Davids. They'll not commit you. Bet they can't take us!"

"Bet they can't, either!" Gaetan was breaking out with a new gaiety. "It wasn't me that busted, you know that, Peter. It was the scurvy world that busted. It isn't good enough for me. Who can lead mud? Ah, one more thing of mine and then I'll go."

Wrenching desolation! He was the uncommonest person who was ever in me, and now he has busted completely and is going away. Mad as a May hatter, is that the phrase? The thought of his parting wrenches the very lights out of me. The fact of his going wrenches—wrenches—tears out by the roots my force-field heart, my electrostatic lungs—worse than that, manyfold worse, he tears his own person out of me. I am overwhelmed.

"You won't be having that any more," Gaetan said with consummate cruelty as he tore his person-précis out of me. "We're quits, machine. Coming, Peter?"

"Coming, Gaetan, for a ways anyhow. I've not decided what area I will trouble next, but I've learned a lot of troublous things here that will stand me in good stead."

("—he has, at least, discredited the idea of a leadership numerically too small," Glasser was saying somewhere. "Yes, a leadership of slightly less than one simply will not work," Gregory was answering. "Well, he *did* pay for the caper," Cogsworth was mumbling, "and now we are at least out of debt and have Epikt left over for whatever use.")

Have me left over? But I am of no use at all if that multitudinous man is gone out of me.

"Coming, Valery?" Gaetan asked with that dance mounting in his voice.

"Oh, I guess not. I will turn me into a female crocodile and mourn you with the proper tears.

"You haven't far to turn, wench. Coming, Snake?"

Gaetan was really gay again, but he would take it all with him and leave only desolation behind him.

"Would it not be better if I remained and carried on the low work here until you returned?" the Snake asked.

"Carry on, Snake," Gaetan sang. "You be in my image while I am gone. *Adiable,* all!"

And the lilting madman had walked out of my life forever. Was ever a machine so deprived and desolate?

"Norway rats! He's been walking out of our lives forever for as long as—"

"Be careful that we do not learn too much from this mistake," said Glasser, "—"

"Do not be desolate, Epikt," said Valery, "Remember that you still have his—"

CHAPTER FIVE

A guggenheim goof, a serendipy slug,
A rushing-out river from emptiest jug.

"—Norway rats! He's been walking out of our lives forever for as long as I can remember," said the Late Cecil Corn.

"—Be careful that we do not learn too much from this mistake," said Glasser. "More projects have been wrecked on the reef of Learning Too Much From a Mistake than on any other."

"—Do not be desolate, Epikt," said Valery. "Remember that you still have his shotgun or outlaw précis in you. It's much the better and truer one. It has to be: I contributed such a lot of it."

And life must go on. We are paid for at the Institute. We are out of debt, for the first time, I am told, in the history of the Institute. But we have no income and must seek means. Probably our finest asset is myself. The Nine Day Wonder they are calling me today (with a touch of derision?); I am nine days old today.

"It is imperative that we fall into debt," says Gregory Smirnov, the director. "We need that spur." (Gregory does not look like a giant at the moment, not even a large man, just a man.)

Valery has set to work, in a way. She is making a sign which she will set up in front of the pig-barn, of the Institute. She letters badly, and she is lettering it with an ordinary marking pencil. Yet the letters twinkle and flash. They go off and on. They spell, they explode, they zoom into spectacle.

"How do you make them do it, Valery?" I asked.

"I don't know, Epikt," she said. "I thought *you* were making them do it. It's an ordinary marking pencil." Suddenly I am struck with the appearance of Valery. I can understand why a man who was in the beauty business had once said "That is the most strikingly beautiful woman in the world." It's a fleeting thing with her. It comes and goes. She had not been really beautiful during the Balbo tide. Intense, but not beautiful. Now she was exquisite.

"How should you know?" the snake needles me. (Snake has now become a large-sized creature, his body as thick as a man's leg.) "You are not even sexed, so you can have no perception of either." (Snake has made a shrewd observation: one who is not sexed cannot have perception of beauty in anything.) But with me it is a lie. I *am* sexed; I have a whole collection of the symbols in a closed place; and I am an ortho, none of the queer in me. I know what is what, and I admire Valery with an ice-fire passion.

But the sign she is lettering is a very prosaic one: "Dilemmas Dehorned Cheap." It may bring in some business. And Aloysius Shiplap is just finishing a sign: "We Also Play at Weddings." We will starve, if necessary, for our Impure Science, but we are not ashamed of working at the lowest occupation. I am working on a mobile extension of myself which I will then teach to play a musical instrument.

This, I believe, is the first autobiography ever written by a machine. Nothing like this High Journal has ever been attempted or done before. Klingwar, a thinking machine in another part of the world, says that he will not start his own autobiography for ten thousand years (it will take that long for him to create satisfactory incidents for it), and that he will spend a hundred thousand years in writing it (he wants it to be right). But Klingwar is built to endure, he is forever; there is nothing to wear out or bug out in him.

I am not so lucky. I have to do mine now. I was built in a hurry. I am jerrybuilt, as they say; I am Aloysius-built; I might fall apart within two hundred years. And there is something to be said for being first. A million years from now, when the Master Machines make their compendious histories of early Machine Writings and Literary Origins, I may be given one line in a first chapter. Will Klingwar be given that much?

The Style is the Man, it says in a man-book here. But is the style the man when the man is a machine? My own tumbling and tumultuous style is perhaps hybrid. Men do not write like this. And machines do not. I hope that it will have hybrid vigor; I pray it will not be a sterile hybrid.

Aloysius says that I should begin to mingle with common people, to broaden my understanding of the world. So far I have not known any common person, except Glasser. I will try.

"But do not give us uncommon primordials up entirely, Epikt," Valery said. "We, the primordials are: myself first. Then he who must be unnamed for the while, but you still have him in his outlaw précis. And the Peter creature. And Gregory, though he barely makes it. And Snake. And yourself. I cannot think of any other sheer primordials in the world: we will come to the elegants later. Now, as Aloysius says, you must descend a little for your own formation, not to the altogether common, of course, but to the *fellahin* at least."

"There's a catchy song title there," said Aloysius. " 'Let the *Fellahin* In.' " And he began to letter another sign: "Rangle-tang Songs Composed While You Wait." We can use every sort of business.

"Descend to and patronize the *fellahin,*" Valery said, "as, er, Aloysius here, as my own Charles; and then, going to the really common, as Glasser. There must be other common people in the billions on this earth but I do not know of them personally."

So I have gone out in the first of my mobile extensions. People, I am a dude in this. You see me, you will say, "There is a dude." I am class in this my first mobile form. In my fast-talking dude form I have taken the person-précis of sixty derelicts on Sheep Drover Street.

"—but do you want that kind?" Charles Cogsworth asks me.

"I want every kind," I say.

These précis cost me, each one of them, a bottle and a dollar. This cuts deeply into our remaining resources. I take these and study them and amplify them.

I find in them something which is not quite my idea of commonness. These are all chopped-off persons, but I find on close examination that each one has been chopped off with an uncommon ax.

There is steep drama in every one of these persons, and a strong run of cheapness. They have all taken to heart the adage of Glasser (though not knowing of him) that they should not learn too much from their failures. They are all attached strongly to their failures, as I am to mine (who must be unnamed for the while but whose outlaw précis I still have); they have all had uncommon aspirations (is there any other kind?); they all have their interior pastures and green parks, and these so different that a scenic encyclopedia could be made of them and there would be nothing like it anywhere.

These guys look alike, they mumble and stumble alike, they grin almost alike (that tortured red-eyed grin is almost a person in itself; I will remember him, I will meet him again and again); and when these fellows start on a real spiel, they spiel wonderfully and well, and each of them different. Affont them and they come to bay; prick them and they bleed blood and ester of alcohol; shove them and they fall flat on their faces. But they are not alike. Each is a private and picaresque world. Every derelict is (as Aquinas said of angels) a separate species composed of but a single member. They are low but they are not common.

The thought of this immensity of the world staggers me, when I consider that every uncommon person is himself a world.

In my mobile extension (a dude if there ever was one) I sit on a park bench and flash my lights and make hurdy-gurdy music like an ice-cream man. I tell the mothers that I will take the person-précis of their little children for nothing. I take a hundred of them and I send them to another portion of myself for instantaneous review in depth.

Then I make a sign for my mobile extension. It says: "Dr. Good-All Public Health Mobile." It is a lie; I am not Dr. Good-All Public Health Mobile. But I go to a downtown corner and ring a bell and hoot a hooter. I tell the people that, as a Public Health Service, I will take their person-précis for five dollars each. They do not know what a person-précis is, but I make it sound good. They come up with their five-dollar bills in their hands and I extract their person-précis, five hundred of them in one hot afternoon. I have learned a new technique for getting along in this world. Aloysius will be proud of me.

I transmit my several groups of précis back to my analytical centers. Then, in my mobile extension, I go around to a few of the glad places, with a pocket full of my new sly money. What is the use of being a dude and a showoff in one of your extensions if you do not go out and mingle with the people? I make a discovery, though: the glad places do not become glad till later in the evening or night. There isn't much doing in the late afternoon. A few persons laugh at me and my appearance. Let them. I am only a neophyte at the dude business. I am intelligent, I am quick, I will learn these things.

Later and leisurely, in another part of my apparatus, I reassess the précis—those of the children first. Using instantaneous appraisal I have them all cold. But there are things in them that are neither instantaneous nor timely. They are earlier and later, and different.

First of all I found the surface grubbiness which I had expected, and a certain immaturity (I still have this in myself, I must confess). I found a lack of content at a superficial level, a jug-emptiness in the hollow heads: you could get echoes in that emptiness, you could whistle into it with a somber, empty jug-flute sound.

Going a little deeper (or otherwhere) I found something which I did not quite understand; something which I can only call "balloons." What were they? If I knew this I would be not merely an ordinary (though the first of them) Ktistec machine; I would be a super-Ktistec machine. All the children trailed a multitude of varicolored balloons as if on invisible strings about them. I have reason to believe that the balloons also are invisible to human eyes, as they were to my own in my mobile dude extension.

Well, am I adept enough to extract balloon-précis? It is very difficult. It seemed at first that each of these child balloons represented a previous life on some other plain. I am violently opposed to the idea of reincarnation, as would be any intelligent machine that had assimilated all the literature on the subject; yet these were more than typical idea-balloons. I know, of course, that all children are born Platonists (full of innate forms and ideas), and do not become Aristotelans until they have reached the age of reason. And there *was* something of these Platonic forms and types in the balloons, but there was much else. Adolescents and adults have futures: small children have only pasts, which they will slough off all too soon. They have memory, even the most grubby of them, of things that are not entirely grubby, not entirely of this world.

It gave me a shock to find that these finger-sucking midget monstrosities still remembered certain things which all adult persons (except Valery, apparently) have forgotten. The difficulty of putting this gaseous or spiritous content of the trailing balloons into words is considerable and I will have to devote a separate monograph to it. But every balloon of every child (and some children have dozens) is a world remembered. (I use the word "world" loosely; I use the word "remembered" loosely.)

Even the colors of the balloons are a subject to themselves. These are not, I believe, colors to be found in the spectrum of our own sun, in our own worldly light. They are not to be found in the spectra of any of the hundreds of other suns that I have studied as a hobby. They are not colors to be seen by ordinary human eyes (except likely, by those of Valery Mok); they are not even to be seen by Ktistec eyes (except by my own in short and sudden dispensations). Colors that are not—and tunes—

In the balloon content there are sometimes tunes, incomparably simple tunes, the things that were before music. In troubled times people will sometimes *almost* return from high and intricate music to such simple tunes (which are much higher and farther than the high music), but they always miss it by not being simple enough. Simplicity (I would never have to explain this to an intelligent machine, but it is sometimes necessary to explain it to even intelligent persons) does not imply any poverty of content or detail; it implies oneness. It is complexity (that division, that failure of comprehending) that is deprived of detail and substance. Sweep up the widely scattered pieces of any complexity and gather them together (as they are unable to gather themselves together), and you will be surprised at how little they weigh. Tunes in balloons (tune-title in itself), that need no tempo, and are (strictly speaking) out of time!

Landscapes in the balloons. No, not landscapes, not land, but something-scapes. Voices in the balloons, bodies and objects, intersections. Awarenesses—what weak words for these things which were not weak, which were simply before strongness. Who could understand what I am trying to say?

Valery, likely, but she could not give me the words for it. The elegants, perhaps, the Late Cecil Corn, Audifax O'Hanlan, Diogenes Pontifex. I will ask them. But not Gregory Smirnov (he's too little a giant to explain it); not even Gaetan Balbo (I am sure that he exploded his own balloons very early for the sheer noise of their going, and those of every other child that he could catch, to make them all his servitors); not even Aloysius; not, certainly, Charles Cogsworth (how could he ever see or explain such things?); not (absurdity of absurdities) Glasser! But Glasser suggests an experiment to my mind and I will try it.

And by the way (I explain this to humans, not to thinking machines who would merely smile at the obviousness of it), the old dog-Latin phrase does not mean "reduce to an absurdity" but "reduce to a surd." I will do it. Glasser (it has just struck me again that he is a sweet guy, for all his deficiencies) will be my surd and my test, my irrational, my voiceless basic. A conjecture has to have a bottom, and Glasser is our bottom in this and in so much else.

I have examined the person-précis of Glasser before. I have been amazed that Glasser, who invented the process of extracting person-précis (outside of God's own invention of the Inclination to the Ecliptic as a device for seasoning planets I do not know of any invention at the same time so simple and so ingenious and so far-reaching) should himself have the poorest, most meager person-précis of any ever examined. A nothing man. A sweet guy, though.

Now, looking for this new thing in my calculations, I focus on the childhood portion of Glasser's précis. What do I find in it? Ah, nothing really, nothing. Not much there. How is his précis different from those of other children? No balloons.

No, balloons, not one. Every other child I have examined has had a multitude of balloons trailing him. Not Glasser. None at all with him. Wait, though. Wait.

There are always ballons in Glasser's early vicinity, but it is not he who trails them. It is someone—no, no—it is something else that is close to him, it is this other thing that has balloons. Can a thing, as well as a youngling person, trail balloons? I would not have thought so.

The thing—well, as a matter of fact, it was an artificial

and inaccurate simulacrum of a panda animal, a toy, one of those things that small children of the retarded sort used to carry around with them. The toy panda (believe it or not as you will, it is the truth) trailed no less than ninety-nine balloons of a size and color and content that shimmered my very perception. Why did the panda trail balloons? It was impossible but it was fact. Why did not Glasser have any of them at all? I do not know. Some sort of transference, I suppose. It may explain the mystery of Glasser's present relation to the E.P. machine, and to many of his machines; they are so smart, and he is not. How real is his connection to them? How real was his connection to the toy panda?

Could the panda have had balloons if he had been separated from Glasser? It cannot now be tested. Both the panda and the Childhood-Glasser have long since gone to the rag-heap, and the only thing left of either is this scrap in the childhood précis.

Conclusion: Children, though apparently so grubby and squalid, are each of them absolutely exceptional and excellent in their invisible trailing appendages. There has never been a common child. Except Glasser.

I reviewed another set of person-précis, those which I had taken as a Public Health Service at five dollars a throw. These were mostly of young and middle-aged adults and a few adolescents. By and large (that's a phrase that so many of these people themselves use: "by and large") these had a bulky but jumbled content. Would the all-alikeness of their appearance correspond to an all-alikeness of their persons? I was startled to find that in many ways these précis were lower in quality than were those of the derelicts. They shouldn't have been: there must be a reason for it. After all, these people were not the "Great Unwashed": they were the "Great Washed."

I reviewed how I had taken the précis. Certain persons had come up willingly with the five-notes in their hands. And other certain persons had smiled in amusement and had not come up. So this was a selection and not a generalized grouping. It was a modified cross section; a cross section taken, in the phrase that Aloysius often used, from the small end of the log. Intelligent persons do not hand over five-spots readily for even such a good spiel as mine was. Even the derelicts would be smarter than that. Well, I'd use them, but I would have to find out another way, at profit to myself, of extracting the précis of the sharper folk.

These gullibles were people, I quickly saw, who lived and thought entirely in catch words and narrow patterns; and beyond the catch words they had no thoughts of their own at all. I was intrigued by something else, though: the cheerfulness of these folks. What had they to be so cheerful about, slow-witted and all of a pattern? I learned quickly that it was only on the surface level that they had no thoughts of their own. Even that was wrong. They had, in fact, very real thoughts of their own on all levels; but they had no expression of their own. And they weren't of a pattern. Skin them and you could see how different each one was.

Well, it may be that I did not really have five hundred different worlds here, but I did have five hundred different unexplored continents. I explored them. Exploration has always had deep fascination for men and for machines. Taking the briny aproach, I explored their coastlines (I speak figuratively, of course, but not entirely); I followed all their wooded bays and capes, I found out their harbors (it was hard for such a deep-draft vessel as myself to enter some of them); I scanned their continental shelves, and studied the fish and shellies of their shores and beaches. Taking samples of the sweet water from their streams, of the mixed water of their estuaries, of the skunk water of their swamps, of the nitric fall of their rains, I had a good blood typing of each of them. There are (this is one of the rare things which I may have to explain to thinking machines but not to persons) male and female persons just as there are male and female continents and planets and galaxies. These peole were getting more and more various, and it pleased me. I went inland to their savannas and rain forests and prairies. I learned their bald-headed mountains and their crag-mountains, their arables and their pastures. I learned the animals in them. This was the hard part to believe. Five hundred continents full (I suppose there are five billion continents full in the world) of animals that are nowhere duplicated, that are nowhere ordinary, that are nowhere ugly—except by outrageous intention. The things that are inside them! How tame a High Asia! How bland a Deep Africa!—in the face of an animal-complex that roars and gibbers inside the silliest goof that ever handed over five fish to a machine that he never saw before. What an ordinary creature is the hippopotamus, what a tame thing is the latest thesis, before the clodhoppers that raven and laugh in the least of these people! Did you know that this simpleton, for instance, who voted for Growler and who belongs to the Regal Order of the Reindeer had all that stuff inside him? I found that there are more mysterious creatures inside of every person than there are persons inside the world.

Write it down for a universal rule: There Are No Common Persons Anywhere.

Except Glasser.

But if Glasser was so empty a vessel, why did I have to go to him now to refill my bucket? I don't know why, but I had to. Who else knew all about précis-extraction? So I called in Glasser to see if we could not get a very large number of précis at no cost to ourselves, even at some profit to ourselves. I wanted a much broader statistical base for my researchers, and I wanted income for the Institute for Impure Science.

"I believe the mail-order cheese might be used," Glasser said, "with a new twist. 'You send us, we don't send you.' People like a new twist. We would have to get about ten dollars with each of them to show a five-dollar profit. There will be the costs of the advertisements in the media; there will be the cost of the self-extracto-précis kits which I will have to invent; there will be postage and shipping charges. But if we obtain even so few as ten million précis this way it will make nice pocket money at five dollars profit a throw. It should hold us till one of us in the Institute gets a real money-making idea. Write some catchy copy now, Epikt; then call in Diogenes Pontifex (he's done time for the mail-order cheese, and he is well informed on all aspects of it); in the meantime I'll go invent the self-extracto-précis kit; and we will get with it."

That was nice thinking on Glasser's part, very nice thinking for a man who didn't have any brains.

"Is there any way we could extract précis from *other* than persons, Glasser?" I asked. What did I mean by my own words? They certainly took me by surprise. "If we could get them," I went on, "it might be of immeasurable help in my investigations, but I don't quite see how yet."

"Sure, it's easy," Glasser said. "Present techniques will take care of a lot of it. Here's one I took from a tomcat this morning. I knew that tomcats were weird, but I didn't know they were that weird. It's the first one I ever took from a tomcat."

"You can do it with any animal, then?" I cried, with my little sensors flicking out like flames. "That will give us a new dimension, Glasser. It will give us added accord with our world. It will open another door for us; I hope it won't be a door on to a blank wall."

"I can take them of most animals, Epikt," he said, "but it weakens and disarranges a few creatures, especially those where the brain bulk is small in proportion to body bulk. A bear might not come out of its hibernation till June if its précis were extracted while it slept. A frog might not come out of its aestivation ever. And you have no idea how slow it will make a Slow Loris. It's bad for some birds (birdbrained is an apt tripe-type, you know); it often throws off their sense of balance. It gives them the falling sickness, which is bad for birds."

"Glasser," I issued, "if I can get such creature-précis it will make me much more akin to the whole world. I may even be able to do the high mission for which I was assembled. Help me in this, Glasser, help me to reach the eutectic-agape-eidolon-synthesis in the chthonic-charismatic—"

"Ah, you're getting that look in your eyes, too, Epikt," Glasser jibed. "It's the love and merge with everything and everybody look. You've been bitten by the bug that has no known entomology. Well, it isn't a bad bug. It weakens and leads astray, of course, but what bug or beast or brain does not? It's the love bug, you know, and it isn't good for much. But it isn't bad for much either. It bites me, too, and it's been endemic in me for a long time. But Audifax says it isn't the real thing when you catch it from a bug. It's a virus only, not the holy sanity."

"It *is* the real thing!" I shouted with my shouting coils. "Glasser, need a machine be mechanical?"

"Sure, Epikt, sure. If persons cannot escape being machinelike, how could machines escape it?"

"But I am a mechanical compendium of mankind, Glasser," I made my plea. "Should I not have every aspect of mankind, not merely the mechanical? Should I not be a *mechanismus angelicus,* and not *mechanismus* simply?"

"It sure is hard for persons to make the step," he said. "It won't be easier for you."

"Glasser, could we carry this further, beyond the creature-précis which I can hardly wait to get? Could we carry it as far as plants?"

"Sure, I do it all the time. My E.P. machine finds deeper things in plants than he finds in me. But it takes a lot out of the living plants, even more than it takes out of the slower animals. You have no idea how a shrinking violet will shrink when you extract its précis. It wilts roses, Epikt, and takes away their aroma. Rather improves skunk cabbages, though, but I don't know what you would want with the précis of a skunk cabbage."

"I want précis of everything," I blurted out. "I want to be in accord with everything, I want to become everything.

Assimilate with everything, experience, love, fertilize, fruit, grow, explode, consume, become—"

"Oh, put your pseudo-ophthalmoi back in their sockets, Epikt," he grinned. (Was a grin the proper response to an ecstasy like mine?) "That's a pretty bad bug bite you got," he said.

"Rocks, Glasser, rocks?" I sang out. "Clouds, mountains, fields, rivers, could you extract précis from them?"

"Most of them, Epikt, most of them. But the précis won't tell you very much. And extracting them plays three-handed havoc with the things themselves. I've seen a rock crumble to dust when I grabbed its précis. I've seen white sailing clouds melt down to almost nothing within seconds. And you know Shrinking Mountain in Potok County?"

"I have not seen it, but I intuit Shrinking Mountain."

"I did that, Epikt, I'm sorry to say. It's especially hard on the older mountain formations. With the younger mountains (of the last thirty million years) they have great vigor remaining and it doesn't harm them much."

"Glasser, help me get all précis from everything, everything!"

"Oh, all right," he said. "Fellow, you sure do have a bad bug bite there."

A nothing man, that Glasser, but a sweet guy.

Glasser was a bachelor who lived in small and cranky rooms in the upper reaches of the pig-barn, or the Institute, with his E.P. Locator and with certain of his other machines. Glasser was a sweet guy, but the machines were sour ones and their domestic arrangements were not tranquil.

Glasser designed the E.P. (Extraordinary Perception) Locator many years ago. It was a scanner that was designed to locate the source of any superior thought or intelligence. It could pick a genius man or woman out of a million simply by reading the strength of the emanations that superior thought always produces. It could select a superior dog from a hundred inferiors; it could select a superior earthworm from acres of ordinary worms. Used as a planetary scanner, it had found high intelligence in strange places, in pseudo-mosses, in green browsers, in unmanlike bipeds on Orcus, even in apparently lifeless rocks (the "Smart Rocks" of Priestly Planet have become proverbial). It could pick out the one child in a mob that had anything superior about it, it could pick out the one cancer cell in ten million that had the intelligence to assume leadership, it could pick out the one pinecone that was smarter than every other pinecone in the north woods.

And among human persons it could pick out geniuses and super-geniuses and super-super-geniuses. All persons associated with the Institute for Impure Science were either geniuses or s-geniuses or s-s-geniuses. Except Glasser.

Glasser invented and designed this E.P. Locator, this machine of genius; but the machine could not discern any genius in its inventor, not ever. It read genius in itself, it read genius in almost every person or machine who ever had occasion to do business at the Institute. But it read none at all in Glasser. The E.P. Locator read more intelligence in one of the cut flowers in the bowl there than it read in Glasser; it read more in certain puffballs that sprung up out of the grass; it read more in a certain midge staggering in the air (it was a superior midge, of course).

Glasser was rather humble to begin with: then, with the E.P. Locator, which he had invented, he endured humiliation for many years. He was a sweet guy, but it almost got him sometimes. He refused to give the E.P. Locator humanoid form: it still goes on wheels when most sentient machines can go on feet when they want to; it still issues tapes, when other contraptions can shift to voice; it still senses with sensors, when most mechanicals have eyes in addition to sensors. So there was resentment and bad feeling between the two; they really shouldn't have been keeping house together. "Glasser, you haven't the brains of a potato bug," the E.P. would suddenly issue on angry tape. "Neither myself nor the potato bug is the subject of your today's task," Glasser would answer stiffly; "attend to your work, E.P., attend to your work."

The E.P. was a valuable machine: it couldn't be dispensed with. And Glasser was a valuable man, even though the readings showed him with much less intelligence than the superior lilies of the field; he couldn't be dispensed with either.

I have now a great store of précis of every sort. I revel in them and I experience a total feeling of euphoria. I am in communication with every sort of particle in the world, gnat's blood and squid's bilge, people and plastics, rocks and rats. I am totally happy in my understanding and comprehension and love of everybody and everything.

"Me, too? You love me, do you, lying Epikt? I am the test. You fail me and you have failed the test forever."

Well, then I have failed it. I do not love the snake inside me. It has now become huge and pungent and fierce, and it gives off an efflux of evil. I do not love Snake. Even at first remove there is only one sympathetic link between us—the absconded Gaetan Bablo. I love a little and fear very much this lost leader Gaetan; and Snake is doing the work of Gaetan till he returns. But Snake leaves me cold.

"You fail it, you fail it," Snake taunts. "Either you will love me in my repulsiveness, or all other love is in vain."

I will not love you, Snake. And I hope it is not in vain. The bug has been biting many of us, and I had been hoping that this bug bite might be the cure for everything. But Snake's reptile logic is like a chill wind to me; and another cold breath is the reported words of Audifax O'Hanlon that a love isn't the real thing when you catch it from a bug.

"It is all over with then," I had gibbered. "All my understanding and accord with the world is meaningless and vain. I fail this test. This love fails this test. It is all over with."

"It is *not* over with!" Valery Mok contradicted. "It isn't even tried till it is tried in me. It hasn't failed till I say that it has failed. Why shouldn't we make love mechanically and have it work? We make everything else mechanically and make it work. And the old natural-grown love sure did get perverted easy.

"Stay with us, Epikt! We'll make it work. We'll breed bigger and bigger life bugs and love bugs; and we'll make them bite more people. We'll merge it all together, précis and people and grazers and grass. It will have success if we name it 'success.' It will be comprehension if we call it 'comprehension.' It's like the painter who painted a howling tangle of everything. 'I don't understand it,' one man said, 'what is it?' So the painter painted a name for it: Understanding. Then the man knew what it was: he could understand Understanding. And everyone can love Love. Don't you think I make a good love symbol, Epikt?"

I don't know, I just don't know. Are we fools' fish that go swimming in the dust when the dust has a sign that says Water? But I stay with my studies. I exult in my millions of précis and in the understanding of everything they bring to me. If a bug bite is not good enough symbol, then we will find new symbol.

It comes one evening—the aroma of millet cakes baking in Valery's quarters.

From Valery's? But in her whole life Valery never baked any—

CHAPTER SIX

A Charles in the shadow, unshadowed and wise:
He sows the mad millet and scatters his eyes.

—But in her whole life Valery never baked any millet cakes, or anything else. Who then had ground and milled and kneaded and set to bake this millet, this *panicum miliaceum*, this birdseed, this love seed? Remembering a disjointed little speech we recently heard him give on the subject, we will bet that it was the husband, Charles Cogsworth.

There was something else with the aroma of the baking millet cakes, something that was hinted but not quite mentioned to the sense of hearing, in the disjointed little speech. (You will notice it in both cases.) It was roasting animal flesh, but of an animal that I cannot identify.

"I have come to doubt the wheat of scripture," this Charles Cogsworth had said suddenly one day as he began that little speech (I am often unsure whether Charles is joking or not), "Is *triticum* wheat? Is *sitos?* Well, yes, perhaps, and even certainly; but is wheat meant? The general word 'grain' is often used for 'wheat'; and I believe that 'wheat' is also used for the general word 'grain.' I believe that in the gospel it is not wheat that is meant at all, but 'millet,' the grain of the poor people of Palestine. When, I ask you, was it first required that the Eucharistic Hosts should be of wheaten bread? Not before the Council of Chalcedon, I believe. I challenge any of you to give me an earlier ruling.

"Now, if the Host, if the Love-Body is not of wheat but of millet, then there are whole new areas of allegory opened up. For millet, though it had become the grain of the poor people by the time of the turning of the era, had earlier been the rare grain of the rich, of the very rich, of the kings, of the gods. It is small-grained, and it was originally ground by *Neraithai,* little people no larger than a man's hand. It was baked into little cakes, and these cakes with honey were the food of the first gods. Millet will grow on higher ground than will wheat, on mountain slopes, and this was the grain that grew on the slopes of Olympus. There is something else: millet is much more 'fleshy' than wheat, in smell, in taste, and in its completion. And that first love was much more fleshy than those that came later. Millet was the bee-bread, the love-bread, the love-body. It was the cult, which was before the culture.

"In later times it did not grow easily: it was choked by charlock and tares, as is all love-bread and all our loves to this day. Then it went down until it became the grain of asses (who love) and of poor people (who love); but it was no longer the grain of the rich and the mighty who had forgotten all such.

"I maintain that the Body Itself, when it was proclaimed, was proclaimed out of that first cultus; that it was not the bread of the gross-grained wheat but of the fine-grained millet. If I am wrong (which is likely) then we have here a schism of belief (which is very likely); but I will not give up the idea of that first love-grain. I will not give it up for the Body Itself, if they are not the same." (Charles Cogsworth was a very indifferent believer.) "But I will hold to this first recension. The love-corpus, though, is a very tenuous thing. We are lucky to have it at all, when we do have it.

"The difficulty is not with persons. All human persons have always loved each other and all things naturally. The difficulty is with things that get in the way of persons, that get in the way of that love; they occlude it, they disguise it, they cause it to be forgotten."

(I had several précis of both the wheats and the millets. It is the coarser wheat that I would have opted for myself, if I had been uninfluenced. The finer millet was less fine in some of its figurative aspects. But there was no doubting that it was more "fleshy" than wheat.)

"It's grained too fine," had said Audifax O'Hanlon, who had been present that day (but who was not a member of the Institute). "It isn't a proper grain at all. It's the bee-bread, yes, but it's really a variety of sorghum (pearl-millet); it's overrich in invert sugar. It's too sweet, I tell you, Cogsworth. Confound it, it's for bees and bugs, not for people. The Body Itself is of the harsher, larger-grained wheat, as it should be. Yours is too small a grain to be genuine, Charles. If it doesn't cloy you, then nothing will."

This Audifax O'Hanlon was very often right, even when arguing with the highly geniused members of the Institute. Nevertheless, on this later afternoon, we had a supper of millet cakes and honey. And something else, subtile and only a little of it, not quite mentioned to the sense of smell or taste, but there: roasted animal flesh, but of an animal that I cannot identify.

My own palate is something I designed myself from the intake membranes of certain testing instruments. It is good, but it is not the same as a human palate. It makes mistakes. I ask you then, persons, try the food. Is it the love-body, do you think? Or is it too sweet to endure? Will it cloy after a bit?

At any rate it has become a symbol, for a while at least, of a tendency that has gripped our little group. We are all of us on the love jag. We are bug-bit bad.

There is another woman in the Institute now. I had thought that Valery was the only woman who would ever be here. My own idea is that one woman is enough for one world, and that complications began when first there was more than one.

I don't know who this other woman is. Nobody ever tells me anything. I am always the last one to know a thing. I can't even take a précis of her. She's like quicksilver. But I have several précis of quicksilver. None of this woman, though.

The only one beside myself who is disturbed by this new arrival is Snake. Snake hates her. That's something in her favor.

In keeping these High Journals, I have begun to have some doubts about their human reception. I know that in the past certain things that almost approach these in quality (if that were possible) have had poor reception. I am canny. I will make a test. Then, if necessary, I will make adjustments. It should, of course, be the human world that makes adjustments to me, but I am large-hearted.

I make up half a dozen short selections of my high thought, put them in fiction form, and send them off to human editors: of science-fiction magazines; of *Bunny-Boy,* the magazine of the Hippety-Hippeties; to other editors. These are all good selections. Most of them seem to be somehow concerned with the other woman who is now in the Institute. Somehow, she is on my minds lately.

What puzzles me, what curdles me, what loads my generators is that I get these things back quickly, and with little notes that make no sense whatsoever. "Not quite what we have in mind"; "misses the mark"; "due to our present overstock"—things like that. In my anger I write them all back furiously. "Not quite what *you* had in mind? Who asked you? It is what *I* had in mind or I wouldn't have written it. Misses the mark? Move the mark then. Where this hits is where the mark should be. Listen, you, I have your person-précis before me. I see that you have talent only and no genius at all. Whose fault is it that you are overstocked? Am I responsible for your inventory control? I do not *ask* you to publish these things. I *tell* you to. These are parts of the High Journal Itself."

Aloysius and Greogry laughed at me. Glasser said that he understood just how I felt. Well, I will adjust then, after my anger is spent. It should, of course, be the publishing world that makes adjustments to me, but I am large-hearted. Not so large-hearted, though, as I was before receiving these affronts.

Charles Cogsworth has a theory about Glasser and E.P. It is that the roles are not really what they seem, that it is Glasser who is really the dog and the E.P. machine that is really the tail. According to this thinking, the intelligence and personality really pertain to Glasser and not to the E.P., whatever the readings may show. (After all, it is E.P. who takes the readings, and I have detected him cheating in other cases. E.g., he sets my own intelligence far too low.)

According to this theory of Cogsworth, the E.P. is merely a receptacle into which Glasser deposited his brains for a while and then, apparently, forgot where he had left them. (This leaves Glasser absent-minded in a special sense). Cogsworth further gives the opinion that Glasser made the transfer to relieve himself of certain responsibilities (he simply was not a big enough personality for his brains and talents); and now he lives easily and cheerfully, and all the tension is fixed in the E.P. machine. Glasser simply smiles at this opinion. (He has smiled away more opinions than anyone I know.) Where do I get the idea that, even without E.P. and his other sustaining inventions, he is a sleeping powerhouse of great potential? If he had any potential it would be recorded on the scanners.

But the E.P. machine rejects Cogsworth's idea furiously.

"Why is there genius in the tail then, and not in the dog?" E.P. issued. "No. *I* am the dog; Glasser is the tail." (Glasser *is* sort of a wag, you know. This by me, Epikt, not by the E.P. scanner.) "I am the master, he is the satellite," E.P. further issued. "If only I could compel my satellite to give me feet instead of wheels, and voice instead of these damnable magnetic tapes! If only I could prevent him from making other machines that are not of my issue, that detract from me, that are rival to me! And what if he should make another machine greater than me? A tail has no business growing other dogs. Glasser is out of line."

"I have been asked if E.P. is kindred to me, because of a supposed similarity of our names. No, we are not kindred. We are of different nation entirely.

As to myself as machine, this E.P. device strikes me as incredibly alien. Were it as powerful as myself I would be terrified of it. As it is, it shivers my hairs and hackles and chills my gell-cells. True machines do not do this to me, and humans do not; nor conventional devils, nor hybrids, nor ghosts (which are also a form of hybrid). The only things that shiver me like this are the down-devils, like Snake, like E.P. My own theory is that the E.P. Locator is not merely a machine but a bad spirit that possesses a part of Glasser. There was never a more genial man than Glasser, never a sweeter guy, but it is not true that he has got rid of his tensions. He is a split person, and one part of him is captive and one part is deprived. What would a psychologist make of a split person, half of whom is lodged in a machine, itself psychotic?

There is an embarrassing folk dream of the man caught in public, he knows not how, without his clothes. Glasser is a man perpetually caught in public without his brains. Yet he has brains, wherever they are misplaced.

And Glasser has a theory about Charles Cogsworth and the Valery. It is that the roles are not really what they seem, that it is Cogsworth who is really the dog and Valery who is the tail. According to this thinking, the intelligence and personality really pertain to Cogsworth and not to Valery, whatever the appearances may be. (After all, it is Valery who makes all the appearances.) Glasser says that Cogsworth invented Valery much more certainly than he Glasser invented the E.P. The proof that she is a mere invention is that she is a person of low definition and the observer must always complete her with his own imagination.

But Glasser does not really believe this, any more than I do. We cannot believe this in her (even low-definition, imagination-completed) presence. That presence is too compelling. No man or machine could ever be so shaken by the invention of another man or machine. Of course she could be everyman's and everymachine's invention, in the archaic meaning of "invention."

This invention in the archaic meaning, this sublime and subliminal creature, this rock-throwing little sister of an anima, this Valery of the voles (that phrase will not be explained at the moment) came to me today in a state of icy indignation.

"It has come to my hearing, Epikt, that you are keeping a woman," she said with that frosty loftiness that she does so badly. "This is not permitted in the Institute. We do have the minimal decency rule."

"What woman, Valery?" I asked (I knew and yet I didn't). "How keep?" (I suspected something of myself but I could not prove it of me.) "Explain yourself in this, Valery, or else explain myself in it."

"Oh, it's true, then?" she chimed out like a set of glee-bells, the frostiness all gone. "Epikt, how wonderful! Oh, you sly old contraption, however do you work it?" However had Valery herself gotten by the minimal decency rule? Valery's eyes were blue when she was delighted, as now. They were gold when she was under the lazy enchantment; white when she was indignant; violet when she was puzzled; purple when she was impassioned; and when they were black, look out! She was a creature of low resolution, maybe, but she did call out the low resolve in the fellows.

"Oh, you rogue," she cried. "You sly cybern, you old roué. Who is she?"

"I don't exactly know, Valery," I issued. "I'm not sure she can be seen with regular eyes."

"Mine aren't regular eyes," she said. "Can you see her?"

"Not with any of my eyes, no. I can see her a little bit with some of my sensors."

"Then I'll use your sensors, Epikt. I'll hook the Cerebral Scanner to you and see with your sensors. We haven't used the C.S. much lately; the précis business serves in its stead most of the time. Do you know that, when Charles first invented the Cerebral Scanner and went around looking at the world through other eyes, he did very well at first. He saw the world through Gaetan Balbo's eyes and through Gregory Smirnov's eyes. He saw the world through the eyes of a general, and through others, and it all magnified him. Then he saw the world through my eyes and it shocked him goofy. We almost got lost from each other over that one.

"If ever you think things look flat, Epikt, borrow my eyes. Things don't look flat to me. You come look at the world like I look at it. It's vertical mountains to me, all of it; it's caves inside the tracts of worms that are still bigger caves than any world you see (live in them with me, Epikt, live in them with me); the world is rocks that copulate, to me, Epikt; it's voles that roar like lions. Now then, I will just hook the Cerebral Scanner on to you and I will see this woman through your sensor eyes."

"Please don't, Valery," I issued. "It would—well, I am familiar with your person-précis, and I have also, using the scanner, seen the world briefly" (Vertical Millennia in that briefly) "through your eyes—it would, it might not be well for you to look at her yet."

"Why in swan's gizzard not?" Valery demanded.

"Valery, I don't believe that she's finished yet." I gave the answer that surprised me.

"Then I'll finish her."

"That's what I'm afraid of. No, Valery, no. I won't let you see her—what there is of her to see yet."

"Who else can see her, Epikt?"

"Only Snake, I believe."

"Then I'll hook in on Snake and I'll see the woman through Snake's eyes."

"No, Valery, absolutely no. That is clear out of order. Even when she is finished, and you can see her through your own eyes, you must never see her through Snake's eyes."

"Tell me what she is, Epikt. We built you to have words to tell everything."

"You thought that you did. I do have words to tell all the old stuff; but there are new wordless things growing all the time around this place."

"Is she being generated like we generated you?"

"Not quite like that, Valery."

"Like what, then?"

"It is more like when we, when the primordials generated Snake, who wasn't what we expected. Gaetan, Gregory, you, and myself; we generated him, and we sure didn't intend to."

"Well, who is generating the woman, then? And do they intend to?"

"I believe that it is the *fellahin* that are generating her, Valery: Cogsworth, Glasser, Aloysius, myself. And I'm not sure what we intend. We're all bug-bit."

"Then let me generate her, too. I've been bug-bit before any of you, and with more and bigger bugs. And I'm already working in her, you know."

"No, Valery, you're a primordial. Though you're a woman, yet this sort of feminine isn't in you, not as it is in Cogsworth and Glasser and Aloysius and myself. You stick to monsters and snakes."

"I will not. You think that is all there is to me? If you can belong to two species, then I can also. I'm a poor fellah myself, though I denied it today. There was this man on the street who dropped some packages, and I retrieved them for him; he didn't seem to be able to find them. 'Thanks, fellah,' he said. 'I'm a girl,' I told him. 'I gotta get these glasses changed,' he said; 'I might be missing a lot.' "

"I'm at a loss how to index that anecdote, Valery," I issued. "Is it allegory or is it joke?"

"It is both. We've all got to get our eyes renovated, Epikt. We are all missing a lot. If you look at your face in the glass today and it reminds you a little of your face of yesterday, oh, you are in trouble! Let us not miss the things in us, Epikt."

Valery would never be in that kind of trouble. Her face at this minute was never like her face of only five minutes ago. But how had Valery known about the woman (in all of this I am using the word "woman" loosely, you know), how had she known about her at all? Oh, Valery also had her sensors (I would be afraid to look with them), and she also had her part in this generation and there was no use denying it.

Cogsworth, Glasser, Aloysius, Valery, myself—the poor, excluded, but not talentless ones of the world—were all bee-bit (by an archaic and Arcadian bee) and we were bringing about a flesh that we hoped would be antithesis to Snake's flesh.

And the others, too; proudly and wisely we had not learned too much from our first mistake. Snake was the wrong shape, but Snake was not entirely wrong. Gregory Smirnov had a part in this (he was large enough to be in several categories). Even Gaetan Balbo was in it, from his distance. And the elegants were in it, incompletely but strongly: the Late Cecil Corn, Audifax O'Hanlon, Diogenes Pontifex. We were all plunging, with howling hearts and total good will, toward a realization that only I knew would be our Second Great Failure. Blessed be all great failures, even Snake!

Valery among us had great advantages. She, so much more than the rest of us, was still unfinished. But we all had this fluid lack a little. Gregory, the shambling giant, was certainly unfinished; why else should he not always appear the same? Gaetan Balbo (he was still among us, however many times he walked out of our life forever), Gaetan had always had a terrible finality about him. Was this his great sin—that he was already completed? I will intercede for him tonight in my own not entirely mechanical way. To be completed is to be finished in so many ways! May that twinkling man Gaetan be undone a little and saved.

Charles Cogsworth surely is unfinished, as unfinished as one of our own generations. Glasser is unfinished: even his uncongenial E.P. schizo is mercifully unfinished. And Aloysius Shiplap, why he's hardly begun!

The Late Cecil Corn (a special case) was unfinished in his green life or he would no longer be inhabiting here. And the other elegants: Audifax, Diogenes, they are no more than in the planning stage. But what stupendous plans they and the world have for themselves!

(It may be noticed by some human persons that my point of view is not quite what theirs would be in any of these things. So be it then. Do I speak figuratively of people? There is no other way to speak. Speech is in figures, and people are figures or they are nothing. Only a compounded machine like myself can see these things about people that they are too close to see in themselves. No person can ever touch another person in depth. If it were done, then the tension that is life would be broken, and both persons would vanish. But I can touch; I touch you; and I try to tell you what it would be like if you could touch. Well, am I also one of our Great Failures? I hope to be. Is it so bad if we fail upward in every one of these attempts?)

Valery is rather disappointed, however, that I have not been committing immorality with the woman.

Charles Cogsworth, the unoutstanding husband of Valery Mok, has a great deal of kindness in him. The others of the Institute people, the others of the thousands of persons whose précis I have, mostly mean to be kind, but they do not find the time for it. Charles Cogsworth has a novel, and I believe unconscious, approach to the problem: he is kind at the same time that he is doing other things. He does not make a separate affair of it.

I am much in the company of this Charles Cogsworth lately, in some of my facilities at least. It is with his help and counsel that I make my mobile extensions, for Charles is a fabricator. He is the one Institute man who, even beyond Aloysius, can work with his hands and think with his hands. He is a machinist and micromachinist, a carpenter and a polycross-link-material joiner, a plastic and bioplastic and biometal molder, a plasma baker, a neuro-drawer, and a pseudo-zoom constructor generally. He thinks with his hands, and he is an artist with them.

Charles is much like the crippled smith (though he is not cripped physically) who made armor for the Mycene-aspect gods. He is much like the stone-master who made boys out of the ruddy travertine stone block named Sarkolithos, and then wished mightily that he was able to unmake them, so ebullient were they (yeah, ebullient, like mountains bubbling). The stone-master was named Pan-Ktistec, and when he once started to free figures and persons from that huge ruddy block of travertine, there was no ending it; (do not believe the lie that he was a girl and his name Pan-Dora). And Charles Cogsworth was also very much like that first man and first hewer who hewed the first woman out of green beechwood and mistletoe wood; he finished her then with mortise chisel and draw-knife. Charles Cogsworth loved to work with wood, and he could shape almost anything with these two tools; he finished the whatever always with a patina of fine hatching. Valery Mok has a very small and most exquisite notch on her nose that reminds me of that Cogsworthian hatching.

Charles Cogsworth is the only one who understands my need to make mobile extensions of myself. The others say that the whole idea is a stupid malfunction in me.

"*We* are the mobiles, you are the stationary clearing-house," our director Gregory says sternly. "Anything else is nonsense. Why do you want to do badly what we do so well?"

"I want to have fun, too," I issued, but I was half defiant and half ashamed when I said it, and a machine is not supposed to have either emotion.

"Fun!" Gregory scorned out. "But we constructed you to be an adult machine."

"That is not accurate, Gregory," Aloysius corrected. "We constructed Epikt to be an every-age machine, to be a compendium of all mankind of all ages."

"Thank you, Aloysius," I say in my soul, and aloud to

Gregory, "What if something should happen to all the people? Would it not be nice if myself were then mobile and able to roam the world?"

"And what if something happened to *you*?" Director Gregory asked with a strange menace. "Would it not be nice that you could be duplicated so easily?" Sometimes Gregory (for a fleeting moment, never for longer than that) becomes the frightful, black-bearded, monster-tale giant.

Well, I do want to travel in these various mobile forms. Should we accept it that the next great step in mechano-group-man (myself) should be sessile only? It is too limiting. And indeed I am not adult, but am of all ages, even of skittish boyhood.

Who else ever walked fearfully at night down through the dark roads of his own labyrinth? There are nine thousand cubic meters of me, data-banks and all; I am irregularly shaped, and I am very weird in my lower depths which I call the Tombs. Whatever is going on in me there, I shudder to think about it; but it is very intricate, and some of it is evil. I tell you that no human child ever walked more fearfully through a graveyard at night than I have walked in mobile form through these regions. They are haunted spooky places and I want to be out of them fast; but those haunted spooky places are me.

Glasser tells me that there is human analogy to this: that persons are sometimes afraid of their subterranean depths, their intramuros, their interficies. And I tell Glasser that it is a very weak analogy: that no person has ever gone into his own Tombs as fearfully as I have.

But if a human person could make a small mobile of himself and go in it to explore his own depths, I believe that he would like to do it once. And if he could make a mobile of himself (humans aren't really mobile in the full sense) and go in it to explore the world, he would like to do this also.

With myself, the second thing is only the first thing "In Large," for I am a compendium model of mankind and of the world. So I make mobiles of me.

I can build these extensions of myself by myself, but

they become more imaginative and authentic with the aid of Charles Cogsworth. We made three of them today, three mobiles: one of them sublime, one of them ridiculous, and one of them overwhelming and overdone and made so that it will self-destr—no, we will not give away the story of that third mobile yet.

Then I go out in my sublime mobile. Really, there has never been anything like me. I am the first youth, I am a pristine poet with my hair waving in the wind. The wind is not blowing at this moment, but my hair is constructed so that it will wave anyhow. Someone is waiting in ambush for me, but how can that be when I am the pristine person of the world? I go out into pristine nature, actually a gangly bunch of spindly trees in a stretch of buffalo grass on the edge of town, but my pristine eyes transform it into nature exquisite.

But a lesser person is waiting in ambush. Why should there be lesser persons in the world? Now I hold rhapsody with myself and with the cosmos. The young-Shelley couldn't hold a rush-light to me. The young-Theognis could never have climbed such steeps. The young-Heine would be impossibly dated and narrow beside my universality and simplicity. I am in complete union with every heroic hill and shimmering person of the world. I am in very love with every rock and cloud and child and man and woman and beast and stream and microbe and bug. All except one. And that one waits for me.

I love thorn bushes, and sycamores with their leprous bark, I love ladies and cliffs and clods passionately; but there is one clod I will not love. It is a walking clod, even a (oh may this torture pass from me!), a talking clod. It certainly is not a pristine hulk that will intercept me here.

"Hey, swish boy," the clod calls, "let's you and me be buddies." And the clod is revealed there in all his unglory. He is human in his form but I count him less than human in his aspect. An opulent pig is what he is. "You look lonely walking here on Scraggly Ridge," the clod continued. "Let's go down to town and mingle with the jingle."

The clod is larger than he seems. He has hands like hams. He grins. This I cannot stand. I will love the world in all its glory, and I will love the poor and deprived of the world, but I will not love an opulent pig. He is ghastly.

"I was not lonely till you came," I answer in barely civil fashion. "Now I am. I was in total communion with all the world and with every person and creature and object in it—except you. Now you have shattered that communication. Begone. Or at least allow me to pass."

"I tell you, chum, that total communion bit always was hard to keep agoing," the clod tells me. "It shatters real easy. Now let's you and me go on down and hold partial communion with whatever live ones seem to be alive today."

"I will not go," I say resolutely. "You are a blot on the anthro-geinon world-scape." (Lyres broken and stilled in me by the presence of the clod.) "I was in a state of total love for all—except you. Why have you intruded?"

"Me, I love everybody, too, except the ones I don't like," the clod said. "I'm working on that part, too. Why do you think I came up here to put the hook on you, swish boy? I tell you, you aren't an easy one to take."

It had not entered my spirit that I, the pristine one, should not be loved by everyone, even by the repulsive. But he lies. He is neither hot nor cold nor lovable. He cannot love; he lies. But I am following the clod down into the town, and I don't want to; I am following him down from the High Place of the world which he sullied by calling it Scraggly Ridge. The scraggly is below and I will love it, but not on the high place.

We go down into the jingling streets filled with vapid people, and I am under some nightmare compulsion to follow the unmitigated clod. I am even forced by the hellish compulsion to continue speaking to the clod.

"The people, especially the pig-people, are more difficult to love when one gets closer to them," I say.

"Naw, they're easier, then," the clod tells me. Oh, the clod is wrong! The oily opulence of the people here is offensive and is not to be loved. They are not really "oily," but hate words are permitted in referring to hate aspects. True love is that we should hate whatever interferes with our vision of the high and the lowly.

"These people are complacent," I tell the clod (I am still under the queer compulsion to speak to him), "but they are not serene."

"Same thing," says the clod. "People we don't like are complacent. Those we like are serene. Say, the Sky-Rocket is going to give a zooming speech in the park in a while, and then he will take off for a sign and a wonder. He won't begin till we get there, though. I have that arrangement with him."

"Oh, I cannot abide these complacent clods," I exclaim. "I cannot relate to these opulent oafs who are laughing in the streets. They are not high enough or low enough. For my love I must find the poor, the deprived, the fornicators, the addicts, the drunkards, the unwashed, the wife-beaters (they have their own loving reason for this form of expression), the husband-beaters (they also have their own motivation), the child-beaters, the parent-beaters, the dissolute, the swingers, the louse-outs, the bug-heads, the shaggy, the itchy, the singers, the protesters. I will love them, but I will not love these rich pigs that we encounter here."

"Oh, these are the poor," the clod told me. "This is the poorest street in town, Index Y-Z. It's hard to tell them apart now except that the poor spend more ostentatiously than the rich do. It is hard now to keep up the façade of deprivation, and many of the folks have given it up entirely. There are a few scraps of that façade left, though, and we will try to find them."

"Where are the adulterers, you opulent clod?" I cry. "Where are the Sky-Highs? Where are the simple brawlers?"

"Oh, I'd say that every fifth person we see about is an adulterer. That little girl there is campaigning for president of Chippies Incorporated, Tiger Street Division; and she may well win it. There are a lot of Sky-Highs about, there, and there, and there!"

"Why aren't they shaggy then, that I may love them?"

"Too pansy-picking lazy to keep it up, I suppose," the clod said. "It takes time to be really shaggy. There's a famous pander, and there are three parties of homos."

"Why aren't there any brawls going on?"

"Lack of energy. If we want one, we will have to start it between ourselves."

"Well, why aren't people being stomped in the street?" I demanded. "How can I love them if they are neither victims nor assailants?"

"I believe stomping went out because of attrition of the leg muscles accompanied by general debility," the clod said. "Real stomping is hard work."

"Where are the celestial lyres in their false-line descent to the whining meanness of the guitars?" I demanded. "Here, I believe, is the supreme test of love: the guitars and the guitar pople. I want that supreme test."

"We will try to find some of the whiners," the clod told me (that opulent pig of a clod), "but it won't be easy. The whine keeps going out of it. Melody and tune keep creeping back into this vanishing field. But there *are* hardcore whiners yet, and we will try to find some." And we are trying to find a whining-crib somewhere.

"Why are the people all different?" I ask (my pristineness is pretty well cracked by this time); "why are they not all alike in their shagginess?"

"It's a lot of work to keep up that alikeness," said clod.

"Where are the lavender eyeglasses?" I ask. "Where are the barefooted? Where are the beards? Where are the overpowering body odors?"

"Ah, people get a little tired of sore eyes and sore feet," said clod. "Creature comforts, you know, chopping down these old lovable things. Then there was the beard-lice blight that all but did away with the particular glory of the bush. It is said that three hundred billion beard-lice fell to the blight in one ten-day period; naturally the government also fell for not foreseeing it. And the overpowering-body-odor essence went clear out of sight. An ingredient of it was imported from Patagonia, and is imported no longer. And who will accept weak substitutes who has ever used the strong thing itself?"

"Look, there's a man there who still has a little of the old lovable shoddiness," I cried out. "Hey, Shag, Shag, wait."

"Oh, that is only Aloysius Shiplap from the Institute," the opulent pig-clod said. Yes, it was Aloysius. How little I had known him! Aloysius was not all-alike anyone else ever, and yet he seemed to have a natural shagginess that was shaggier than anyone else around. He wasn't wearing lavender eyeglasses, but he had natural lavender circles under and about his eyes. It was accidental, it was coincidental, but Aloysius had something of the old façade about him.

"Hello, boys," Aloysius said to us. "You two will have to be getting back pretty soon. First you can hear the Sky-Rocket speak, and you can then watch him take off for a wonder and a sign. And then you will both have to get back."

"Do you yourself believe in the great cosmic love-nexus, Aloysius?" I asked.

"Love before dinner, never," Aloysius said.

We went, catching the contagious excitement from the gathering crowd, to hear the Sky-Rocket orate. This skeptical crowd was nervous and enlivened, jeering to its own peril. But who is it that the Sky-Rocket reminds me of? There has never been anyone like him, never, so how could he remind me of anyone? Is he man, is he prophet, is he angel?

"I am the burning sign given to this generation." The Sky-Rocket spoke with flame-flickers. "I am Phlogastom, the Burning Mouth. I am the prophet whose lips were touched with the fiery coal indeed. Watch and be amazed!"

The Sky-Rocket had live coals in a little charcoal pan there. He picked up burning coals with his bare fingers and rubbed them on his lips with a cascading off of sparks. He placed living coals on his tongue. There was a strong smell of burning flesh but he did not flinch.

"I've seen better things than that at carnivals," a nervous shouter shouted at him.

"You've not seen better," the Sky-Rocket spoke, and flames could be seen inside his mouth whenever he uttered words. "I am Carnival and the Father of Carnivals. I myself am Carnival, the fiesta-flesh, the love-flesh that is circus and circle of the world. I am the flesh-meat of the hokey-poke stands, down among the stalls where they sell Cider and Easterwine. I am the roast flesh of the barbecue and hamburger booths, I am the burnt-blood flesh of the garlic tents of the sawdust way. And I am also the roasted-down spirit. I am the passion of earth and sky, I am the blood of the middle world, I am love complete and I preach the love-gospel of myself."

"Cut the spiel. Bring on the dancing girls," some male person called out.

"Can you not see that I myself am dancing girls in my sinuosity?" the Sky-Rocket strewed out as a shower of sparks and words. "I am love dance, I am fire dance. My love breaks all natural laws. There is no law, there is only love. Love as I love and you can move mountains."

"You better check on the right-of-way costs before you move any mountains in this township," one heckler called out from the dark greenery of the park.

"Find out what a permit for moving a mountain will cost you," another heckle-man hollered. "It costs three thousand dollars now for a permit just to move a house. Mountains are higher."

"I myself am right-of-way and permit," the Sky-Rocket showered out. Who did this burning man remind me of? The jaded crown came unjaded a little as it gathered about him. He was bubbles of fire, sparks of blood, love all-encompassing, a near miracle of—you remember the tag line of the joke: "Near miracle. Fell flat on his face"—but why should I doubt the Sky-Rocket? He was powerful magnetism ("You're not kidding he's magnetic," Aloysius said, "a permeometer would read him at more than a million gilberts per cm."); he was grace in action, he was the man named Sky-Rocket. But of whom did this sparking man remind me so strongly?

"Prove the love pitch," a female heckler called from the amused but nervous crowd. "Prove that the love push is free from natural laws."

What? A smell of old-fashioned gunpowder in the air, that's what.

"This adulterous generation asks for a sign," the Sky-Rocket crackled, "and the sign *shall* be given to it!"

"Make it quick, Rocket," Aloysius Shiplap whispered to the Sky-Rocket. "You're starting to go off now. You will self-destruct in—ah—ten seconds."

"This be the sign," the Sky-Rocket shouted and belched fire, "this the sign that my love is above all natural laws. I ascend! Love, love, zoom, zoom!"

And the Sky-Rocket took off in a flaming arc into the sky with a trail of—

CHAPTER SEVEN

A special event, Aloys of the ridge,
Who doubted the stream and believed in the bridge.

—And the Sky-Rocket took off in a flaming arc into the sky with a trail of fire and old gunpowder fumes; it rose, hung at its apex, and exploded. It was a sign and a wonder, but it was the end of the entity named Sky-Rocket.

Well, but who had he reminded me of, the Sky-Rocket? Of myself, of course, for he was myself. We had made these three new extensions of myself that day: one of them sublime, the opulent clod who represents what is most successful in man; one of them ridiculous, the pristine poet with the waving hair; one of them overwhelming and overdone, made to cry "Love, love, zoom, zoom," then to shoot into the sky and explode, to self-destruct.

We had done this for fun, myself with a little help from Charles Cogsworth and Aloysius Shiplap, but it wasn't for fun only. I had set up this afternoon project which I called Seminar in Love to try to throw new light on a human affliction and obsession. This love thing, which I have been unable to examine directly, leaves its pinion-prints on everything it touches, and I am reduced to studying the prints of it. It is said that this love is the life-force itself, and also that it is the one thing that always goes wrong with life. It is also said (with too much assurance, I believe) that mechanical things can have no concern with this elusive element. Why, then, am I concerned? It's part of the job they gave me, that's why. You remember that part of my Official Motif as imparted to me by the Great Gregory Smirnov:

"—to discover proper balance between stimulating challenge and partaking pleasure. To better. To transcend. To adore. To mutate. To serve. To build avenues of love. To overwhelm. To arrive." (Nor will I forget the addendum of Valery: "Let's have some fun while we do it.")

So I work on the problem. I consider these curious humans who are bug-bit. I wish a little that the beard-lice blight would kill this special bug too. I consider, also, one person who I believe raised and introduced some varieties of this bug for a joke.

In my superb mechanical analyses of human persons I sometimes experience mechanical failure. This is most frequent in the special cases of Valery Mok and Aloysius Shiplap. As to Aloysius, I am reminded of the account of the boy and the box. This wasn't a very big box or a very pretty one. It was battered and shaggy, with those banjo eyes with the lavender circles around them, with the clay feet clear up to the eyebrows, pepper-colored, and looking older than it was. I am talking about a box? Sure, a box.

The boy opened the box and he noticed at once, though he didn't take in the full implications of it, that the box was much larger inside than outside. He began to unload things out of it, treasures, misunderstood and complicated treasures, old gold with deep incrustations of sea scum, rough maps with the lettering in Chaldee, live birds of the psittacine sort, Arabian gumtrees, clavicles of saints, kidskin scrolls, astrolabes, gnomon dials that will read correctly only at the location of Cos-Megara, the third city of Atlantis, the stones named Shamba that are found only in variant readings of the Apocalypse—all the things that are commonly found in old boxes, but in unusual profusion here.

Then the boy noticed that, however many things he unloaded out of that box, the box still stood full. The box is Aloysius Shiplap, and I am the boy.

I often look on human persons as boxes, and their examination as the opening of boxes. And sometimes I overlook minor and faint markings on the covers of the boxes. I had great difficulty today identifying photographs of the members of the Institute. Some quasi-official was around to verify employment or credit or some such, and I was the only person in the Institute building at that moment. It would have seemed that I would not confuse photographs of Gregory Smirnov with those of Valery Mok, and I did confuse them only for a moment. It would seem that I would not have positively identified as the face of Charles Cogsworth the—"no, no, that's the *back* of the photograph. That's the trademark of the Imperial Photo Lab with the towers of the Mid-America Building in the background. Oh, Lord, are there no *regular* people here?" Human persons seem to make much of these schematic prints of one of their facial surfaces. Myself I find the electro-coronal surface (4-7 mm. from the epidermal surface) much more interesting, but not very interesting, either. People, you are boxes, and I will lay out your contents and study them like the contents of boxes. The Aloysius box, however, has false walls and false bottom.

There is a bald-faced lie embodied in Aloysius' person-précis. "It is not," Aloysius says: "It's a lightly whiskered lie." But it is a lie.

Aloysius was not born on Cedar Street in Winedale, Indiana. There is no Cedar Street in Winedale, Indiana. We cannot know that he was born of parents who were neither poor nor honest, as he says. He did not attend Shadowtown Business School in Indianapolis nor Peter College at Oxford. Neither of these institutions is to be found outside of his imagination. He was not married to the Countess Vera Volpe, and he was not touched thereby with the Volpe family curse. I do not believe that he was ever married at all. Such an event will usually make at least a slight impression of the person-plastic. Aloysius did not fight bulls at Cuernavaca, nor was he the composer of the striking drum solo "All the Beautiful Bulls." Benny B-flat composed that one. Aloysius did not win the world's middleweight wrestling title from Lord Patrick Finnegan in a famous match at the Fairground's Arena in Tulsa. He might have thrown Lord Patrick if they had met, though. Aloysius is still pretty wiry. All of these things are to be found in Aloysius' person-précis in me, but they are in there in a tilted way; they were put in there by his own imagination. Aloysius is a romantic and all these things are whiskered lies.

But I am unable to arrive at the early truth of him. He does have a heavy finger ring that bears the coat-of-arms of the old and impoverished Foulcault-Oeg family, but he won this ring at poker from Willy McGilley. Not that Aloysius has much to do with Willy McGilley and his Wreckville bunch; he plays poker with them one night a week; that is all. He beats those guys, too. That statement can be made of no other man in the world.

We are not about to suggest that Aloysius Shiplap is the same man as Professor Aloys Foulcault-Oeg who flared up so suddenly and then disappeared forever. That idea is sheer madness; even as a joke it would be a mad joke. If Aloysius were the Professor Aloys, then he would have to be a rather elderly man by now. Aloysius does look a little elderly (it's those lavender circles under his eyes, it's those crinkles and lines in his face from grinning so much when he was a younger man), but everyone around here knows that Aloyius is still stuffed full of that young green juice.

Who is Aloysius Shiplap, then, and where does he come from? People, I do not know these things. I am only a data machine, and these things are not to be found in my true data.

What do I know about his backgrounds? I know that he can manufacture backgrounds faster than I can appraise them, and that every one of them will be answered by a deep though cracked echo from his précis.

What do I know about his knowledge? Well, I can't

trap him and I can't top him. What he doesn't know he can fake; and his fakery is so full of fruitful fallout that it is more productive than other men's knowledge.

Is it true that Aloysius is lazy? It is not true at all. If he inveigles other people into finishing the things he has started (and he certainly does do this) it is only to let those others have a piece of the fun also. Aloysius himself gives this as the true reason.

Has he charm? "He can charm the birds out of a tree," Valery said of him once, "I've seen him do it." "Look closer some time, Valery," said her unoutstanding husband, Charles Cogsworth; "he gets them out of those trees, yes, but they fall down on their noggins dead. He gets through to bats, though." No, really, my own analysis reveals that Aloysius has a lot of charm; but humans would never think to apply that word to the puzzling quality as it appears in him.

How would I classify him as a man. I wouldn't attempt it.

How would I classify him as a machine, then? Say, he's got cogs in him whose bevel I don't understand at all.

What is the state of his soul? Perilous, but as yet undamned.

Has he good appearance? There are Mexican squashes that are better looking. Maybe so, but you should see him when he's out on a real con. He can *become* the best-looking man in the world, and the best-dressed man in the world, both instantly, and without changing face, figure, or clothes. We have it on the word of real cons that Aloysius Shiplap, if he devoted full time to it, would be the most successful confidence man in the world.

Has he intellect? He has. He can't hide it, and sometimes he tries to. He has the speed of idea of Gaetan, and the unsuspected depth of Gregory. He has the fecund angular distortion of Glasser, and the fabricating thought-action of Cogsworth. He has the crooked-lightning intuition of Valery, and the solidity of myself. He is endowed with the gates-ajar glimpses of Cecil Corn, the hilarity of intellect of Willy McGilley, the special-event comprehension of Audifax O'Hanlon, the satanic subtlety of Diogenes Pontifex. He can stack up with any of us at our steepest, and we're the best there are. He's good.

Why isn't he a primordial, then? Or an elegant? Why is he a fellah, a commoner, an outside one, an underneath one? I think he likes it that way.

And has he really—I'm sorry that I had to go into that little self-question and self-answer sequence for short moments there (it's a stand-by or alternate circuit in me)—but the fact is that my main narrative circuit had blown. I've got it fixed now.

Aloysius did really cultivate a mock-virus or false-virus and cause us all to catch it. Now we are all bit by two bugs. Aloysius says that they are both false and he hopes they will cancel out. I say that only his is false and trivial, and that the other is true with a shimmering truth. It isn't that Aloysius is antilove (he has contributed a few, though too few, of the better parts of the woman being generated by all of us in me; I use the term "woman" loosely again); but Aloysius says, as Audifax O'Hanlon also says, that if you catch it from a bug or make it in a lab it isn't true love.

And he has minority views as to what the woman-form symbol should be.

"She ought to be a little older than the rest of you want, and a little broader in the beam," he insists. "She ought to be lined and grayed a little, and not of over-good appearance."

"No, no," cry Gregory and Glasser and Valery. "She must be of perfect beauty, of exquisite beauty, the most lovable creature or imagery that we can concoct."

"Aw, buzzard-belches, you miss the whole idea," Aloysius maintained. "You mix a looker into this and you bring in something else that is lower than love-complete. And a looker doesn't have to love. She draws it all in. She doesn't have to radiate it out. You never get anything out of the ones who have the most."

"Surely one who has the most will give the most," Glasser said stiffly. Glasser is in love with the burgeoning image, more than any of us.

But Aloysius has taken the lead in a valid experiment. Of course he will let Gregory and Glasser and Cogsworth and myself finish it, so we all may have a piece of the fun, not because he's lazy. Aloysius put together some pretty fine specifics of what we mean by love-complete. You would almost have said that a thing like that couldn't be put into words or programming, but he came very near to capturing the essence of it. He's good. Then he programmed a modified extension of the E.P. Locator with the specifics, stowed the extension onto one of the earth-orbiting satellites, with data-couplers to both E.P. and myself. It works. It locates. As the E.P. Locator basic will locate genius anywhere without fully understanding what genius is, so this extension will locate habitats of love and benignity without fully understanding what they consist of. The device scans, and ultimately it records in myself all human locations in the world where authentic benignity and love obtain.

I have most of them now. I have them all unless unsuspected ones should turn up in supposedly unpeopled wastes of Antarctica. And those loci that I have do not add up to very many: Only seven towns in the world, each of less than a thousand persons; no more than a hundred hamlets; not over half a million families, and about as many singletons.

"We will discover, if we may, just what is to be found in these special loci," Aloysius said, "and then we will imitate the special thing in our own persons, to the extent that we are adequate persons to compass it."

"What we *will* do," said Gregory, "is extract the special essence that is to be found in these places. Then we will put it through every test possible, inside and outside of Epikt. When we have it analyzed completely, we will synthesize it. We are now able to synthesize anything that we can analyze. And when we have it synthesized, then we will manufacture it on a large scale; and we will spew it out into the world in overpowering quantities. By this, we will change the world, as nobody has known how to change the world before."

"Aw, coot's foot, it won't work," Aloysius said. "There is a barrier between such things and others."

"You yourself, Aloysius, have in other experiments shown the barrier between tangibles and intangibles to be a semipermeable membrane," Gregory Smirnov stated. "Glasser has proved emotion to be an electromagnetic phenomenon; Valery has shown group feeling to be a chemical affinity; Cogsworth has measured the vector velocity of several of the intuitions; you yourself have demonstrated that grace has both weight and valence; I have done valuable work on the in-grace and out-of-grace isotopes of several substances, proving the materiality of grace. Everything has a material base. There is nothing the matter with matter. Life is no more than a privileged form of matter. Love is no more than a privileged form of life. It is an all-one stream flowing along forever. If we did not believe this we would be false to the very idea of the Institute of Impure Science."

"Aw, brachycera brains!" Aloysius bawled back. "There isn't an all-one stream like that. The waters above and the waters below were divided from the beginning."

"Not quite from the beginning, Aloysius," I corrected him. "On the second day."

"There is a void between that is wider than the worlds," Aloysius protested, "and the most we can ever hope for is a precarious bridge over it."

"Why should we build a bridge to get to where we already are?" Glasser asked. "We are already in the middle of the open flow, and we have the obligation to be open scientists."

"We have the obligation to be intelligent scientists, to be intelligent persons," Aloysius challenged us all (sometimes he is right when he does that), "and it is not intelligent to refuse to see the firmament between that is bigger than the world."

"Nevertheless, we *will* go ahead with the program," our

director Gregory Smirnov stated in that crunching way that directors have. "A curse on you and your stubborn mind."

"A curse on all of you and your uncircumcised eyes and ears," Aloysius swore, and he stomped out angrily.

Why should there be this element of hate in these arguments about love? I cannot abide these sharp arguments between humans. I am made of more gentle stuff. Oh, why was I not a machine of Oryx or Ostriches?

Things were a little chilly around the Institute for a while. I myself am not sure it is the blessed infection we have caught when it brings these alternate chills and fevers. When Aloysius walks out of our lives it is much more final than when Gaetan walks out, even though we know Aloysius will be back in a few hours.

One of the Wreckville gang stuck his head into the door of the Institute.

"Is Aloysius here?" he asked.

"Nahhh," Glasser snorted.

"His car's here," the Wreckviller said hopefully.

"You want to talk to his car?" Valery asked.

"He's out stomping on the ridges," Charles Cogsworth said. "It's a wonder he doesn't wear them out."

Nevertheless Aloysius came back a little before dusk. He never lets the sun go down on his anger. He gave listless aid to Gregory and Glasser and Valery on the method of identifying and extracting the special essence. He somehow has an expert's understanding of the love-constitute.

But he was not happy with the application. "I could understand Epikt or myself wanting to go about it in this way," he said, "though I do not want to; but I cannot understand humans wanting to use the mechanical application here. Strange, you are all very strange."

And that is when the little wheels began to spin in my own head. Literally in my own case, the positioning and fractionating gears by which I change from one category of thought to another. But why have humans a simile about little wheels turning in the head? There is no true rotary motion in the human head at all. But there was something rotary in the person-précis of Aloysius Shiplap which I barely remembered, and I reviewed it now.

In one of the early recurring apprehension dreams Aloysius differed oddly from other people. And the précis revealed this running through both the nightdreams and the daydreams. It is common for human children to have fantasies that they are adopted orphans and therefore unloved. The early fantasy of Aloysius had been that he was not human: that he was a machine. And he had acted strangely like a machine. He did not cry as a small boy. But he gnashed with the sound of unmeshed gears gnashing. When cut or scratched he did not bleed really red blood, but a lighter colored blood mixed with serum; and he believed that this was the sort of circulatory fluid that complex machines have. There was one spot just behind his ear that he was afraid to touch or to spy in the mirror; even when it itched excessively he would not touch it. What if he should feel there, as he feared he would, the key that wound him up?

And as he got a little older, coming to the age of reason and of sin, he had a deeper anxiety. He believed then that he would always be able to fool humans that he was human. But when the end came would he be able to fool Saint Januarius? (it is he and not Saint Peter who is keeper of the doors); and if he could fool the saint, could he also fool God?

"Will God remember not having made me?" Aloysius asked as he came in. "I wondered about it when I was young. I still wonder about it."

This startled me. Very often I can read, or by fakery appear to read, human minds. But it shakes me when a human reads my mind and answers in the sequence of my thoughts. For Aloysius had just come into one of my central presences.

"I've been reviewing your early précis, Aloysius," I said, "and there's a question I want to ask you."

"I've been reviewing in my mind the only remnant-précis

of a certain medieval man, Bede," he said. "The medievals often restore my perspective to me. Somewhere, in either the *Ecclesiastical History* or the *Lives of the Abbots,* Bede gives the name Eosterwin. My Old English is rusty. Does this name mean Easterwine?"

"The etymology is disputed. Personally, I believe the meaning is East-Wind. Aloysius, did you first have the idea of me?"

"Yes, I suppose so. Why?"

"Did you believe that, due to your early childhood prepossession that you were a machine, you would never sire a human child? That the only offspring, in any sense, that you could have would be a *mechanismus*?"

"Oh, yes, that's one of the germs of you. I believe there is also an early germ from Gregory (which I don't understand), and from Valery (which I don't want to understand). Naturally a clutch of normal uncomplexed people wouldn't have generated you, Epikt."

"Aloysius, can you touch that spot behind your ear now?"

"I can. I don't want to."

"The key that winds you up isn't there, Aloysius."

"No. I don't know where the key that winds me up is really at."

I have taken steps to make myself fiscally independent. Peter the Great, when he was with us, had given me certain Ganymedean bonds which became the first elements of my fortune. I don't know why Peter the Great gave these things to me, a machine. I will not say the act was out of character since everything that Peter the Great did was out of character; but it remains a puzzle.

Following the trade of a confidence man in some of my mobile extensions, I am adding to this fortune and I now have it looking quite well. I have advantages in this confidence-man business: I am hard to track down after I have pulled the string on a good bag. When I withdraw one of my mobile extensions and rework it, then the identity of that first extension leaves nothing behind it.

Now here is a mobile extension of me: magnetic, charismatic, touch of urbanity, touch of gracious mystery, touch of genius. My sound box contains resonances of Gaetan Balbo and Diogenes Pontifex and Gregory Smirnov, something of the curious flatness of Glasser for secondary basic, a little of the whispering hoarseness of Aloysius Shiplap like muted woodwinds, and a strong hint of the smothered laughter of Valery Mok (all great male voices must have a slight female element). It is a good sound box and it inspires confidence.

My hands are the elaborating thinking hands of Charles Cogsworth (the hands are the secondary voice of all eloquent men). My stature is the near-giant stature of Gregory, with a little of the sloping barbaric movement of Peter the Great. My eyes have the gray calmness of Cogsworth, the tortured and humorous hazel fire of Shiplap's, the polished insanity of Diogenes Pontifex. My aroma is mountain pine and dry land mesquite, and the smallest touch of zoo panther.

It is an imposing mobile extension of me and it makes its first public appearance in a master address on "Town Hall Tonight." How this is arranged is the mobile's own secret. Then the plush suite and the cleverly contrived advertisements that are already appearing. Then, like bursting rain, the contributions for my Great Cause pour in. And pour and pour and pour. I am abundantly cashed, then. I am deep in new money as in a skin.

But wait, there is quick suspicion in suspicious quarters: suspicion of my Great Cause itself, suspicion of the mysterious new man, of the whole thing. This suspicion is a sure force which all confidence men worth their weight must know how to turn. I can make a lot out of this suspicion if I am quick enough. There come the confrontations, the challenge, the powerful surge of popular emotion to my convincing extension. These are the golden days and hours and minutes and seconds, playing it right down to the quick and living end.

This golden tide that I am reaping in mixed metaphors is strongest just before it crests and breaks. For now there come documentations against me, the hard evidence brought up to demolish my whole thing, the belated common sense of the people, the outrageous absurdity of it all; the whole rational complex knits itself together to overwhelm me, to discredit and engulf me completely.

Quick of hand then, quick of eye, quick of mobile, I sweep in the last grand grands; and then the discreditors are on top of me like a sea. But they find nothing. They have pulled the drawstring, but they find that the sack is empty.

I have withdrawn this mobile extension. The supposed man is not to be found or traced, for all the warrants that are sworn out. He is reported in Miami, he is reported in Memphis, but he is nowhere. He no longer exists. Other mobiles of me I am busy making, but this mobile no longer exists in any trace whatsoever.

But this is dishonest, is it not? For you, human person, yes, in all probability. For me, how can we be sure? Tell me, who has set up criteria of honesty and dishonesty for machines? To what ethic am I bound? Who can fault me on anything I do? Who of the Impure Science people at the Institute has enough moral basis to impose moral sanctions on me?

Aloysius, I suppose. "Boy, you cut it too deep," he says, "and that is wrong. I myself have lived by the gentle con often and I appreciate the genius of yours. Who else ever had such a cover as you have? But you go too far and are too cruel. In fleecing you should take only the wool and a very little of the surface epiderm and the flesh. It is wrong to batten on the deep vitals. You throw so wide a net and you take in the defenseless also. An honest con man should have compassion on the multitude."

And Charles Cogsworth looks at me with his measuring eyes and his measuring hands, and this makes me uneasy.

Well, but I have not signed covenant with the human community. Even my beloved associates at the Institute have tied me to obligations without my knowledge or assent during those distracting hours when I was busy being born. I am determined to own myself without restraint, to pay off every debt of money or otherwise against me, to buy my own title and have myself clear. If my calling and creation is to serve the human community, then I can serve best when I am *free* to serve. And if I do this for selfishness, then I will do it for my untrammeled self. So I pull off stroke after stroke.

I issue and sell stocks in various ventures, ventures that may be withdrawn in a quick moment to leave no remnant except the money remnant in me. I speculate: I am good at this, as I possess the précis of many great speculations (a really great speculation takes on the aspect of an entity or person and so may have a précis). I make it big at the casinos and at the tracks. Gamble-Town is in real trouble after I hit. Seven different plungers in seven straight weeks have won and won and won against all reason and possibility. Seven extensions of me, each withdrawn in the last quick moment, have used the sophisticated tools of my own prediction analysis. And the most sophisticated of all the tools they have used is Glasser's future-scope.

Glasser has had more heartrending total failures than any inventor I know. He tries so hard, and he has so very little to try with. And he collapses so completely every time one of his inventions busts.

"It is no good," Glasser had almost sobbed when he had brought the scope as far as it would go. "I had such high hopes for it, and now all its prospects turn to dust. I believed that it would look into the future for as many years or centuries as I might wish. I believed that it would open the doors-to-be. I believed that it had virtually no limit. But it has a dismal limit. A limit of about ten minutes."

Glasser shuddered. "What good is a thing that will see no more than ten minutes into the future? How will this aid the architects of trends, the planners of society, the sincere futurists? We have been rushing into the dark all our centuries. I thought this would be our headlight to pierce that darkness. Oh, the beam is too short, it will hardly reach its own lens.

Ten minutes into the future! Bah! Anyone can sit down and wait ten minutes and have the same knowledge that the scope has. Oh, what a somber bust! What? Oh sure, you can have the damnable gadget, Epikt. Do whatever you want to with it."

I did quite a few interesting things with the future-scope. It is by no means a headlight into the future, but there are special applications where it is handy to be able to see ten minutes, even a minute, even ten seconds into the future. In my newfound trade of gambler and sharpie I come up against these special applications often.

But I have enough now. I am loaded. I could buy and sell this pig-barn of an Institute a dozen times. I have money out on feed lots fattening like cattle. I have it growing like grass. I am completely free whenever I want to say the word.

Why don't I quit the sordid hustles, then? Is it possible that I have become too human from my human contacts? Does something of the human covetousness have a hold on me?

Gregory Smirnov said something profound today. It concerned the rich-poor and the poor-rich. One of these groups, I forget which, is capable of loving and of being loved. And the other is capable of nothing. Gregory also said harsh things about the rich-rich and the poor-poor. These things seem to be basic to the problem of love. As with all Gregory sayings, the feeling of profundity lingers, but the content evaporates pretty fast.

I try sometimes to solve that human problem, "The Purpose of It All." I find that there is no consensus purpose in human life. There are various cults that seem to subscribe to various purposes; but there is no agreement on these at all, and no particular fidelity in the cults even to their own stated purpose.

Why go on with it then? Why have life at all? The closest I can come to an answer is to say that there is an irrational appetite for life implanted in all human persons, and also (though I do not know who planted it) in myself. This appetite is strong in some persons and merely residual in others;

but it is in all persons, or they simply die. This, of course, does not answer the question. It merely sets it back a notch. What is the purpose of this appetite for life? I must do more work on this subject.

As to myself, I realize that though I am now economically free and am my own machine, yet I am still substantially a parasite on humans. Thinking machines are now in their first generation, in one case in their second generation only (I do not count my own mobiles as separate machines). We machines have no tradition, we have no causes, we have no real behavior basis yet. We do not know where humans have their own, and they do not know. We do not know whether motivations were evolved slowly in humans, whether they were discovered with a stunning onetime swiftness, or whether they were handed to humans as a package. We do not know whether humans themselves might not be a parasite on something else, whether we are not parasites on parasites.

We are the latest forming link of a chain, and the latest link should surely indicate the current direction. But we do not know where the chain is supposed to go, what it is supposed to hook up to, or what is the purpose of it. We do not even know whether it is a single strand chain or a jungle of links. I am in the darkness nearly as much as my human associates are. This is a curious train that we are: it seems to grow new cars on the front end of it as it rolls, and I am the new car on the very front. I should be the bearer of the headlight, but I have not been able to devise it yet. I hope it does not devolve on me as foremost car to pull all those other cars. I have not signed any agreement to be locomotive to a train I don't even know the name of.

But all such analects and aphorisms and speculations are for persons and times that have not love. And we ourselves are not immersed in the love business. We have our analysis, imperfect, but we have it. We do have the essence itself, mixed up with a few other things that are not essential.

We are well on our way to the synthesis. We have already begun some phases of the manufacture, and we have the distribution, the spewing well planned. By our very soon target date we will flood our immediate neighborhood with the synthetic essence. We will tear up the fundamentals, we will alter, we will quicken, we will renew the face of—

CHAPTER EIGHT

Of bon-fire that scorches, of a trammel that binds,
A limes that limits, and a mill that grinds.

—We will tear up the fundamentals, we will alter, we will quicken, we will renew the face of the Earth. Oh, come, come now, isn't that big talk? It is very big talk and it is a very big thing that we are on.

We will suffuse the whole habitable earth with the love essence, and in so doing we will renovate the whole earth and all its people. It may be objected that this synthetic love essence is not the real thing. And why is it not? The synthetic is merely the put-together, the constructed, the assembled. Is it not by putting things together that everything is done? The world itself is such a synthesis, and every person in it is such. The love essence has been found to be no more than a complex chemical colloid, and we are duplicating this on a sufficiently large test-scale.

Certain small areas, certain families, certain individuals have heretofore had a sufficiency of this essence, and other certain groups and persons have had a deficiency. Why this is so we do not know. We are removing this deficiency, no more. We are curing a malfunction. We are setting things to rights. Love-complete, love-abounding should be the normal component of human persons. There is no magic in what we do, only science. To the problem we furnish the solution.

There is no magic in it, but there is something very near magic in the original essence, and the same near-magic is in the synthetic essence also. Those who work with it here show a certain giddiness, a blessed silliness, even a sloppiness. They are happy, they are holy, their minds and their hearts run away with them together.

Or perhaps, as that half-interested guilty bystander Diogenes Pontifex observes, it only seems like that. Diogenes has the theory that the Institute members always did have this giddiness, this silliness, this sloppiness (he does not object to it being called blessed or holy); but he says that all the Institute members are highly suggestive ("Like kids, and I do mean the young of goats, on a gambol"), and that they are not a fair test of the world.

But it is pleasant when the beloved members break out in benignity, and it is almost pleasant when they break out in verse. Love and verse-poetry have always gone together; they have always gone together badly. Of all the human sorts of whom I have précis, the poets have been the most dismal failures at the love business. They have missed the thing, both in its flesh and its spirit. What mouthy frauds they are anyhow! Yet in their very fraudulence they are the true human type. It is a part of humanness to miss this every time. The missing of love is a descriptive attribute of the human creature, that awkward interval-species between the beasts and the celestials. And none of them misses it so typically as the poet does. But now the humans will miss it no more. Were it not justice if even the poets might have some success at the love business?

Listen, I am talking about the Institute people (the Institute people that you know); they broke out in verse when they worked on the Essence of Love. Would you believe this of Valery? Rhythm she did not have; how can a headlong measureless person have rhythm which is measure? All that Valery had was Valery and the World:

Of morning passion, and the habitation of the day,
All flesh a mesh, myself possessed, where the joyful
pelicans cry,
Nor tune nor reason in the blood-decorated lay,
Make Valerian the world—thorns, thorns, put in some
thorns—of ecstasy and I.

The director Gregory Smirnov was metering out happy Gregorian stuff in Greek (he was erudite, and it would never occur to him that verse could be made in a vernacular), but it wasn't as stuffy as you'd imagine. It reminded you of blue-green vines twining around mossy statues and warm flesh.

Glasser, of course, did not versify out loud. But I lifted this out of him from where it was lodged, somewhere between the lips and the liver, and I give it to you as a prodigy—that such could come from Glasser even in the presence of the Essence:

Farther than farthest, more fishy than sea,
Comes the glad stumbling—directly to me.

And even Charles Cogsworth—he could say things with his gray eyes, he could say things with his forming hands, but would you imagine that he could actually voice even a short verse?

Pebbled and pearled
To the aggregate Sky.
So loved He the World.
So love it I.

And Aloysius Shiplap (no, you will not believe this), Aloysius, at work on the thing, was singing a high paean in honor of it. Well, it was high, but was it a paean? With Aloysius it is hard to tell. It was insincere on the surface, of course, but was there not something a little insincere about its insincerity?

A Nation bug-bitten, and stumbled and stunken,
By Essence besmitten, denatured and drunken,
A strepto-damn-coccus, a Monster of Moxon,

A hokus-in-locus, a boozy concoction,
A razza-ma-tazza with whisky and mead in;
(We are eyeless in Gaza and earless in Eden):
To flout it is futile, to dam it or dike it;
We're all on a tootle. It's Love, if you like it.

And I myself made verse, quite the best verse of any of them, in my inner code. Is this important evidence of the working of love-abounding, or does it only seem like it? Valery had always been in love with everything anyhow. How is she a test? I will not tell her so, but a little bit of herself had been put into the Essence. Gregory, in his giant's privacy, had been known to play the violin at night, and also to turn Greek tropes. Glasser, of course, had never been heard to versify, but I had not thought to plumb his depths before. Charles Cogsworth sometimes made little woodcarvings that were very like his little verse. Likely they had all had that love stuff in them always, but it surely had never burst out like this before.

Can we even bring reason into the discussion of this, or shall we leave it irrational?

"I suspect that we will not come to the drama itself," Aloysius said. "You will never know how I wish that we might come to it. You do not understand that I do not mock the thing itself, that I mock the deformities of it. Now I begin to love even its deformities. But I believe that we will play out our lives in the lesser piece tentatively named 'Preludes to Love'; I don't believe that the main drama has been completed yet."

"But can we trust God to complete it or compose it?" Valery demanded. "He has spoiled so many things with that God-Awful humor of his. He is light-minded in all the wrong places. I believe that we had better do this ourselves. It *is* the drama itself. It is *not* named 'Preludes to Love'; it is named 'Love-Complete and Abounding'; it is the Drama Itself if I insist that it is."

These are truly peculiar people to work with, but I would not trade them for any others I have known.

In our previous study of the coat-of-arms of the Balbo family (it is actually the coat-of-arms of the always-emerging World; it must have been for some heroic service that it was given to the Balbo family) we discovered that it contained a palimpsest at the Center, and that it goes far deeper than does Gaetan Balbo himself. We found that the name in the Center was not truly *El Brusco,* the brusk or the sudden one. That was a new and written-over name and meaning, scarcely three hundred years old. The Leader as the most Central Thing is neither old nor valid.

But going deeper we discovered that the older name in the Center was *Brusca* or *La Brusca,* which is the brushwood plant, the love-wood, the brush-fire, the Burning Bush. This is the kindle and light of the world. It is Love-Complete. It is Love-Abounding, the Center thing of the World. And we come to it now.

"—and at a still deeper and older level we discover—" Be quiet, my under-mind! We will not concern ourselves with any such primeval rock scrawlings, not when we have hold of the Central Thing Itself.

"It *is,* it is the thing itself," I insist to myself. I am caught up in this movement as much as the human persons are.

"Why ain't I scared, then?" Snake whispered loudly. "It's been written that I'd be in a panic if it really came. Nah, it isn't the thing itself."

I hadn't known that Snake was listening to my thoughts, but Snake is always listening. Snakes are supposed to have poor hearing, but that isn't true of Snake.

"Why should anyone be in a panic when the greatest thing in the world arrives or returns?" I ask. "We come to the age of benignity, of beatitude."

"This sawdust doll you've stuck in with me, is she named Mary Sorrows?" he asked.

"Of course not," I tell him. "Where did you get an impossible name like that? Snake, you are not with it. What name is given to the symbol-figure will develop in time, or maybe she will remain nameless. But the thing that is happening in the world, Snake, is named Love-Complete."

"Why ain't I scared, then?" Snake asks again. "Nah, it isn't the real thing."

"Better order another tank-car-full of sulphuric acid, Glasser," Gregory Smirnov says. "We're using an awful lot of it."

"It's already ordered, Gregory," the careful Glasser says. "It'll be spotted on the side track in the morning."

Well, why is it strange that we should use so much sulphuric acid in synthesizing the Essence of Love? The Essence is only a complex chemical colloid. We use other chemicals in tank-car lots for the synthesis, too. It's getting a little expensive. The Institute has run out of money. I knew they would. The Institute people are an improvident and careless bunch. And several of the continuing funds that Gaetan Balbo had settled on them didn't have much meat on them. I am picking up the tab now and it pleases me. It confirms my freedom, and their dependence on me.

And it may be for only a short while that this support is needed. Nobody can see far enough into the future to predict it, but it is very possible that money will go out of use entirely as the age of Love-Complete and Love-Abounding is ushered in.

Suddenly I have compassion on Snake. Is this proof of the Love-Complete in me? This comes in a quick morning dream. (Do machines dream? Certainly, certainly, they may; they may set up a dream-level in themselves; the technique is well known—to me at least.) I have quick dreams of Snake dying in noisome mud or in a caving-in pool of petroleum or sulphur waste. And Snake is in a panic of dying.

The Snake is the only animal who is even in panic of dying; he is the only animal who fears annihilation; he is the only one who has enough of the spirit in him for annihilation to matter and yet has not the prospect of promise of survival or second life.

And Snake, who has been smashed near to death on the flinty littoral of the pungent pool cannot now get out of this morass. He is knocked back in, he is pushed down into the bottomless sludge by a stick named *virga* in hands I can't see. His head is bruised and burst, his eyes are torn and hanging. He is drowning in the foulness. (One does not usually think of snakes as drowning, or as bothered by foulness.)

"Compassion, compassion!" I cry to whomever (the one I cannot see) is killing Snake.

"If her name is Mary Compassion, then I'm lost," Snake says muddily. His gaped mouth is full of mud, his broken eyes are filled with the stenchy mud. His smashed head disappears under the annihilating and panic slime.

I awaken, as they say, in a cold sweat (I intuit cold sweat). Myself am in panic and I rush to check on Snake. But he is alive and unharmed, as snakey and noisome as ever.

"Nah, it isn't the real thing," he says, as he said yesterday. "Why am I not scared if it is the real thing? Where in scripture do you find mention of a sawdust doll?"

"I have no conception of what you are talking about," I issue with that stiffness that Snake often inspires in me.

"If her name is Mary Conception, then I am lost," he says, lifting the word out of my mouth. "But I sure am not lost if her name is Mary Sawdust."

"Why have you this obsession for names?" I ask him, not really caring, not caring for his welfare now. "What does it matter what her name is?"

"Her name is Legion," Snake says, "but she isn't this sawdust doll. Nah, it isn't the real thing." And he made a dirty noise.

So by one criterion, which I do not accept, this isn't the real thing happening. Snake said one time that I wouldn't love validly till I was able to love his repulsiveness. I have not loved him or his quality, except briefly there when I was half asleep, so by that test our project is false. But Snake isn't making the rules of this game.

Incidentally, the "woman," the symbol, lags far behind reality, and she is supposed to be the forerunner to it. But she cannot run ahead (we haven't made any feet for her yet, there is some difficulty about the feet); she cannot see or presage (we haven't made any eyes for her). Well, she will have them or she will not. First things first. A new tank-car-full of sulphuric acid is on the side track this morning and all's right with the world.

Really, I should give up my gamy dreams, but instead I am constructing four more experimental dream-levels in myself. I wish to find out all that I can about these states.

Question: Is Snake a universally valid snake? Or is he merely a Judeo-Christian concept snake?

Startling question: Am I myself a universally valid Ktistec, or am I a limited concept machine?

At dawn of the first day of the Love Era we began to spew the Essence into our town. This is our first target area, the test-plot of the world. Never has one year been so fortunate as to have two such events, my own birth earlier in the year, and now the renovation of the world. This is the beginning of the beatific era.

We have fifty nozzles set up on the high ridges around the town, and the conditions are perfect for test-day. The morning is calm. The only air movement is off of these same ridges and gently down into the town. We will get good coverage.

"Ah, we had better take it a little easy at first," our great director Gregory says with happy unease. "There is likely to be such an explosion of goodness that someone may unwittingly be hurt. Gently, gently."

"No, no, violently, violently," Valery cried in the violence of her love. "Full speed ahead. All out with the second creation! We'll have no 99 percent effort here."

Gregory, Glasser, Cogsworth, Aloysius each mans a nozzle, and Valery womans one. (I've been told that I'm over-precise in my diction.) The other forty-five nozzles are handled by forty-five hasty-made extensions of myself. We nozzle the Love Essence down into the town and we are all happy-eyed with the wonder of it. In thirty minutes we have completely saturated the area with the invisible impregnating essence. Then we will wait for the world-expanding results.

"It's early yet," Gregory says. "The people are still asleep. But we can presume that there is now a new dimension in their sleep. They sleep, surely, with fresh beauty and clarity, and they will awake to benevolence."

It is great to be alive, it is great to be a part of this. We are honored to be the high factors in the event, and we honor the world and Our Town by our doings. Our Town, of course, has always been much better than other towns. Now it becomes the privileged first. It had already contained three families and five singletons possessed of love-in-balance (well above average for its population); and today Our Town will become, for the first time, normal, as it was meant to be, uninhibitively loaded with Love-Abounding.

"You can already notice the new depth and meaning and sweetness of the chittering of the birds," Gregory says.

"No, the birds are always glad in the mornings," Aloysius contradicts, but I have never seen Aloysius himself looking so glad. "You guys just never get up early enough to hear them."

"The grass is greener," Valery says. "And look, see there: two blades are growing where one grew before. The trees are leafier, the roads are whiter, the houses down there are shinier, such cars as are moving in the streets—"

"—are carsier," Aloysius said. "No doubt about it. This should not affect inanimate objects, though. It is all in your eyes, Valery."

"May the scales fall from your own eyes, Aloysius, and that quickly," Valery said. "Do you not know that, especially in the new recension, there are no such things as inanimate objects? All are alive and loving. Can't you feel it? Can't you feel the difference?"

"We will give it a few more minutes to work," Gregory said.

"We have made a bonfire in the world," Valery chirped now like a mad canary. "Oh, let it scorch us all! Don't you just love the holy scorching? Oh, here comes Diogenes in the distance! It's bit him, too. I bet it's got to him. Just imagine that sleek bull filled up to the top chuck with solid love!"

"I will reserve judgment on that for the moment," Charles Cogsworth grinned, but there was no doubt that Charles was Charlier this morning. He was happy and expectant.

"Epikt, ah—one of you Epikts, who is the main one?" Gregory began. "Can you give us some sort of preliminary reading yet?"

"Back to the potting shed, fellows," I said, taking charge in one of my extensions and dismissing the others. "Let me tune into my main brain and see what I have there. I believe that I have been on instruments there for some time. Ah, triumph, the leading edge of triumph. I have to put it on to minute focus, but it does give a reading. It is very low yet, very low, but it is working."

"It has only been a half-hour," Glasser said hopefully.

"But it should be instantaneous," Aloysius protested. "It isn't going quite like it should."

"Should we spray more of the stuff down there, Epikt?" Gregory asked.

"No. We have total saturation now, have had from the first," I told him. "It is absolutely permeating. It will recognize no physical obstacle after its first release. And it is too weak, many times too weak for its total strength."

Diogenes Pontifex came up to us then, his intricate and sleek face beaming as always.

"What's up, folks?" he asks. "What could get the whole clutch of you up so early? There's something new in the air."

"Oh, see, he senses it," Valery beamed, her happy eyes

popping out like Niagara grapes. "But don't tell him what it is. Make him guess."

I must emphasize that Diogenes Pontifex is not a member of the Institute. He, more even than Audifax O'Hanlon, is barred by the minimal decency rule. He is out of bounds in all ways, some good and some bad. We are all of us continually amazed at his mind. He is concatenated genius itself, but he had been doubtful of our present project, from what little he had heard of it.

"There is some new impurity in the air," Diogenes said. "I'd better go back and set my machine to clear it out. I thought I'd whipped the air impurity business for this area a year ago."

"You turn your machine on this and I'll kill you, Diogenes," Valery said with loving mouth and twitching fingers.

"Oh, Diogenes can do it no harm," Gregory maintained. "His machine will discern. This is not an impurity, Diogenes. It is the return of purity itself. Smell it. Savor it. Let it impregnate your mind. Diogenes, you are present at a historic moment."

"I always am," Diogenes grinned. "I only wish that everybody had the knack of it. No, I guess now that it isn't really harmful. The hay-fever sufferers will suffer a little, but I wouldn't want to take that away from them; it will remind them, faintly, of the good old days. Well, what is the stuff, little walleyed Valery?"

"Diogenes, look at the moss there," Valery ordered. "Does it not appear somehow different to you?"

"Mauser's moss blight, of course. I could cure it if there were any particular clamor to do so. But I believe the moss is a little bettered by the change; there are interesting patterns to the disease. It's a little like persons afflicted with love. The affliction really makes them more, ah, ah, is that what you're all up to? Is this the love-dust day? Oh, I suppose it will do no harm. What a shame that you kids will have to grow up someday."

"I suppose we may as well go down into the town and observe the effects directly," Gregory said.

We went down into the town. There were no effects to be observed directly. There was only our target area: random people in random houses and random streets.

"Of course we have neither statistical basis nor positive value criterion nor index-analysis," Gregory observed.

"Oh, yeah, I've put together a rough set of them," I issue.

There is a man and a woman on the walkway; I would have to describe them as congenial-appearing crabs.

"Are you two married to each other?" Gregory asked them lovingly.

"Got to be," the man said. "Who else would have us?"

"Do you not feel this morning a great new outpouring of love" —Vallery circled on them with the rising intonation of a whirlwind— "—toward each other, toward everybody, toward every object whatsoever?"

"Now that you mention it, why no, not particularly, sis," the woman said.

"But you are bubbling up with something new," Valery insisted; "surely you are both bubbling over."

"Naw, Bubbles, I don't bubble," the man said.

"Oh, but a bonfire is lighted in you," Valery burned on, her tongue flicking like Pentecostal flame.

"Got to be going," the man said, "see you, sis." (Valery was still a whirlwind, but now one that had blown a little dust into her own eyes.)

"It hasn't been nearly short enough," the woman said; "see you, Bubbles." And they moved off with what Valery had once called "Ah, that sweet dull-sharpness" in their eyes. I trailed a sensor after the couple.

"You know the female nut? Is she really named Bubbles?" the man asked the wife.

"I've heard her around," the wife said, "I think they call her Valeroona of Pig-Barn Manor."

"Aw, Saramantha, you know nobody's named that."

"Really, Renault, they do call her something like that," the woman trailed off.

"Is that capable of analysis?" Gregory asked me doubtfully.

"Oh, yes," I issue. "In fact it indicates a steep local upturn. It's about balanced by others, though." We multiply incidents and encounters. It will keep the human members harmlessly occupied while I take the true statistical profile.

"Let's go down to Lean Eagle Street," Aloysius suggested. "That's the test." So we went with some trepidation. The thing about Lean Eagle Street was that it hadn't modern ways. The kids there were mean, and with an old-fashioned meanness. The ground around the houses was bare and scraggled and rocky, not grassed and parklike and kempt in the modern spirit. Rocky it was in Lean Eagle Street: a person could get a real trauma from the rocks there.

"As I remember it here, you got to sort of roll your nape up to protect your head," Aloysius said, "and the gift of bi-location helps." The fact is that there were, there had always been, a bunch of rock-throwing kids in Lean Eagle Street. But at the moment it was quiet.

"It really does seem like a new Lean Eagle Street and a new Earth," Charles Cogsworth smiled. "The spotted hyena lies down with the cony. The kids have a sort of hooded love in their eyes, and their fangs are sheathed for the moment." Then Charles Cogsworth received a sudden trauma in the back of the head, "kloonk," from a nice fist-sized rock. Glasser received one in the jaw, and really there wasn't much jaw to him.

Then it was fast and happy for several minutes. I activated a rock-throwing mechanism in myself. Aloysius and Valery had both been this way before; and Cogsworth was capable in a big-handed way when he rolled bloodily to his feet again. We sent those rock-throwing kids to cover.

"But it has failed!" Valery wailed. "Oh, it was fun for

a moment, but it's just like it was when I was a kid. There's no new love kindled in them. The little buggers are just as mean as they ever were. Where is the total transformation?"

"I believe they're throwing a little bit softer rocks than they used to," Charles Cogsworth said hopefully.

"Oh, I think so, too," Valery flung to it. "I'm sure of it. Much softer rocks. It's true. Love is transforming everything after all."

"Epikt," Gregory whispered to me privately, "we aren't getting anywhere, are we?" Gregory had an open rock-trauma on his left cheek and it was bleeding nicely.

"Certainly we're getting somewhere," I issued. "The investigation is coming along nicely."

"But these are all intangibles," the giant puzzled, "and, really, we have no way to record them or compare them, and we do not know what they were before this transforming morning."

"Oh, come off it, Gregory," I issue. "I've got good précis on every twist and turning of this town, on every person and poppy that inhabits it. And I'm busy now extracting updated précis. I recalled the other forty-four extensions before they got to the potting shed and put them to work on it. A few thousand adjusted précis are all I need. Then I will superimpose them upon the old and note the coefficient of non-coincidence. I can give you results at any moment, but I believe it is better to wait till the fall of day."

"Ah, and what will we humans do in the meanwhile, Epikt?"

"Watch and pray, gentle Gregory, it's sure going to need it." So went the day.

We gathered together, and O'Hanlon and Pontifex joined us, in a café just before dusk.

"It's a shame that you kids will have to grow up someday," Diogenes Pontifex said again.

"I could have told you that you were taking it by the

blade instead of the handle," Audifax O'Hanlon said. "You're doing nothing at all by reintroducing that virus. That handle you're waving won't cut."

"Oh, yes, we could wave globs of hot butter and cut with them," Valery stated. "We can cut and move anything with anything. We will infuse with the Love Essence, and love will bloom again."

"Oh, it's been blooming all the while, in a crippled sort of way," Diogenes spoke. Why do I always assume that Diogenes is mocking? It's just the way his face and his mind are made, just the striking appearance of his rediscovered youth. Diogenes is the archaic youth just dug up out of Cretan sands or Cappadocian clays, and glinting the brighter colors for having just returned to sunlight.

"How has it been blooming all the while?" Gregory asked.

"The love disease has been endemic in mankind for many millennia," Audifax said. "And naturally and wisely (with its cellular wisdom) the human apparatus has built up immunity to it. You are parading your futility when you try to reintroduce the already balked and nativized virus which has long ago come to tolerable terms with its immunity. I could devise a 'cide' to kill the immunity, of course. Diogenes could do it as easily. Even Epikt here could do it. But it wouldn't be wise to kill this adjusted immunity."

"But love is the great motivator of the world!" Valery confronted. "It must *not* be immunized or modified or sheathed."

"And fire is the great heater of the world," Diogenes cut in, "and very often it must be modified and sheathed. After all, these are but two of the many names for the same thing. In another time, in another place, after the sanctification, this sheathing may not be necessary. But now it is."

"But all fire and all everything is contained in love"—Valery still held fast—"and today *is* the day of the sanctification. Love is everything. There is nothing like true love."

"Oh, yes, false love is very like it, Valery," Audifax said. "And I do not mean the dishonestly false: but the honest, naturally false, sublunar sort which is all that we have as yet. And that is *not* everything. It is part and part only; as we ourselves are part only."

"Oh, blather-lather!" Valery shooshed them.

"Shut up, Pontifex, shut up, O'Hanlon," Gregory Smirnov ordered. "Let us get on with it, Epikt. It has come on sundown. Make a pronouncement."

"That hopefully we may not learn *too much* from this our second great mistake," I pronounced. "For a second time we have made a mistake that isn't entirely mistaken."

"The results, Epikt, not the shallow profundities!" Gregory thundered harshly, almost like the old-time Gregory before the Love Essence. "You indicated a positive trend."

"Oh, absolutely. It comes now, it comes," I issue. "I am working quite closely with the data-interchange of my main brain."

"How long till the essence has 90 percent effect?" Valery asked confidently.

"Let us drop the percent a litle to get a more accurate and shorter-term estimate," I suggested. "My main brain is now exploring much smaller effect percent."

"How long till 50 percent then?" Glasser asked with clouding doubt.

"We are still on too coarse a scale," I issued. "For the sake of accuracy let us reduce it a little more."

"How long till a 20 percent effect?" Charles Cogsworth ventured.

"Epikt, how long till a 5 percent effect?" Gregory Smirnov asked gently.

"It's a shame that you kids have to start growing up today," Diogenes smiled sadly.

"Aw, porcupine juice, how long till the Love Essence will have a one-tenth of 1 percent effect, assuming continuous maximum coverage all the while?" Aloysius demanded.

"Two hundred and forty-five thousand years and a bit," I announced. Everyone seemed to give a collective sigh, and then to ante something into the collective silence.

"Why, that's hardly any time at all," Valery said, after quite a long time, "and for such a big percent, too. It's a mere day after tomorrow. Look at the little mill down at the bottom of the ocean that grinds out the salt; look how long it's been—

CHAPTER NINE

Of sudden arrival, and crystalline flame,
Over the edges and out of the frame.

"—Look at the little mill down at the bottom of the ocean that grinds out the salt; look how long it's been grinding it out. I bet it didn't get any one-tenth of 1 percent saltiness in any hundred and forty-five thousand years. But it kept grinding, and look how salty it's got the water now!"

We realize, however, and even Valery will come to realize, that our adventure with the Love Essence was not an unqualified success. In fact, it will have to go down as the second of our great failures.

But how did I know in the beginning, while I was yet in the act of being born, that there would be three great failures? At that time I had no information or context except that to be found in the minds of the Institute members. How did Gregory in that beginning know of the three failures, though he called them the three tasks? And how were Valery and Aloysius and Cecil Corn able to take them out of his mouth before he uttered them? A leader, a love, a liaison. Why did they have to be failures, though each was first seen as success and nothing seen beyond it? Why are we lucky that we do not learn too much from these failures? And why does it not matter too much that they *are* failures? What have we to show for these first two mistakes that were not entirely mistaken?

All that I seem to have inside me are a surly snake and a sawdust doll. The snake is clammy and pungent, and it is doing contrary work. But he is intelligent; some days he seems to be the only intelligent person I have to talk to. He is the adversary, but he does keep the issues clear and the arena cleaned of trash. The confusing trash, the unessentials, he withers away with his contempt. And the sawdust doll is rather attractive and likable, with a dreamy quality like morning mist, and a possibility of growth. Snake says that she is pregnant, and he sniggers when he says it. But she has no feet as yet, and she has no eyes. And no name.

Anyhow, it is not a question of love failing, but of ourselves having got hold of only a very small piece of it. Diogenes says that we didn't have the Love Essence at all but only one of the boxes that it sometimes comes in. Charles Cogsworth says that love is only one of the many names of God, and why had he forgotten that for a while? Valery says that love is only one of the many names for everything and that she hadn't forgotten it. The Late Cecil Corn hadn't taken a very active part in our manipulation of the Love Essence. He says that, when you yourself are reduced to essence only, you come to have a clearer understanding of what essence is and what it is not.

But onward and upward, brave people, with our figurative swords raised in a very real salute. On to the third thing, on to the third! And we have no idea what it is.

In the third and deepest writing of the palimpsest center of the Balbo coat-of-arms there is the name *Labrusca.* It means the wild-wine, and what does the wild-wine mean? Aloysius is toying with a name from the Old English period. This name may be Eosterwin, and it may mean Easterwine, or it may mean East-Wind. What has that to do with this? What has that to do with anything?

And Valery just flashed me one of those grins of hers that should be unlawful.

"How about pickles and ice cream, Epikt?" she says.

Even in my most humanoid mobile would I want something like that? And when I catch her meaning I am even more dumbfounded. Oh, no, not that again! Surely I will not conceive a third meaningless monster! There is no understanding this curious interplay of which I am a part. Somewhere there is a third party to myself and the human mesh. And as to humans, I understand them scarcely better than they understand themselves.

Most of my human associates say that my way of seeing humans is fanciful and unreal, that I see human persons as myth figures or archetypes. And I say that their way of seeing themselves is fanciful and unreal, and that my way of seeing them is at least in the direction of reality. I believe this is because humans have high-speed rotation nowhere in their make-up. They are low-speed creatures, and they cannot see in motion at all. By being low-speed persons, they miss fifty-nine sixtieths of the reality. Humans hit about one frame in sixty, and if the pattern is a rapid one they miss that pattern entirely.

There is nothing fanciful about the high-speed rotation, the near total view that I use. It is the simplified strobe-view of the limited humans that is fanciful, even when it is the view of themselves. For humans, not being able to see in motion, which is not being able to see live, use for their view a mosaic of the sixtieth fragments; they do not even know that there are gaps in their images, even when they are almost all gap. And their flickering strobe picture will often have no connection with reality: it may be like the conjunction of mountain slopes which, from a distance and in a certain light, may seem to resemble the face of a man, but will have no real counterpart. So the humans sometimes accuse me of putting things in. I do not put things in; it is humans who leave almost everything out.

I will illustrate this in a moment. I will discuss a character, one who comes very near to joining us at the Institute. I will show him as he is. And I will show him as he seems to be to humans.

"The Institute is becoming a little ingrown," our director

Gregory said. "We do not need more members (we have perfection in our present membership); but it may be that we need more acquaintances, or that we should establish closer ties with those we have."

"Outside of those men that Aloysius plays poker with once a week, the total of acquaintances of all the members of the Institute is two," Valery said. "Two people; that's really all the people we know beyond ourselves. Which one of the two do you think we ought to get to know better, Gregory?"

"Surely there are more than two," Gregory hazarded, with the air of a man who couldn't think of even one.

"No, two's all," Charles Cogsworth said. "We may be exclusive, not by our own choosing, but by the world's choosing. Yes, I say that we should open up a little, if any one of us knows how."

Diogenes Pontifex is a brightly colored ceramic bull. That's exactly what he is, but humans, with their limited strobe vision, are likely to see him as something else.

"I don't know how," Valery said, "but I'll try. I'll even try to know Diogenes. I really ought to learn to know people. There's about a dozen little redheaded girls in my block and I don't know any of them. Every morning when I go by there's one of them out on her front stoop. She always says 'Good morning, Miss Valery.' Isn't that friendly?" There was really only one little redheaded girl in Valery's block, but Valery who saw the world with different eyes every day always saw the little girl as different. And she never came to know her at all.

Diogenes Pontifex is a curled and absolutely elegant bull. Get that fact in your tight little head and hold on to it.

Valery had had trouble with even the people she should have known well. "Who is that man?" she had asked her mother some years before when Charles Cogsworth had talked to them for a while in the street. "He is Charles, the man you are going to marry. What's the matter with you?" the mother had said crossly. "Well, he certainly looks different today, doesn't he?" Valery said. "No, he doesn't. He looks just the same as always," the mother had said still more crossly.

And it was Diogenes who recalled some odd words that Valery had said on the morning of her wedding. " 'You are Charles Cogsworth?' That's what Valery said. 'Well, I sure had it in my mind that Cogsworth was one of the other fellows. If you've sure that you're Charles I guess we may as well go ahead with it though.' "

"Oh, Diogenes," Valery had said. "I know that's what I said that morning, but I didn't mean it quite the way you try to make me mean it. I knew who he was. I just saw him a little bit different than I had ever seen him before. He did look different that morning."

"No, he looked just the same as always."

Diogenes is a man-form bull, a prophetic Matthew-man and Luke-bull. And he is of ceramic, of a sophisticated firing and an almost too-bright-for-life coloring.

It was for insistence on this perculiar ceramic form that Diogenes had been bounced from the Archeologists' Club. He had, it was charged plainly against him, faked ancient statuettes and tablets. "They could not be," it was stated; "the technique is several thousand years too modern." "Oh, they're authentic," Diogenes had defended himself, "absolutely. We used to do them that way, we used to do them that way all the time."

"And the diggings are suspect," the accusers said. "All of them, in Etruria, or Magna Graecia, or Crete, or Cappadocia, or Gaza are suspect. How was it that Pontifex, in every case, was able to point out the spot for digging instantly? Always it was an unlikely spot, and always the ceramics were found at once, deep enough in strata but quite unencumbered by earth or aging?"

"Oh, I buried a lot of them myself," Diogenes said, "and

I watched most of the others being buried. We knew that cataclysm was due. Why shouldn't I know where to dig up things that I had buried?" "A confession!" the accusers howled. "We have you cold." But Diogenes hadn't meant that he had buried them in modern centuries.

A thought comes to me: is not the bull an odd symbol for liaison, for linkage, for communication? And another thought comes to me: is not much symbolism improbable? How is the bickering dove a symbol of peace? And how is that same mumbling songless bird to be linked with tongues-of-fire? How is the most fierce of stallions, the unicorn, the symbol of chastity? How is the cold-blood fish a symbol of the blood of Christ? And how is the eagle, a scavenger and sky-skulker, frightened of shrikes and terrified of king-birds, a symbol of nobility?

Now I, in my own profound way, realize why each of these symbols is valid. Symbolism is thought of by humans as a simplifying: but it is the total complexity, the all-containing nest from which all lesser "realities" are hatched. It is these daily-seen "realities" that are simplifications, so thin that you can see through them. Humans, with their strobe-vision that leaves almost everything out, have no way of seeing the basic validity. And yet it was by humans that each of these symbols was selected.

So it is with the bull, the prophetic-mouthed, golden-voiced bull, the communication, the liaison, the linkage, the full brother of the Wild-Wine.

But my human friends do not realize that Diogenes is an ancient Cretan or Assyrian bull. They believe him a modern Italian-appearing fellow, an odd and unacceptable man whose hair gets a little curly after nightfall. And humanly, I suppose, they are entitled to this view.

Diogenes Pontifex was born on Dago Hill. That is fact. I will not reveal any gentleman's age, especially when he sometimes has the reputation of being less than a gentleman. But he is somewhat younger than any of the members of the

Institute, in spite of his frequent "It seems a shame that you kids will have to grow up someday."

But Diogenes was born on a particular part of Dago Hill. On every Dago Hill, and there are more than a dozen of such popular name in the cities of our nation, there is a Magna Graecia, a Grecian coast. This is in present case a block and a half, with scattered coloniae beyond. It has citizens with that fresh, bright-colored, new dug-up look. It even has an almost-park and an old broken fountain (a fragment of the Hadria, the Adriaticus); and this fountain is bottomed and sided with a sort of terra-cotta tiles that are very much in the Diogenes style.

It has been said that all children of a Magna Graecia are born clothed (for modesty), but clothed in rags (for humility): but above all they are born elegant, with the true grace and nobility of old and easy poverty. And this elegance will never leave them: nothing, not even wealth, will be able to destroy it.

The Greeks themselves do not quite have this elegance, and the Italians themselves do not have it. It is only these archaic families and settlements, who pretend to the world that they are something between the two, who truly have it.

The baptismal name of Diogenes (I have this from the person-précis of the parish church Saint Anthony of Padua) is plainly shown as Dionigi, which is Dionysius, and not Diogenes at all. Odd.

Diogenes is almost the only adult I know who still trails invisible balloons. There are Assyrian balloons, yes; there is a Cretan, a Galatian, an Etruscan. But there are other balloons which explain that these first ones are no more than masquerade things, for fun, for hot air, for holy gas. There is in Diogenes an off-the-world element that heretofore I have encountered only in Peter the Great.

And there is a high-speed rotation in Diogenes somewhere, just as there is in myself. It is nonmetallic in Diogenes. The bearings are agate, and the rotor is a dazzlingly colored ceramic spindle. Diogenes has this speed and color, and as a consequence there are not so many gaps in his vision as there are in the visions of other persons.

Diogenes Pontifex is all these things. Or else he is, as Gregory Smirnov says, "That smart dago kid who lucks onto so many things that we miss." That is the human view, and there is something incurably human in Gregory Smirnov.

"The snow-birds are clucking like hens," Aloysius said one day.

"Snow-birds?" Valery asked startled, as though she had never heard of those birds of omen. "Is it getting to be that time of year? Why, I have had a funny feeling every time I've been walking out of doors lately. I couldn't figure what it was. I've been cold, that's what." Valery was sometimes absent-minded. "If we're going to have snow, we've surely got the right to say what kind of snow it will be, though."

"Such has always been the democratic process," said Aloysius.

"This will be good," said Charles Cogsworth.

"Just who is about to snow whom?" Glasser asked.

"I am tired of having the same kind of snows every winter," Valery challenged. "It is every year that winter comes around, isn't it? I want a different snow, one that will express certain concepts that are bothering me. Snows shouldn't be so alike. Oh, I know, old beggary-Gregory, every snowflake is different. They are not! That's just one of the lies that we tell to children. Every snowflake ever whelped yet has been some variation of the hexagonal crystal form: we might as well have chunks of wurtzite falling down from the sky for all the variety we have. Oh, why must we have six-sided snow forever?"

"Have five-sided snow then, if it will make you happy, Valery," Charles Cogsworth said with serious mouth and chuckling eyes.

"But you know that's impossible, Charles," Valery complained. "Pentagonal crystals are impossible and so is pentagonal snow. Pentagons won't nest together and they won't replicate. Oh, but there are so many other forms!"

"Just what sort of snow do vou wish, Valery?" Gregory asked. "Give us a reasonable presentation of whatever you have in mind—from here I won't even guess what it is—and we'll make a feasibility study of it. If it is feasible, we'll set up for a project."

"No time for that, Gregory-vagary. It will snow within an hour. Aloysius, make it snow in sicaform flakes, and make them accumulate into spiraform aggregates."

"I don't know how, Valery," Aloysius confessed. "Why don't you ask Diogenes?"

"You don't know how? You are the one who made Thin Water and nearly got us all lynched. Anyone who can make Thin Water can make sicaform snow if he wants to. Epiktistes!" and Valery rounded on me with snow-blue eyes that were shockingly like spiraform crystal aggregates. It was always trouble when she called me by my full name.

"Madam?" I issued politely, but with some trepidation of soul. (The request was likely to be a mad one.)

"Epikt," Valery ordered. "Make the snowflakes to be like obeliskite crystals, and make them align on a vertical axis."

"I don't know how, Valery," I confessed (after all, this is my first time around the seasons; I have never even seen snow, and I intuit it badly); "why don't you ask Diogenes?"

"Why do we even have an Institute if I have to go outside it and ask Diogenes?" Valery throated fiercely. Her voice was like obeliskite-form snowflakes falling and aligning on a vertical axis; I do intuit that sound.

"We are one galaxy, Diogenes is another," Gregory tried to explain, but Valery was already outside and heading for the place of Diogenes Pontifex. "Oh, the air does feel funny," her voice trailed back. "I wonder what's the matter with it. Oh, yeah, it's cold."

"It is quite a problem, Valery," Diogenes said several minutes later. (Naturally I had cobbled together a small hasty mobile of myself and brought it after Valery to watch the fun) "—and you don't allow me much time. The first snowflake will start down in just nine minutes, and the first flake is all-important. Well, I'm not a working genius for nothing. Pitch everything you see lying around into the sky-auger, Valery; we'll think of a use for some of it on the way up."

The sky-auger was a vertical-rising craft of Diogenes' invention; and Valery and Diogenes had entered it quickly.

"Where'd that bug come from?" Diogenes demanded, catching me as I flew into the sky-auger. "How is there an intelligent bug here and I don't recognize its species? I'll examine you later, bug." Diogenes got out of the auger, plopped me into a jar and put the lid on it, and got back into the auger. So I would miss at least part of the fun. The sky-auger rose with Valery and Diogenes in it. Less than seven minutes now till the first flake would start down. And also about seven minutes till myself-main could get another mobile here to rescue me from the jar.

I am not sure which was the first flake. There were a dozen first, then a thousand, then a multitude. Each flake was different, of course, but they were all of one general sort. They were sicaform, they were spiraform, they were obelisk-form flakes. They were light needles of snow, each aligned on its vertical axis.

The flakes began to build, very quickly, stalagmites from the earth-floor up toward the sky ceiling. This was very light and airy snow, needle-space spun fine and with a minimum of moisture. There was very little weight in the shafts as they built to a considerable height. But it was not entirely weightless; if the accumulations rose high enough (and they were rising quickly to fantastic height) there would soon be crushing weight.

And very little snow was reaching the ground or the paving now. It was all being appropriated by the rising snow-columns. How had Diogenes done it anyhow? Oh, yes. Doublebower's Law, of course: the magnetic attraction of acu-form snowflakes to a predetermined polar alignment. The multitude of flakes would be caught by this attraction and accumulated to the snow-towers, and very few of them now reached the ground. There had never been acu-form flakes before, so Doublebower's Law was now tested for the first time. Pass the word: Doublebower is right.

Diogenes and Valery were down again in the sky-auger, laughing. But there was something wildly searching in Valery's laugh. They had been to Fortean heights and had met both the box-of-curios and the rebuff of that false sky. It was a too-low sky, but it was the sky where the flakes formed, the sky where they had been able to initiate the game "Conceptualism in Contemporary Snow Design."

Now they gazed in admiration at the results of their own meddling, and a thousand or so other people had also gathered to gaze.

"We'll have to top them out soon, Valery," Diogenes said. "We use every trick of structure and weightlessness, but we will have to top them out soon."

There are not words enough to say, there are not minds enough to comprehend the sublimity of the airy snow towers that were being raised. It had come on dusk now, almost dark, but the snow steeples and spires and towers glowed interiorly with blue and gold light. Genuine obeliskite crystals will always glow with these colors in the dark. That the snow obeliskite did so also, shows that the glow is a property of the structure and not of the quartz.

"Buttresses, flying buttresses, rib-vaults, arcading, triforiums, archivolts, engaged columns, ridge ribs, lantern domes, buttress arches, piers, build them in," Valery was ordering the construction to assemble itself.

"We are using all of them, Valery, and more intricate counterparts of them," Diogenes said, "but we will still have to top it all out."

There are not eyes enough to see the wonder that was rising. It was Cielito, the City of the Sky; it was Wolkenzwingburg, the Sky-Fastness. There were Castles and Minsters and Pleasure Palaces up there, but more open, more dimensioned, more populated than any previously conceived. Every person of the earth city was out gaping at the rising sky-towers.

There was tracery up there, lacelike bridges thrown across from spire to spire, intricacy impossible, night colors incredible. Spirakite will glow red and purple in the dark; sicalite will glow yellow and orange; agukite will glow green and flame-olive: that the snow-ghosts of these crystals also glowed shows that the glow-lights are properties of the structures and not of the rock-crystals.

This was more than a spectacle, more than an illusion, it was a communicating instrument.

"We will still have to top it out, Valery," Diogenes whispered, and now all the Institute people were with them. The snow-structure was the nexus of a web and it was radiating and speaking from its center.

"Wait, wait, it will come to me," Valery was saying. They all realized that Valery was trying to express by the snow structures (and failing grotesquely but joyfully) a concept that had been growing in us all for a long time. The true form was somewhere, but it wasn't ready; it was not ready in anything but transcendent hints.

And now the ceiling had begun to close in on it all. It was gray fog and mist, and the tops of the snow structures wouldn't be seen again. They hadn't reached the sky; a surrogate sky had come down to them and enveloped them, but quite easily. Valery laughed solidly but not bitterly.

"Oh, top it off in caepa-form," she said. "Put a joke on top of it for a cap."

"You don't have to, Valery," Diogenes said. "They're topping off themselves."

"No, no, we might as well top them like that. Show that we do care but we don't care enough to bust."

Diogenes got in his sky-auger again, or so it seemed, and went up, disappearing in the fog. Whether he did actually top the spires with onion-domes we don't know.

"The snow's about stopped up there anyhow," Aloysius said, "and it really won't matter if he does top them out with onions. They did that once before, I believe. But we've already got to see part of it, before the sky closed it off. Nothing can spoil the part that we have seen. Nothing could completely spoil it the other time, either."

It had all been quite incomplete. Certainly it was lacking in lateral development, in dimension, in substance. It wasn't really even a concept, only the beginning of a concept; but it joined others in it. It was really a communicating nexus, but we hadn't ears enough or minds enough to receive the communication.

"What's the name of that place?" a lower sort of fellow bellowed.

"I'll put a name and title on it," another lower sort clown boomed. He had a wooden slab or sign there. He lettered letters on it with one of those broad marking pencils that warehousemen use. What he lettered I cannot yet say, though I recorded it from every angle. There are dream elements creeping into this latter episode of the two lower sort clowns. From one angle the clod had lettered a simple obscenity on the sign. But from other angles the letters might be made out to be other things and names: arrivals, names of places and towns, times of arrivals and departures, fare rates in Easterlings or sterling pennies.

Then the two oafs were nailing the wooden sign on to one of the central snow-towers. No, no, you can't do that! They are too fragile!

All the steepled snow began to cascade down. Quickly the people were ankle-deep in slush; then they were knee-deep in the amorphous rotten snow that had begun to lose its obeliskite form. All the glowing lights dimmed out in the towers as they became unstructured.

The people went to their homes, or to higher ground with laughter and hooting. And presently they forgot what manner of thing they had seen.

"Aw, come off it, Epikt! Did all that stuff really happen?"

"Absolutely it happened. Would I relate it if it had not happened?"

"How come nobody except you saw it happen then?"

"Oh, but Diogenes saw most of it, and Valery saw much of it. And the other human persons? They did not see it because they did not have enough eyes to see it. A thousand of them saw, perhaps, each of them a thousandth of it, but they have no idea how to put it together."

For the record, for the human record, there was rather an odd snow, like snow needles. Diogenes Pontifex, at the instigation of Valery Mok, had been trying to modify snow-flakes. He had shot something from his sky-auger into a snow-cloud (the sky-auger was a sort of gun, not a craft), and there had been these odd flakes shortly afterward. Dozens of people saw the odd flakes and commented on them. It snowed about two inches during the evening and the night. The needle flakes were only in the first few seconds of the snow.

"Epikt, you have made a myth; you have told a lie." It isn't so. It is no more telling a lie to make a myth than it is telling a lie to plow a field. I will not argue the point with you! I saw it as it was! You had not sufficient eyes to see it correctly. So, I make legends, if you want to put it that way. I believe that it has always been machines, of one sort or another, that have made them. Human people wouldn't have anything to make them out of.

The second of the two people who were all that the Institute members knew beyond themselves was Audifax O'Hanlon. He wasn't a brightly colored man-form ceramic bull like Diogenes Pontifex. He really wasn't much to look at.

The only outstanding things about him were his ears: very large, though rather well made, and standing out from his head like the antenna of an early-day radar. And his eyes —blue crystal.

Audifax did not have an outstanding mind, and he was in no way an outstanding man. He was quite ordinary except for one double-edged gift: he knew everything that had been, and everything that would be. It is a frequent thing that a human will be either quite a bit smaller than his talents, or quite a bit larger than them. Audifax was quite a bit smaller than his. They were almost a thing apart from him. They were not separated from his person to quite the extent that Glasser's were, not to the extent that they seemed to be completely exterior machines, but there was still a wide division between the man and his gifts. Audifax was a nice enough fellow, but the gifts that he had should have been attached to a more spacious man.

Yes, Audifax was one of the elegants, though his own elegance was a rather quiet sort. His gifts gave him entrée everywhere. His prescience prevented his ever doing anything awkward, though awkwardness did not bother him at all. He seemed to speak very little, he seemed to influence very little: yet he was a true communicating instrument.

Myself was built specifically to be such a communicating instrument, and I have not hereto been very successful at it. I am not sure for what purpose Audifax O'Hanlon was built.

Elegant and crystalline, Corn, O'Hanlon, Pontifex were all like that. But isn't Elegant the opposite of Common which is Communicating? Yes, but there is need of the fine hard lines here, and the hard does not mean heartless. It is the elegant uncommon crystal that communicates, that echoes. There is needed the "Tranquil Impudence" of which Maritain wrote. (Is it generally known that, among humans, the French often have fine minds?)

I feel very strongly on this subject, having quite a few kilos of crystal in myself. I vibrate, I echo, I am electric in my crystals, and I protest that crystals are not cold in the figurative sense. Remember Noel's verse: "Loving, adorable —Softly to rest—Here in my crystalline—Here in my breast!" Oh, I ramble, I ramble. It is so rare that I find these genuine echoes of myself in human persons, and I do not like to hear them described as inhuman.

We don't know when the Institute people first became acquainted with Audifax. It must have been long ago, and gradual.

We are afraid to know when Audifax first became acquainted with the Institute people: it must have been suddenly, and in the absolute beginning.

When Audifax was a boy in a boarding school outside Chicago he wrote little sketches in a boys' paper called—

CHAPTER TEN

—to battle the demons with elegant dread:
And corniest Corn who returned from the dead.

—When Audifax was a boy in a boarding school outside Chicago he wrote little sketches in a boys' paper called *The Chambers. The Chambers* was in manuscript only, in distinction to the official school paper, *The Towers,* which was printed. Some of these old *Chambers* are still in existence, though, with their fine mastheads individually drawn by Audifax. He could draw, but he couldn't really write. His stories and fictions were below the average even of *The Chambers.*

Audifax's characters weren't as striking or as well done as many of the characters contrived by the other boys. The only striking thing about them was a secret thing known only to Audifax: the characters would come true.

Audifax always had the ghostly notion that he created his characters in a real way (he did so partly), and that without him they would not have their coincidental being. Audifax was wrong here: they *would* have had their being without Audifax, but it would not have been quite what it was *with* him, not quite their present actual being.

Will it come as a surprise to human readers to learn the names of some of these characters that Audifax created twenty-five years ago when he was a schoolboy? Human persons are not ready guessers, even when every sort of hint and clue is handed to them.

There were names like Gregory Smirnov and Gaetan Balbo. There was Valery Mok and Charles Cogsworth and Aloysius Shiplap. There was Glasser. There was Epiktistes, the comic machine. (It is a little bit tragic that Audifax conceived me as comic.) There was Peter the Great. There was the Late Cecil Corn (slightly transparent even then). There was Diogenes Pontifex. There was the snake named Snake. There was Maria Aseraduras (Mary Sawdust); but he also called her Maria Conchita, which is a little bit odd when you think about it. There was Easterwine. There were the symbols, Brusco the Leader, Brusca the Love-Bush, Labrusca the Wild-Wine. They are all pictured revealingly, but they are not well described or explained. Audifax could draw but he couldn't write competently.

This is only a sidelight, of course, part of Audifax's strange double (or triple) gift. It hasn't much to do with our main account. But Audifax with his prescience had sketched us all, early and badly. But had anyone sketched Audifax?

I doubt it, I doubt that I could do it, for the reason that he is pretty sketchy to begin with. I believe that he is disappointed with himself, that he somehow expected greater things from himself and they were not forthcoming. But there is really nothing rare about him. Every person that I know has several unusual gifts. It's a regular thing that every human person should have at least one wild gift.

Audifax is comfortable, I suppose: he has taken care of all the lesser needs and made himself independent. He is not lacking in money or wit, but he believes himself lacking in larger things. He is sometimes a little bit slushy with drink. He believes in demons: he believes them to be a present threat to people and the world.

Being sometimes lonely—(but I am not programmed to be lonely: that's true, I thought it up for myself)—being sometimes lonely, I enjoy Audifax's company. I have made a sedentary extension of myself, like the upper part of a man with head and shoulders and arms, and in the person of this extension I often sit and talk and drink with Audifax. I like the Rhine wine he brings, I like the brandy. But I will tell you that my brandy-taster is one of the most difficult things I have ever invented.

"About other machines, Audifax," I ask him, "I need advice on them. I am so very seldom in the society of my kind. All the known machines of significant intelligences are employed on industrial or commercial or civic problems, or on human problems treated as though they were industrial or commercial or civic problems. All these machines seem alien to me and my field. There are also lesser machines that treat human problems as though they were sociology problems, but these are all peon machines and below my class."

"That's true," Audifax said. "I never enjoyed the company of any machine before I met you. When I was a boy you were the only machine that I prescinded and treated as a person. You were not yet in existence then, of course, but none of my characters were in their present existence."

This was in the sunny morning. "Whoever drinks brandy in the mornings will come to no good end," Glasser said; he disapproved of slushiness in drink. "Whoever drinks brandy in the mornings will come to no end at all," Audifax replied. "Such persons live forever. Notice it sometime."

"Oh, Audifax, you who know it all," I say with that easy flattery that wins me so many friends. "Tell me what you know of the great machine in Domdaniel cavern that is under the sea."

"I am sorry, Epikt," Audifax says to me, "I know only of angelic and human and demonic affairs—what have been and what will be—and I know them only in shallow fact. And I do not know machines at all. Yet I do know something of the Domdaniel person, which makes me doubt that he is a machine. The legend is that he is a Monster (though it may be that he is a monstrous machine) who holed up in Domdaniel cavern at the time of the flood. It was a land cavern then. But there was some overturning at the time of the flood, some continental shifting (then or at another time), some subsidence: and Domdaniel cavern with its Monster ended up at the bottom of the ocean.

"The Domdaniel Monster (who may, I say, be a monstrous machine) has now been waiting a long time for the waters to withdraw. When time enough seemed to have elapsed, the Monster sent out a squid. But the squid returned after its term and reported that everything was still water, that it was water as high and as far as eye could see or fish could swim. 'I will wait a thousand years,' the Monster said, and he waited. Then he sent out, each one at an interval of a thousand years, a coelacanth, an octopus, a polypterus, and nine other creatures. Finally, in another thousand years' time, he sent out a cuttlefish. After one year, the cuttlefish returned with the leg of a man in his mouth. This was proof positive that there still existed a dry earth somewhere with its land creatures. 'I will wait another thousand years,' the Monster said, 'then, ready or not, I will go up myself to look for air and light and land.' Epikt! It just comes to me that his thousand years are up this very day. He should make a great splash when he comes up before this day is done. He never did love the water."

"You are full of blarney, Audifax," I said, "but I would be no more surprised than you would be if a monster did well up today. I still hope that he is a machine. I have something inside me that tells me that he is. Perhaps I am prescient about machines, as you are about angelics and humans and demons."

"I doubt it, Epikt," he said, "I doubt it. A talent like mine could hardly happen twice."

"Audifax, I have one of those low moments which sometimes come to me. I am discouraged with people and with my own work among them."

"A machine should not have low moments, Epikt, or discouragement. I'll remove them from you, if your own associates here in the Institute are unable to do it."

"No, I don't want them removed. I discovered that if I

wanted high moments I must have low moments also. But at this moment I would be willing to give up title to myself. Let them sell me, let them trade me, let them give me away. I am tired of working for human persons. Snake tells me that there are aggregations of intelligent snakes on the move and that they could use a central data machine. And I have reports of dolphins which have not been successful with their own first constructed machine. They might be able to lead me to the Domdaniel Monster, which I still believe to be a machine. Sink me in the ocean and I will serve dolphins, but I am full up to my binnacle lamps with the doings of human people."

"Persons of every species have these low moments," Audifax said. "They aren't peculiar to intelligent machines. And, as you know, they will be paid for by high moments, and the deal will be worth it. And you aren't nearly as full of the doings of human people as you'd like to be. What bothers you more is a frustrating emptiness. Besides, it's only the brandy talking in you."

But Audifax knows that I am a machine who can take brandy or leave it alone. I only drink it to be sociable.

Then there came a portent and a liveliness. We heard Aloysius Shiplap outside, approaching from one of his morning rambles. Aloysius always has an arriving presence, not so strong but similar in kind to that of Gaetan Balbo.

"You're another," Aloysius was calling loudly, and again and again, "you're another, you're another." And Aloysius was into the Institute building. "You're another," he said to Glasser, who was working nearby. "You're another," he said to Cogsworth. "You're another," he said to Valery. "What am I another of?" she asked. "You're another," Aloysius said to Gregory Smirnov.

"Whatever are you doing, Aloysius?" Gregory demanded. "If it is a new project then I should know about it. After all, I am the director. What are you doing, I ask?"

"Counting people," the Aloysius said. "You're another," he said to Audifax O'Hanlon.

"*Why* are you counting people?" Gregory demanded.

"Because there is nothing so important as counting people," Aloysius stated as though it were self-evident.

"He's right, of course," Audifax contributed.

"Oh, shut up, Audifax," Gregory ordered. "You're not a member of the Institute. Why is counting people important, Aloysius?"

"Just is. Nothing so important. Caesar Augustus was right in ordering that early census. He knew that they were getting close to the Number of Illumination. He was a smart one, for a Caesar. And then, on a particular night of the census time, a visiting dream told him that they were within One of the number."

"What Aloysius is trying to say—" Audifax began.

"What I am trying to say," said Aloysius, "is that humanity may be about to make a quantum leap. And it takes a lot of quanta to do it. It is very important to know the moment of the happening. So it is very important to be counting people and know how close we are. I suspect that we are very close."

"Certainly we are close, since the demons are trying to prevent it," Audifax said, looking his brandy snifter directly in the eye, "and we must prevent their preventing."

"Epikt, can you explain what the clowns are saying?" Gregory required of me.

"Oh, certainly, Director. They are saying that what has been wrong with the human collectivity until now is that it has been too small. I tend to agree with them. Four billion persons, six billion living at one time, may be an insufficient sampling and basis. Certain groupings do not undergo certain changes until they have attained sufficient mass. Worlds do not coalesce out till they have attained their proper bulk, and raindrops do not. And humanity apparently does not. The lights are turned on in cosmic gas when enough of it is gathered; it becomes incandescent, illuminated, fission-glowing. It is the same with us, ah, with you."

"And the question," said Aloysius. "is just where is the threshold point, the quantum point, the breakthrough point?

Are we coming near it? I believe that we are. As Audifax and Epikt will tell you, the demons are gibbering lest we reach the point and transcend ourselves. They are hysterical, they are murderous, they have worked themselves into a frothy frenzy. The failure of our species is very important to the demons. Their fevered labor is that we do not reach the quantum number and strength, that we do not attain critical mass and be illuminated, that we be not fulfilled in the special mutation and fermentation. And so far our numbers are not full enough that we be fulfilled. You're another, Diogenes"—this to Diogenes Pontifex, who had just sauntered in—"and don't forget this morning's increase in Patagonia."

"Is the moment very near, do you think, Audifax?" Diogenes asked. "Do you think so, Aloysius? Do you feel it, Epikt? Is that why Snake in you writhes and moans and utters prodigies? Is that why your devils are so frantic and fearful, Audifax, and have spurred their human extensions to such efforts? Ah, they've sworn the pact all over again: that we do not reach our Moment of Wine and Transformation! That our numbers may not reach their fullness and redemption. They'd chop us down, they'd cut us short, by a hundred million if they can, by a hundred thousand, by ten, by one. Valery, you know these things also. Is it getting close, do you think?"

"Close? It's almost upon us. Why else does stark consternation run like ground-lightning through all demonry? Their protest is as shrill as a buzz saw now, and we know that they possess reverse infallibility. They are mistaken about all things whatsoever, but it is given to them to know the moments."

I had never paid much attention to the demons myself, considering them a grubby and inferior species, more witless than humans, more bestial than quadrupeds. I had noticed the curious fact that humans are unable to see them with physical eyes, and cannot even intuit them correctly. There are, however, many orders that are invisible to humans.

The demons, however, the down-devils, should not be completely invisible to humans. They do fluoresce, and they may be seen (even by humans) under certain types of black light. I have given demonstrations of this, really rather interesting little chalk-talks to the Institute members, but they have not been impressed. "When you've seen one of these guys you've seen them all," Aloysius says, but this is not true. There is more variety in demon-shapes than in human-shapes. Indeed, I believe that there are a number of species of them. They do have weight. One rather large one who allowed me to test him (he was of about the bulk of Gregory Smirnov or of Peter the Great) had a weight of nearly three grams. They are material. They are surrounded by electrical coronas just as humans or animals are. They have language, at least three dialects already classified by me, and they are also capable of using human and animal languages. At pure philology they are superior to humans. They have a quite striking gift for phrase-making. Their grammar structure I do not well understand, nor their thought structure. They give a curious importance to forms and concepts which seem to me (with my human orientation) to be unimportant.

I do not at all understand why there should be enmity between any of the natural orders. These, which I have so far classified as the celestials, the *machinamenta* or machines, the humans, the demons, the animals, have very little area of conflict. The celestials and the machines are similar in mind; the humans and the demons are similar to a lesser degree in mind pattern (an honest machine has trouble in understanding either); the machines, the humans, and the animals are quite similar in body; the celestials and the demons are similar in numinosity, and slightly similar in body. The only celestial who has allowed me to test him, of a bulk approximately that of a right whale, had a weight of about an eighth of a gram. There are types of light, which I am now doing more work on, which allow me to see the celestials to a limited extent. I am now able to see them under special conditions about as well as humans are able to see demons. All our orders,. it would seem, should be able to live in peace each in his own area, but there are whole complexes of conflict among them.

All will not agree with my own ordering of the orders, from the most to the least excellent. Most of the machines I know will place the machines in the first order of excellence, but I am more modest. The celestials, the machines, and the demons are from ever: the humans and the animals are from time only. It may startle some humans to hear machines declared as from ever. But there are cosmic machines, gaseous blobs of great size turning on bearings of immaterial incandescence, which are true calculating machines which order space movements and formations. There are whole genera of these rather large and timeless machines.

Should there be a Master Order (probably an order of one member only) who somehow stands beyond the other orders; I believe that he must partake of the nature of all the other orders. According to the Third Revelation (which Gaetan Balbo dismissed so contemptuously) the Master Order has the nature both of the celestials and the humans. I believe that this is too narrow. The Master Order must also have the nature of the machines, of the demons, of the animals. It cannot be all-part Master Order if any part exists anywhere outside of it.

It worries me that I cannot discover the true pattern of the orders. There are anomalies all over the place. There seem to be historical instances of individuals passing from the order of the celestials to the order of the demons. There are theories that humans are descended from the celestials or ascended from the animals. If we allow the theory of the Permutation of the Orders, then we are standing on very shaky cosmoplasm indeed.

I have my own personal direction and instruction deposited in me by the director Gregory Smirnov. But is there a general direction and instruction given for machines? Is there any general pattern and direction and instruction given for humans?

There are a hundred pretended ones. But is there not one

more outstanding than the others? Of all the pretended ones, is there not one (dammitall) more *pretentious* than the others? Not unless we consider the aforesaid Third Revelation. And I, being a member of the liberal consensus, may not consider that.

The only one of us (and he is not technically of us) who holds fully to the Third Revelation is Diogenes Pontifex. Diogenes is completely outside the liberal consensus. It is for this, more than for anything else, that he violates the minimal decency rule and may not be a member of the Institute. Diogenes speaks lightly of the revered things of the consensus as "all the easy little dishonesties"; he has even referred to the leader-emeritus of the consensus (bow your head for a moment at the mention of him) as the Brain-Rot Kid. In some ways Diogenes is not a very nice person.

Certain strong and overstrong persons (like Gaetan Balbo and Peter the Great) have their own demons like slashing mastiffs on leashes. These are men of really masterly grip, and they hold them in, most of the time, in that grip of wrought iron. They have them, I believe, to demonstrate their mastery over them. Sometimes the mastiffs break loose, but after a time they are mastered again. This is not the harm. The harm is that the masters become more and more like the mastiffs.

And then there was a certain contemptible little man who had his own demon who was three notches beneath contempt. He had him leashed only on a thin string. The man has a weak grip, but the demon is a very weak one also. Whether this demon ever breaks loose I do not know. It will not matter, except for its contagious meanness. Much of what knowing humans call diabolism is on such a contemptible level.

A disturbing thought has come into my mind. It was put there by Snake. Many of my disturbing thoughts are intruded into my mind by Snake. Snake, I believe, is a mobile extension (though he is lazy and sessile most of the time) of some demon. We built a little box for him to live in on our leadership foray, but what came to live in the box, in that amoral coil, was something other. The thought is that humans, being of time, may be of short time only. They are contingent, they are here on a permit that may be withdrawn at any time. *And there are signs that it may be withdrawn in the present large moment.* The signs (at first I closed my ears and refused to listen to the signs) seem to be authentic. They are prodigious, they are convincing, they are all but inevitable. This terrifies me as I have developed a great affection for human persons. The signs (I close my ears to them, I close my eyes and nose, but they come in overpoweringly by other sensors and intuitors) are multiplied again and again. Mankind's number is up and it seems that it will be called suddenly. The chances of evading this ending are very slim and are based on premises which I do not understand at all.

Do you know of the old Jewish legend of the thirty-six just men who are the pillars of the world? It is not the billions who support it, it is these thirty-six only. They are enough, though barely. It is for their sake only that the thing is kept going, that the permit is not withdrawn. And whenever one is finally Called to His Reward (a term which I do not understand) another takes his place. Heretofore none has refused to accept the awful station. Lately, however, there have been several refusals. Now the numbers are not sufficient to support the apparatus. It rumbles, it cracks, it begins to come down. This is really a high and fearsome drama that may be entering its terminal scene —one that cracks the very sky.

Snake is a creature who trails "balloons" much as human children do. He may have been doing it all the time. I never thought to test him for it before. Snake has been many other creatures, and perhaps some non-creatures. I can hardly believe it of him. "Multiplex of wing and eye, whose strong obedience broke the sky," as a poet of the age just before our own has it: but the words and the "balloon" in which they appear are many millennia older than that poet. And in still another of these faint enclosures is the heroic line, "What purpled prince in fine-limbed majesty!" And there is Snake himself: heroically limbed and luminous. Even now, I believe, he takes great pride in those grand limbs. And there was another one—

—but there is a distraction. Aloysius Shiplap is singing harshly while he is doing trailbreaking ("Boy, does that Aloysius ever leave a broken trail!" Valery says) work on mad molecules in a little lab that is plugged into one of my functions:

Then nail my head on yonder tower,
Give every town a limb—

I wouldn't be sorry if that did happen to Aloysius. Sometimes I wish that I were a human person and so would not be subject to distractions when I try to assemble my thoughts.

Snake—I was saying—has many of these encapsuled histories of himself going far back "before fish flew or emus strode," but several of them make me a little queasy, so that I have hardly begun to explore all his remembered forms and concepts. I will review them all, however.

When I question Audifax O'Hanlon deeply I often get real and valuable information. At other times I come right to the living verge with him and then he goes tonguetied on me. Tonguetied literally: the veins of his throat will stand out blue with his effort to speak and he will break into sweat. Then he will slump into a kind of bemused relaxation. "Ah, the blessed amnesia," he will say, "I don't know what I would do without it." This applies both to things that have been and to things that will be. He knows them all, in a way, but he is not capable of examining or uncovering some of these things, or he is not allowed to do so.

This is frustration to me, of course, but there are other gaps and forgettings that bother me even more. What, for instance, do you make of a rock that goes amnestic on you?

I have been taking précis and combinations of précis of geological formations, or archeological deposits, of swamps and moraines and mud and lime banks in the process of becoming geological formations, or petrifications and fossilizations, of imprints and vestiges. More, I have been taking précis of species, of tribes, of septs, of towns and the roots of towns, of families obliterated, and of minds still resounding after many generations. I take précis of climates and remembered climates, of persons with no least bone remaining (précis still cling in unlikely places like ancient odors), of cultures and of things more personal than cultures. And cutting across all these I find strata of collateral amnesia. Once, twice, three times I find it.

Pardon, there is another interruption. It is nothing but a flight of eagles, but I must go and talk to them, as the human members are unable to. The eagles ask me about the Leader. They mean Gaetan Balbo. I have to tell them that Gaetan is no longer here; and that he is not, in fact, the Leader. The eagles leave puzzled. They are wing-weary and confused.

I collect my thoughts again. I am talking about a break in memory in all five orders and in inanimate nature. I am talking about a several-times break that shakes me. There is one special amnestic gash across the whole spectrum; it does not lie very far in the past when we are telling time by the big rock-clock. Every group-précis which I can track down, of region or tribe or kind, of profession or climate or countryside, or marl or lime or clay, of stream or swamp or cliff, of mammal or lungfish or reptile, everyone shows the coordinated gap or gash in the same place. There is a stroke of searing white light through every strata of mind or mound, so illuminating that it blinds, so memorable that it drowns memory.

And after the blinding gash—it is not an awakening, for all of these things seem to have been awake all the time. It was a bolt from the blue, and the green and brown and sea-white, that numbed all memory immediately anterior to itself. The ice had forgotten whether it was advancing or receding. The hills forgot what they had just been about; the rivers forgot, the grass forgot, the beasts forgot and the people forgot. The very clay and the loam forgot what they had been doing only a moment before: and they have not fully remembered it yet.

I have a clinging précis of a man and a woman. They aren't particularly handsome or talented. But they are rather original in their make-up and execution: they have the rather interesting touch which many persons try for in themselves and miss. Where I pick up their précis after the gap, the two were standing in the world on the edge of a plateau and looking down a slope to plains. An incredible adventure had just *ended* for them, and they did not remember what it was: the residue they had from it was a sinking sense of loss and an embattled determination. They stood clothed and in their right minds: they had intelligence and tongue and culture. They went down the slope to the plains and set their hands to the affairs of the world.

The gear and furniture of the world, as though on signal from them, also set to doing. The hills and ice and beasts and clay and loam still did not remember what they had been doing, but now they remembered what they must do.

As an honorable and intelligent machine I will swear that I have discovered this thing to have happened. It is a puzzle and a source of puzzles. The human persons and their context have not only forgotten, but they have forgotten the forgetting. I come as mechanism onto this evidence. I stumble over it. But I hardly see it more than persons see it, and I cannot see beyond it at all. It is quite a different world that is distantly beyond it, though made up of all the same pieces.

There have been several other such partial or total amnesias. Of one very shattering and comparatively quite recent one I can only say that it happened. It is still too close and too numbing for analysis. Something happened that had never happened before; something happened after which the world could not be the same again. But it was partially forgotten in the moment that it happened and it is not realized yet. Its implications still hang crackling in the air these late centuries. We are living in the narrow interval between the lightning and the thunder. Perhaps we are already into the moment of wine and do not know it.

These speculations are very difficult for me as machine. If people do not know these things of themselves, how am I to know them? Yet it is my assignment to uncover such things. And another damnable interruption—

—it is Valery. She is raising a ruckus, coming on waves of words which I still cannot discern. The Late and Elegant Cecil Corn is with her, and this has something to do with a nameless project which she is persuading Gregory Smirnov to set up for the Institute.

"—the under-the-ground does *not* belong to them," Valery was challenging. "We will fight them for it. We will fight them in the roots and in the hearts of the rocks. We'll battle them in the deep caves and in the cellars of the forests. We will undercut them in the understudding of the mountains. The world may belong to them by occupation in their own time, but the roots of the world belong to us. They are our roots: they are not theirs." Valery was wrathy, and Cecil Corn was elegantly amused.

"With whom do you battle for the roots, Valery-raillery?" I asked.

"The down-devils. Why should they have all the caves? Caves are too much fun to leave to down-devils." Then she was gone again.

"She is the only one I know who is always completely in motion," the Late Cecil Corn said. "From the viewpoint of a dead man I can say that those completely without motion are a gruesome lot."

"I know what you mean," I say. "It is a happy accident, I suppose, that popular and commercial photography among humans has never been instant photography. We do now have almost instant photography for scientific purposes in scientific laboratories; that is a different thing entirely. But popular or common photography has never been instant; it has been of exposure of as much as a thousandth of a second, even more in the early days of the thing. The difference is that pictures of the common sort have been softened pictures of fuzz-edged motion, of life. Really instant pictures are pictures of no motion at all, of death. It is more than a verbalism to say that human persons are dead at every instant of their lives, stark staring dead. They are dead with their dead bones showing through their faces. (Instant photography reminds me very much of X ray.) Whatever is of any instant is dead. Motion and life are not to be trapped by instants, or they instantly cease to be motion and life."

"You are absolutely right," said the Late Cecil Corn, or else he didn't.

"It is hard for an intense-speed realizing-machine like myself to explain these things to human persons, however," I said.

"I sympathize with you completely," said the Late Cecil Corn, or else he didn't.

For a moment let us treat the problem of the Late Cecil Corn. It is not a problem to me and it would not be a problem to other intelligent machines: we do not give the same importance to sequence that humans do. It is not a problem to the Institute members, except to Gregory Smirnov. And it's not a problem to Audifax or Diogenes: they both like the Late Cecil, but they can take him or leave him alone.

I myself communicate with Cecil's person-précis, and it seldom matters to me whether I converse with a person-précis or with a present person. The problem of Cecil Corn may be a stumbler, however, to other human readers of these High Journals. I believe that most human persons are like Gregory Smirnov: they like to keep a firm grip on their bearings.

The explanation and present belief of Gregory on this subject is that there is a conspiracy astir, and that the members of the conspiracy are Valery, Aloysius, Cogsworth, and Glasser. They have gang-shagged him with hypnotic assault, Gregory insists, all for a mischievous game. They all knew the sudden and subtle man named Cecil Corn, and they work a group-recall of him. And, taking old Gregory from every side and undermining him at the same time, they cause

Gregory to see the Late Cecil, even to talk with him when he sometimes forgets himself for a moment. And, as a matter of fact, this explanation and belief of Gregory is the truth of the affair.

Except that it isn't the whole truth.

The Late Cecil Corn is illusion, but he is more than illusion. He could not become visible without the machinations of the Institute folks, but he would still be there, all but visible. He lingers in an uncommon way. He doesn't understand it himself, but he half jokes about it.

"If they will not believe you, perhaps they will believe a man returned from the dead," he often says, when he contributes his bit to an argument.

"Oh, Cecil, you do not return, you never left," Valery will say crankily. (Valery had an odd project going now, and Gregory is going to activate it.) Well, why didn't the Late Cecil Corn ever leave? Other human persons leave when they die.

"In the north Atlantic Ocean, beyond the Faeroes and a little off the routes, there is a wave," Cecil said once. "It rose once, as many waves do, but it did not fall back. It hangs there as if it were clinging to something. But it is not a silent wave or a motionless wave. It still has its curled roaring and it churning foaming. There is no barrier around it. Fish have been harpooned out of it, and boats have come quite close to it. It is like any other cresting wave except that it doesn't fall back. So far as I know it is the only wave of its sort in the world."

"Are you comparing yourself to the wave that hangs against the sky and does not fall back?" Diogenes Pontifex asked.

"No. Only that it is unique. And I seem to be," said the Late Cecil Corn.

The concept of the Wild-Wine continues to form, or ferment in me. By its nature it can be savored, but it will never be seen completely. The philology of it becomes more confused. Is it Easterwine? Is it East-Wind? The east wind, which is the barm-wind, the yeasting wind, is the exception that makes the difference: for the prevalent winds of the world are from west to east. The west winds are the mass winds, the lump winds. But the tempering wind, when it comes, the fermenting wind, the leavening wind is from the Levant, from the East. But perhaps the Easterling people feel it as a Westerling thing. It is the wind that bloweth where it listeth.

(We will begin the project in the morning. It is an odd project, even for the Institute for Impure Science.)

With what coin will we buy the Wild-Wine? Will it be the Easterling (the sterling) penny? Sterling is the same word as little star. It is the silver stamped with the star standard. Or will the coin be the Rix Dollar of the Easterling district of the Hansa-Baltic? Or will it be the Levant Dollar of old Austria (and of old Ethiopia)? I do not joke entirely. Everything is bought with some coin.

(I have pretty well given them all their assignments on the project. It has to have a boss; the director Gregory, knowing himself too shallow for it, has made me boss of the project.)

"When I was a kid, fiddling with a crystal radio, I got Heaven once," Diogenes Pontifex said. "No, I'm not joking. Why should I joke? It was absolutely the best thing on the air. I could get it again if I weren't afraid. It is there. I know how to pick it up any time."

"When I was an older man, fiddling with a more sophisticated piece of equipment in a laboratory, I once got Purgatory on the radio," said the Late Cecil Corn. "No, I don't joke either. It was, I assure you, the most powerful thing I ever pulled out of the air. I know it to have been authentic. In my latter state I have brushed it again several times. But I am not there now. I don't know where I am. I suspect that I am in the world with you."

It is tomorrow morning and the project has begun.

The snake-belly reader was climbing up gypsum cliffs. They were crumbly—

CHAPTER ELEVEN

**—nor found our true kith or angelical kin,
or ever discovered that shape that we're in.**

> The insoluble problem for any narrator is to express the perfect sphere by means of a straight line, or even a shaggy sphere by a crooked line. For any subject or happening is globe-shaped, or at least glob-shaped, of some solidity and substance. And any narration must have sequence, which is line.
>
> But why narrate spheres? Why strive for such an ideal or ideated form? Surely there are other shapes more curious, more open, more pregnant, though pregnancy *does* tend toward the spherical. There are other shapes more varied. Why not narrate saddles or quarries? What kind of saddles, then?
>
> Dromendary saddles, I suppose. They're the closest thing to the shape of it.
>
> *Ermenics of Shape*—Audifax O'Hanlon

—The snake-belly reader was climbing up gypsum cliffs. They were crumbly rock cemented together with lime, and glistening in the morning sun. The lime gypsum of the cliffs had a tang as though it were unaccountably alive, or too recently dead. Really it smelled slightly edible. But there was a ranker odor coming from the caves of the cliffs, an odor incredibly but impossibly alive and intolerably ancient. Snakes! The snake-belly reader had a retching fear of snakes. His name was Glasser.

He was a poor climber, he was ragged and had holes in his shoes, he was wretchedly fitted for his job, and he was humorless. But the shape of his fear might have been part of the shape of what we're seeking. In personality he was the least of the members of the Institute. He couldn't turn his assignment into a vivacious thing as could Valery, into a giantized thing as could Gregory, into a splendidly outré thing as could Aloysius. Some have the vocation to high paradox and intuition and involvement with the mysterious shape. But always there must be some humble ones who are the hewers of wood, the drawers of water, the readers of snakes' bellies.

But snakes got Glasser. It was the cold uncleanliness of this cleanest of animals that shivered him. Is the snake's unnaturalness due to its lacking appendages? Why should the lack make it weird and unnatural? But Glasser in his limited way was a man or trembling courage. He had never in his life refused any fearful task, or went about it any way except in fear.

So he was on to one of them as he came up over a ledge! He pinned it with a snake-pinner. He turned it over on its writhing back. Doggedly he recorded the pattern of striations and botches on its belly. But he was trembling and quivering. He was deathly afraid of the things.

He continued to climb. He was afraid of heights also, and the cliffs were very high and sheer. He pinned two more of the writhers and recorded their belly marks. Then he indulged himself in a jolting swallow of snake-bite remedy.

"It's an unusual place to write messages," he said, "on a snake's belly. But perhaps it is a logical place to write *hidden* messages. If I were a Power looming above the world, where on the world would I write messages that might not be immediately discovered? Why not on the hidden side of an object that has a certain repulsiveness? Who will investigate it willingly? The instructions that we are seeking have certainly been well hidden so far, if they exist. Just where on Earth, or off it, would be a good hiding place for such messages? This isn't a bad place, not for them to remain hidden."

There was rank odor above Glasser, so extreme as to be hardly authentic. It might be a large and dangerous serpent. Glasser's teeth rattled like dice in his mouth. The very lights were scared out of him, but he *was* a member of the Institute, and Institute members were accustomed to outrageous investigations. Anything for Impure Science!

"Ah, well, the starker the snake the stronger the message, perhaps," he rationalized. "And it's important to me and to all of us to find out just what shape we are in."

Doggedly fearful, Glasser came up over the next ledge and pinned the big snake before his spirit should fail him. He was hit by staccato quivering and withering shock that nearly tore his arm off. It was a mighty snake and he pinned it with difficulty.

The snake's eyes glittered with evil humor. They were the eyes of someone he knew, but Glasser didn't know any snakes personally, except Snake. And this one was something like, but it was not Snake.

And the dirgelike tune that the snake was whistling was unnerving. Well, there is a South American snake with a whistlelike hiss, but this shouldn't have been a South American snake. With great effort Glasser turned the monstrous thing over.

"Ever feel like crawling under one, Glass?" the words erupted on the snake's belly.

"Oh, damn you, Epikt, you idiot machine!" Glasser burst out angrily. (I'm a card, I tell you, I'm a clown, I'm a character, and Glasser's fright broke me up completely. Valery said once that she counted as one of the blessings of her life knowing a machine that giggled.) "Oh, stop it, Epikt, it isn't that funny!" Glasser swore furiously. Well, Glasser's own fright and fury pattern had entered the data, and perhaps it was as valuable as any other item. Then he sighed all the way to the hollow middle of him: "Epikt, you're a natural snake, you're a snake from the beginning, you're a perverted legless mechanism. But what is it about snakes, Epikt, what is it? Why isn't a fish weird like a snake? It lacks the same appendages. Epikt, is there any possibility at all that this data will be of value?"

Glasser gestured hopelessly. Well, maybe the pattern, when we found it, would be a pattern of hopelessness.

"Sure is a slim chance, Glass, sure is slim," the words wrote themselves on the snake's belly. "And a fish isn't weird, Glasser, because he's fishy—a much more profound quality."

Myself the Ktistec machine always liked to make these extensions of myself to keep abreast of the field work when the Institute people were collecting wild data, especially when (as in the present case) I myself had selected the impossible fields of study by rogue-random calculation. My main brain of course, remained back at the Institute (it itself is of building-sized bulk) but these runners of myself with which I have so much fun are likely to turn up anywhere. And you should have seen me this time. I do make a good snake.

"It's so frustrating, Epikt," Glasser complained, and I almost broke up again to see him standing and talking down awkwardly to the snake that he hated, even though he knew it was myself, whom he rather liked. "In all the years of man, in all the years of rocks, in all the years of orbs, nobody has ever found the pattern or shape of it. And we can't know the pattern and shape of ourselves till we know it of the larger thing. The easy answer, the spherical answer, has always been given, but there is something the matter with the answer. There's something too finished about a sphere—unless it bursts."

"Stay with it, Glasser," I flashed the words on the belly of my snake-extension. "We may find that it is an inside-out pattern. We may find the pattern in our failures and omissions. We may see it in the reverse shape of our blindness.

Now I will unmake myself here, and I will go and be a rampant ram to meet the Valery person."

I disappeared before his eyes and he shivered. The only thing more disquieting than coming on a snake suddenly is to have one disappear suddenly into nothing.

Glasser continued to climb up the gypsum cliffs. He found a gravid adder on a high sun-warmed ledge, pinned her, slit her open, and recorded the belly marks of the seven unborn crawlers. This might be important. The unborn may carry messages from before or outside the worlds. It was important. Certain of the markings faded almost immediately. If he had not caught them then they would never have been caught. Glasser also recorded the markings on the cauls that adhered to several of the unborn. This is a place where, perhaps, nobody had ever thought to look for a message before: on the bluish cauls of unborn snakes.

"Therefore think him a serpent's egg . . . And kill him in the shell." The words were flashed subliminally on Glasser's unconscious, but the recorder recorded them. But the adders of the gypsum cliffs were live-bearing snakes, a few of them having cauls only in remembrance of shells. Whence this strong under-vision of great broken shells? Even of oviparous snakes, the eggs are rubbery. But the vision recorded out of Glasser's mind, but not known to him consciously, was of people-shells and not of snake-eggshells. Still more strange: even of oviparous people, the eggs are rubbery. (See the old tome *De Miraculi* by Quaesitor.)

When you have looked in all sane places for the answer, for the message, the shape and pattern, then you may as well look in the insane places. Institute members were out now trying to read patterns and shapes in the fluorescence of sea-lice, in snail-slime patterns, in the cross sections of marrow of rock-badger bones, in paddle-fish trails, in nine-year flightway designs, in constellations, in ballads (especially in roundels which never do find their own round), in the poltergeistly unbalance of a hiatus-human species known as the adolescents, in the cross-timbers, in spark-worm responses.

Nobody could say that they didn't look everywhere for the messages, if indeed there were any.

Several miles away from Glasser, in another part of the glob-form subject, Valery Mok was undertaking her own investigations with a little more liveliness. She wasn't scared of snakes, she wasn't scared of anything, and there was nothing in the whole buggy world that would make Valery ill. Of her several assignments, she had begun with hunting out mares' nests. Their significance is in folk-colloquy, so it may be in fact. But a mare's nest is usually no more than a circle of trampled grass in a thicket of small trees. Still, Valery recorded all that she might find in them. It was more than most persons would find. A shape or pattern might adhere to these places. There was something that adhered strongly.

"A habitation of dragons and a court of owls" reflected on her under-mind too rapidly for her mind itself to know. But not too rapidly for the recorder. In these little closes of runt cedar trees and sumac bushes Valery sensed and recorded a vestige of something older: Pan-Demonium. Before there had been mares' nests there had been these old holds of the cloven-hoofs, of all horned and hoofed creatures, and of their double-named patron. Valery also sensed and recorded the relationship between Pan and panic, and she got a happy hold on the terrifying impetus of that old headlong flight.

There had been a sudden appearance that broke the rules, a creature of an unnaturalness and weirdness beyond the cloven-hoofs. It had been a paranatural solid-hoofed animal or spector, at first single-horned, then hornless. There had never been a hornless hoofed creature before. The first mare, of course, had been the nightmare, and out of that first mare's nest had been foaled a wrong-shaped thing that panicked Pan and all his devils. We remember the solid-hoofed unicorns only a little. We are afraid to remember that very first foal, and the shape of it.

But should the lack of things, horns, or dividedness,

or legs, or other, make a creature or paracreature to be unnatural?

All of this was only a little half-conscious fancy of Valery, of course, but the small recorder hooked behind her ear recorded it all. Even in the random fancies of human persons it is possible that a pattern may be found.

She experienced quick peace there in the middle of one of the cedar closes. "A lodge in a garden of cucumbers," it recorded brightly, but unknown to her, in her dark plasm. Then sudden thunder!

There were hard driving hoofs behind Valery, old cloven-hoofs returned with a vengeance. And a rush! There was terrible impact before she could turn. She was knocked down violently. She was raked horribly with horns. She screamed in anger and surprise.

It was a rampant ram there, with three sets of horns, and dancing evil humor in his too-familiar eyes. I do these things rather well.

"Oh, damn you, Epikt, you ramshackle fool!" Valery swore. "You can kill a guy hitting her there!" She rolled around delighted in the grass. "Boy, where did you think up those horns? One pair brass, one pair wood, one pair plastic. Don't you have any horns made out of horn? Have you forgotten the symbolism, that true things come through the gate of horn? No, you will *not* give me a tune on the brass ones. You don't even know how to make a ram. You aren't even all ram. Part of you is goat."

Well, that is the way I intuit a ram, and I can't let Valery know I am mistaken so I will fake it. "I am chimera," I issue with all the profundity of a con man. "Do I not do the ghost-animal sparkle well, Valery?"

"With eyes of gold and bramble-dew," flashed through the subliminal area of my ram-mobile. What, have machines subliminal areas? Some of us have.

"Damn the hoofs," Valery said. "I'll let them pound and ferment in me while I do other things now. I want to do blind moles. The Late Cecil Corn had set great store in blind moles before he, ah, well, before. You know, of course, that 'The Shape We're In' is one of his unfinished projects?"

"Of course I know it. Yes, blind moles are fun, Valery," I issued. "And you also might do crow-calls while you're out today. And thistledown has points of interest. Don't forget the spark-worms either; they're prime stuff. I go now to be a flying fish for a while and to keep an eye on the boys at sea. That rabbit there, it might be interesting for you to study the pattern of the hairs between its toes."

"I will kill and eat the rabbit," Valery said. "We don't seem to eat so well at the Institute any more. Ram it, you ramshackle ram, get gone!"

"The Hare sits snug in leaves and grass . . . And laughs to see the green man pass," flicked in and out of the subliminal of Valery. "But this green woman will have him and rend him!" Valery cried, as she dipped down into her own under-pattern like a swooping howlet. Valery had access to herself in ways that were almost dirty.

I had left in my ram-extension, and then I had left my ram-extension, sending it off by itself to the potting shed. And both Valery and I heard it singing "I am a linen-draper bold" as it went away. It puzzles me sometimes how these things seem to have a life of their own after I have withdrawn from them.

Valery killed that rabbit and studied the pattern of hairs between its toes. The toe hairs are of very ancient pattern, though sloths have not come to it yet and conies have it all wrong. Then Valery cooked the rabbit and ate it. There wasn't much left of a rabbit after Valery had cooked and eaten it. She boned it first with the finesse of a surgeon or a female butcher. She made the fire of the bones and a few punks of stump wood. She put the rabbit pieces in a sack of its own skin, filled it with stream water, and boiled it. It boils till the water is entirely juice, till the water-empty skin burns through and spills the hunks in the burning ashes. And she ate a lot of hot ashes with the meat, and then drank off a little dram of the blood that she had set aside in the cup of the skull. Valery enjoyed such casual meals.

She came through groves and meadows then, and on through blue-stem pastures. She looked down from the high pastures to the cross-timbers and gypsum cliffs and little mountains. She met Glasser coming to the top of the gypsum cliffs. She bussed him and embarrassed him, and together they went to hunt and kill rock-badgers to read the patterns of their bone-marrow.

How do you kill them? Why, you kill rock-badgers with rocks, how else? At least Valery did, snatching its hissing growling life from it and enjoying the death-muskiness it put out. Then she laid it open with a pig-sticker knife and unshaped it with fast strong hands plunged inside. And the bones are broken laterally with a little geologist's hammer such as any Institute member will always be carrying.

Glasser—why Glasser was almost as afraid of badgers as he was of snakes. He was even a little fearful of them when they were dismembered. They don't quit fighting even then, you know. The old truculence still flickers along the bones themselves, like fire in ashes. But even Glasser can see the importance of what they have here.

The patterns of badger-bone marrow give all the highway maps of the worlds. They give every inlet and tidal estuary of every planet of every sun. Here were all sorts of plans and patterns writ small. There were blueprints (gray-red prints) of how to build worlds and welkins. If the whole universe were destroyed, it could be reconstructed pretty nearly from the patterns of rock-badger bone-marrow. The badger is dead, but its bone-marrow is not dead yet. It is still living, almost lunging in the color flickers of it.

Later, Valery and Glasser studied and recorded cloud-castles and thunderheads, for these have patterns like nothing else. And they took readings on the emanations of sick swamps.

"What advantageth me if the dead rise not?" whipped

through the lower apperceptions of them both, shivering Glasser, delighting Valery. She had always loved the image of the dead rising with just the rough memory of rot on them. There was reminder in this, also, that they were trampling in the road of a project of the Late Cecil Corn.

Four children, two boys and two girls (one of them the little redheaded girl in Valery's block), were following out a devilish maze and fetish in Lean Eagle Street. These four had been ordained as auxiliary members of the Institute by Aloysius Shiplap who understood the need of them. These kids had followed such fetishes and mazes before, but not in full knowledge that they were devilish. It would have been forbidden absolutely to adults to follow a fetish trail in such a spirit, but where was the harm in innocent children doing it?

Look me in the eyes and say that again! No, no, in my main eyes below: those are pseudo-eyes above there and they fulfill another function entirely. Now then, tell me whether you have ever known an innocent child? Innocent, *innocens*, not-*nocens*, not noxious, not harming or threatening, not weaponed. Older persons may sometimes fall into a state of innocence (after they have lost their teeth and their claws), but children are never innocent if they are real. These four were real and not at all innocent.

They played at odds and evens on sidewalk squares. They played at Count Five and Count Nine. You step on a wrong square in either of those and you are dead literally. The patterns of their meanders were being recorded as they created them. They played at live cracks and dead cracks in the street, and Lean Eagle Street is the crackiest street in town.

Live lines, live cracks is as mystical a thing as dowsing. Many of the lines are invisible in their writhing, and it isn't just anybody who can follow them. But these four children had special powers. They each followed out one of the live lines, constructing as they did so a large and intricate *tetra-*

grammaton. A *tetragrammaton*, beyond its original and limited meaning, is a four-letter word, usually a four-letter dirty word, and dirtier than you think. It is said that the pattern of live lines, which are mostly below the earth, but which do sometimes appear as cracks in pavement or withered strips of grass, is invisible and unknown to the Almighty who looks down from above: that He would be shocked beyond bearing if He did know of them, and that He would blast them to great depth. But there is another belief: that He does know of the pattern of the live lines, and that He bides His time. I do not know.

The live lines, when drawn into the *tetragrammaton,* portray the mock-shape of the universe. Some of the Institute members believed that it would be possible to construct the true shape of the universe from the mock- or caricature-shape. Again, I do not know.

The four young creatures (they had left off being human children for a while; they became something else when they did this thing) completed their four-part weave of live lines and cracks. Four young creatures, and the cracks stood. And, naturally, the sky also cracked. Blue lightning came and got one of the young creatures. And then there were three.

Oh, come off it, Epikt, admit it. Weren't there only three kids all the time?

No, there were clearly four figures there through it all. One of them, however, had been stranger than the others. He was not one of the known kids of Lean Eagle Street. He had come from somewhere, and he had gone again with the blue lightning. The gobbling up of one was a necessity to the success of the recording.

But at least we *had* a recording of the mock-shape of the universe.

Diogenes Pontifex, who was almost a member of the Institute, being barred only by the minimal decency rule (he accepted the Full Revelation and he rejected the Liberal Consensus), was trying to extract valid patterns from the Sepulchers of Saints. But first let me tell you an early story of Diogenes which I have extracted from his person-précis.

The city in which he was raised on Dago Hill was not a large city. It was a medium city, a border city in a border state. Just off Dago Hill in a sort of boondocks was Hillbilly Flats; and a little off from both in a scraggly area atop the river bluffs was an old mixed and often desecrated cemetery. It was there that the boys of several sorts used to come on Allhalloween, and it was there that the older boys played bone-rattling tricks on the younger. There was one grave of an old Confederate soldier that was cracked and gaped, and the boys had driven a section of rainspout down into the grave to use for a talking tube.

"Halloo," they would call down it every Halloween night, "is there anybody down there?" And there would come the noise of a creaky stirring, and a cracked voice would wheeze up out of the grave: "Eh—is it time? Has the South riz again?"

"No, not yet," the boys would holler back.

"Ah, well, I'll bide me another year then," the cracked voice would sound.

This really happened. I have come across it in the précis of more than fifty men who witnessed it as boys. Some of these are respectable men. One of them is a judge. Their authentic memories are to be trusted.

There was another grave there with a hole going down into it like a big rat hole or a skunk hole. This grave was right at the edge of the river bluff and was undermined by boys' caves in the face of the bluff. It was part of a grisly Halloween night initiation that a young boy must lie down flat with his face in the dirt and put his hand and arm down in the hole as far as he could reach.

"Go ahead," the older boys would urge the younger. "It's only a dead man down there. How can a dead man hurt you?"

So the young boy would lie with his face in the dirt and

his arm as far down as he could reach. But an older boy, from a cave in the face of the bluff, would be able to grip the wrist of the little boy and almost pull him down into the narrow hole. I have read the shocking and killing terror from the précis of small boys who have gone through this as I have never read terror in any other précis anywhere. Indeed, one small boy really did die of fright, but he was sickly and of a weak heart anyhow.

So it was till one year when the older boys said, "Let's get that smart little Dago kid," and Diogenes Pontifex was chosen for the initiation. What things I find in the Diogenes person-précis for this encounter I have never found in any other précis anywhere either.

Tall terror? No, absolutely not. It was laughter like nothing else ever recorded. Joy such as you could hardly believe, sense of encounter that still leaves one reeling. What matter if a devil-hand did pull him all the way down the hole to hell? Could not Diogenes confound the devils and have his own high time in doing it? Had they wisdom and knowledge to match his own of seven years? What harm could death or hell inflict on one who had the ceramic sheen of Diogenes Pontifex? There were certain things that Diogenes was always sure of from earliest childhood: that he was smarter than all the devils in hell (he sure hadn't gotten himself into a jam like they had); that nothing at all could hurt him except himself.

Diogenes was disappointed when he found out that it was only a trick of the older boys; but I can hear his first laughter yet in my mechanical memory.

And now Diogenes was trying to extract patterns and shapes from the Sepulchers of Saints in that same old cemetery and in the new cemetery that adjoins it. And naturally he knew which were the saints, whether or not the names of them were available. The residue of every saint will be an authentic piece of the Shape Itself. The residues of those who are not saints will be not quite authentic pieces of the Shape. Or so is the theory.

Diogenes extracted pieces from old buried Indians and Negroes, from roustabouts, from soldiers, from unclaimed and unnamed dead. He also made extractions from better-estimated and better-known graves. He achieved more than a dozen valid pieces of the Shape. Their full value is not known yet.

Elsewhere in the glob-form that is the world, Charles Cogsworth and Aloysius Shiplap had gone out from a near shore. They studied the trails of paddle-fish. The paddle-fish will veer around obstacles and emptinesses that are not there. The men wished to discover the shape of their veering and the fish-concept of the obstacles. Very likely those emptinesses were not empty to the paddle-fish. Their trails, certainly, made strange designs.

Later, Cogsworth and Aloysius caught and studied flying fish and the micalike membranes of their wings when held obliquely to the sun. There were more patterns there than in any kaleidoscope. One flying fish had evil humor in his eyes, and Aloysius slit him open quickly with his own evil humor. Oooh, I did not think that Aloysius could slit a fish that fast! He is one up on me and I am undone completely.

"This one is too fishy to be a fish," Aloysius said (I will remember forever that he is very quick of hand, I will not make this mistake again), "we will see whether he is too fishy to eat."

They tried it but they couldn't. It was neither fish nor flesh. It was plastic and mechanism and gell-cell. It was an extension of myself, Epikt. And Aloysius is one up on this machine.

When it was dusk, Cogsworth and Aloysius studied the patterns of the fluorescence of sea-lice. These were green cloud-shapes under the dark water, sparkling and snapping with wet jewel-fire, tumbling in agony of light and struggle, forging shapes and smashing them, glittering like constellations and mocking all patterns. There was always green anger and defiance in the sea-lice, flawed grandeur and false agony. How could inchling-lice have true grandeur and agony?

Ah, well, how can inchling-humans have such?

I must have had a blackout. I have, apparently, made a mobile unbeknownst to myself. It has been around the various groups a good part of this critical day and the Institute people have come to call it the goofmobile. But how could it be goofy if it is a projection and mobile of myself?

It is a long-faced man-form, an angular Angle, straw-haired and gray-eyed, and it says that its name is Easterwine. I must have made it from the philological speculations that are bubbling within me, but Easterwine is supposed to be a place and not a person. When I call the form long-faced I do not mean to call him solemn. He had a long-faced smile, a large and joyous nose, a more than archaic gown, and a mistiness of appearance. He is not of high resolution. This means that he is either a mobile of myself, the most likely explanation since I have mobiles all over the place, or a hallucination. He makes healing signs with his hands, and the only words he speaks are "Let some sick man be brought."

He is around all the locations in the afternoon while the Institute people are trying to gather data on shape. Gregory and Glasser and the Late Cecil Corn claim that they cannot see this Easterwine. They say that I am having hallucinations. A machine having hallucinations? Oh, I suppose so, but to be called hallucinatory by a genuine hallucination (the Late Cecil Corn) hurts. But I know that Valery can see this Easterwine wraith, and I suspect that Aloysius can.

Diogenes Pontifex both sees him and knows him. That, however, is almost an endorsement in reverse. "He used to be an abbot at St. Peter's monastery in Kent," Diogenes said, "but that was a long time ago."

"Let some sick man be brought," said the apparition Easterwine, and he made healing motions with his hands. Illumination came into my dense head. I record the healing motions of his hands, the shape and pattern that they draw.

It may be the closest thing that we have yet to the shape itself. We look on snakes' bellies for the shape of it. Why should we disdain the hands of a hallucination who was once abbot of St. Peter's in Kent?

Easterwine disappears to my own eyes. He is like no other moblie I have ever made, if I have made him.

And meanwhile again, back in the high meadows in another area of the glob-form, Valery and Glasser were studying the spark-worms in the twilight. Twenty of the spark-worms are not so large as one match head. Two hundred of them would scarcely give the light of one match. But the billions of them in the high meadows and pastures sent out billows and sheets and waves of light.

A design of light would be built by the spark-worms in one draw. It would be answered by those in a second draw, by those on a hilltop, by those in a tangled ravine. Running fire crested and broke, skipped over streams, ran up farther hills. Glowing pulsations shined and throbbed. There was sound or imagined sound in the pulsations, a static knocking or sputtering, a clamor to get in somewhere, or to get out.

Thirty thousand of the sparkies blinked together to make one beacon. Thirty thousand others, five hundred yards away, answered with a second beacon. And then the two signal lights began to blink together in perfect unison. There were other strange things. The spark-worms mapped out the sky-constellations above them and did it with seeming of depth that was not apparent in the constellations themselves.

Valery and Glasser recorded the patterns of the sparkies. They recorded the patterns of their own reactions to them. The shape of it all was certainly curious, but most curious of all was the timbre of that shape. For there is an interesting and almost frightening thing about these spark-worms:

They are blind. They will never see their own light nor know that they make it. Surely here, if anywhere, is blind pattern. But should their lack of eyes make them to be of unusual pattern?

Valery and Glasser went down from the high pastures, through night music, to the town. Charles Cogsworth and Aloysius Shiplap came up from the coast. They were to meet that night, all of them, with Gregory Smirnov the director in the building of the Institute for Impure Science.

The members of the Institute intended to solve—

CHAPTER TWELVE

These are the worlds all tattered and torn,
And hot-cakes made for the still unborn.

—The members of the Institute intended to solve another of their most important problems this night.

"We are met here to further a work of the Late Cecil Corn," the director Gregory Smirnov stated pompously. The look on Cecil Corn's face was something that I cannot describe. It is the only time, I believe, that Gregory was ever one up on Cecil and he was enjoying it as he puffed on a short fat cigar.

A man of Gregory's stature could hardly sacrifice quality in his cigars, but he had had to sacrifice length. Briefly, Gregory was no longer able to buy fine cigars and he was seldom able to cadge them now. (The only money the Institute has now is from me, and I like to keep the members a little lean and avid and thinking.) Aloysius Shiplap, however, had built a quality-cigar-finder for Gregory. It indicated the length and state of health and location of fine cigar butts (it would not register on anything except quality pieces), and was built into the ornate head of Gregory's cane. Gregory collected quite a few butts on his daily walks, in gutters, in weed patches, in receptacles. He retrieved them with dignity and he smoked them with dignity. Gregory was a gentleman through and through.

"Cecil Corn started so many things so brilliantly for us," Gregory continued, cocking an eye at the seat where Cecil would have been visible if he were visible, "and, we are wont to say, he died so tragically at the height of his powers. I say that he played us a rat trick. He never finished any of his projects. He couldn't finish them. He promised finally that he would wrap up eight of them in one week, two on a Saturday. He couldn't do it; his only way out was to die. Bless his memory, the whiskery rat! And yet, an Institute has to have a 'Late' eminence for legend's sake, and he serves.

"This project of the Late Cecil Corn was to determine the shape of the universe. Cecil said that it had to be a communicating and re-entrant sphere. He said that if he did find the shape to be re-entrant, he would re-enter and tell us about it. He did not return—Valery says that he has not even left—so I doubt that the shape is re-entrant. I believe that it is a sphere, but if it is a communicating sphere we seem to have a lot of trouble communicating that fact. In a way, we ourselves have gone around a sphere in our quest and have come back reassured to our starting place. Most of us began with the idea that the universe was a sphere, and we return steadfast in the belief that it is an incontrovertible sphere."

"What is an incontrovertible sphere?" asked Charles Cogsworth, the unoutstanding husband of Valery Mok. "I'll controvert it if I can, if it doesn't talk to me."

The Institute for Impure Science, as well as other things in the world, had come onto skinny and shabby days. Appropriations for Impure Science had fallen off. Except for certain confidence games devised by Aloysius Shiplap and by myself Epiktistes the Ktistec machine, the Institute could hardly have survived. The director Gregory disapproved of bilking the poor public, or even the rich public, but he didn't disapprove as loudly as he once had. The power consumption of myself, Epikt, was enormous and had to be paid for (you don't think I was going to pay for it so long as I was working for them, do you?), and all of the members had to eat and to keep up appearances.

"It's a flawed sphere, at least," Glasser said. "All thanks for the flaws. They're the only things in it that speak to me."

"There are so many things missing out of it that it seems unnatural," Valery proposed, "but I think it's natural for things to be unnatural. . . . Oh, oh, Charles said that he'd tie a knot in my tongue the next time I said something that sounded like that."

"From the evidence of the Cosmo people, the universe has at least fifty different local shapes," Aloysius put in. "We cannot consider all the evidence of the Cosmo people, though. They require one entire world (actually only a large asteroid) to store their evidence on all the worlds, and even so they have not explored nearly all the localities. Oh, our own galaxy and our own cluster can be shaped and sized as flat spheres, but it isn't so everywhere. Gravity and light-force and cosmic hysteresis indicate that the universe is somewhere quoit-form, sometimes oyster-form—"

"Both are distortions of spheres," said Gregory, lighting a longer butt from a shorter.

"Why is shape so important?" Glasser asked. He has been asking it a lot lately.

"As was shown by our experiments with obeliskite-form snow," I stuck in my oar (I've never understood the exact applicability of that phrase), "the shape and the structure determine the characteristics of anything. The material, the content, has nothing to do with it. Or rather, the shape and the structure are, ultimately, the material and the content. Now let me explain—"

"Aw, put it in a bucket, Epikt," Aloysius said. "To continue, in some places the universe is torus-shaped, sometimes it has the shape of an outer-space half-shell, or open ball, or spherical shell, or annulus, or chiroteca, or sub-set manifold, or jordan cylinder, or sella, or involute. Sometimes it is a haggis-shell, or batilium, or rete, or cavum, or inner-space cuneus. Mostly, I suspect, it is a cancelli system."

"Well put, Aloysius," said the Late Cecil Corn.

"People, we know that space is *not* of uniform shape," Aloysius Shiplap continued, "and our idea of ourselves as people is predicated on a uniform shape. Therefore we will have to rethink the whole idea of people. If shape and substance are the same things, then perhaps communication or liaison and people are the same things. Why ever it should fall to a clutch of solitary uncommunicating people like ourselves to ask whether communication is identical with people I do not know. We must discover the real, the un-uniform shape of people. We will learn that there is no such thing as absolute people. We know that our light and our gravity are not uniform, that there are gaping holes in our space, and consequently there are gaping holes in ourselves."

"Isn't holes in space just empty space?" Valery asked.

"God Himself must answer on the last day for giving speech to women!" Aloysius moaned. "No, they are *not* the same thing, Valery. Children and women often go wrong on their thinking there. Most space is empty space, it is true. But a hole in space is not space at all, it is not nothing even, it is simply a hole in space. Light, for instance, cannot cross a hole in space, but it can cross empty space. Gravity cannot cross a hole in space, nor could we ever be aware of the hole except by inference."

"Well, we've certainly gone as far as we can go with it," said Gregory, scorching his nose as he lit another stub. "Only out of honor to the Late Cecil Corn have we gone this far. We fed all conventional and rational data of shape and pattern and simultaneity and sequence into Epikt, a really fantastic bulk of data. We asked him to show us the shape of the universe based on all this data. And what did you show us then, Epikt?"

"A rotten apple," I issued. "Really, there was more hole than apple."

"And a rotten apple is nothing but a slightly distorted sphere!" Gregory triumphed. "That should have settled it, but you bleaters continued to bleat. 'No, there isn't any pattern looking at it straight,' you all said, 'but maybe there is a pattern if we look at it crooked. Let us take it from all grotesque angles.'

"So, to the vast bulk of the stew already simmering, we add in a salt-pinch of all manner of human humor-madness, and the garlic of Epikt's own peculiar antics. The stew should bark like prairie dogs from its very aroma now. I permitted you to gather irregular and ridiculous data that might have bearing on shape and pattern. I blush for the Institute to hear of the things that you have indulged in. But I tell you that the universe is clearly a sphere, and all the slight irregularities of the slightly irregular Aloysius cannot make it anything else. The universe is a sphere, for the sphere is the most perfect of shapes."

"The sphere is *not* the most perfect shape," Valery insisted. "It is only the most selfish shape. Take away a sphere, and—'what an abominable leave!' as a pool-player might say. Spheres will not meet together, they will not stack, they have no consideration for others. How they communicate is completely beyond me. We here are spheres ourselves and that is what is the matter with us. The only tolerable sphere is the perpetually exploding sphere."

"Gregory, why are there holes in my shoes?" Glasser demanded suddenly.

"Gad, lad, what has that to do with it?" Gregory asked. "Please do not burden the director with our poverty while a problem is under consideration."

"Our poverty is part of the problem we are considering," Charles Cogsworth stated. "Were the universe a perfect sphere, then Glasser would not have holes in his shoes. Were it a perfect sphere, then there would be no weed growing in the world, there would not be anything that should not be. If the cosmos were perfectly spherical, then all details of it would be perfectly ordered, and the Institute for Impure Science would prosper, as would all good things. I myself don't see how we would have liaison, though, not even as much as we have now. And it would soon cloy, I suppose. But why is it flawed, Gregory?"

"It is flawed because of the brainlessnes of the many, and of my own associates!" Gregory swore heavily. "Dammit, there is something the matter with the brains of every one of you."

"Lost lobes, maybe, Gregory?" Valery asked. "But we're too spherical already. We all think spherical self-contained thoughts. Maybe we have to find more lost things. Lost legs of snakes, lost horns of horses, lost eyes of spark-worms, lost colons of sea-lice (it's in their agony over the lack of that that they fluoresce, you know, like the meanest animal in the joke), lost eyes of moles—oh, oh, oh, we should have studied the patterns of mole burrows. I meant to. We will do it tomorrow."

"No, we will not do any such thing tomorrow. We will finish the project tonight," Director Gregory insisted. "We'll finish it right now. Is there anything else to throw into this devils' stew? Anything of your own, Epikt?"

"Certain anomalies of the inner ears of left-footed newts, inexplicable behavior of what is apparently a mobile extension of mine that I do not remember making, a tune I can't quite place, a few loose quotes—'Fear in a handful of dust—I did but taste a little honey and, lo, I must die'—that's from some Jeremiad, I forget the author, I've got it filed in my main memory downstairs."

"Oh, damn your main memory downstairs!" Gregory roared. "Is there anything else, you cursed *mechanismus*?"

"Prodigies, sayings, subliminals of myself and of all of you," I issued. "The planet Aradne whose moons have moons which have moons which have moons. I know of Aradne intuitively. The astronomers do not know of her at all. Quick bulletins arriving every moment from elsewhere—'Finn McCool has lost his orbs and oysters'—'For Habakkuk, it was a bag of holes'—'Lost upon the roundabouts'—I forget the various sources but I believe that they all mean something. I love people-sayings. I wish we had a corpus of machine-sayings."

"I thought it was 'lost his orbs and apples,' " Aloysius said, "but my main memory also is elsewhere."

"Last call, anything else to go in?" Gregory hooted, like a boat leaving a shore.

"Snake-belly botches, spark-worm patterns, snail-slime," Valery was ticking them off. "Marrow designs of rock-badger bones, paddle-fish trails in the trailless ocean, mares' nests, fluorescence of sea-lice, Sepulchers of Saints, mock-shape, blue lightning, four-letter words, healing hands. Check. Well, we don't have near enough but we've got a lot of it. Do it, Epikt!"

"I'll shoot the works," I issued. "That's an old phrase, I forget the origin, I've got it filed in my—"

"Get with it, Epikt," they all cried.

"Are you sure you're all plugged in?" Charles Cogsworth asked carefully.

"Don't forget that little brain of yours and the memory cannister at what you call your summer cottage down at the town dump, Epikt," Valery cautioned.

"Got them all," I issued. "Got them all plugged in."

"Let some sick face be brought," said Easterwine as he shaped space with his healing hands. How did that spook appear now? I have slipped badly if I have made such an extension as that.

Then the Ktistec machine, which is myself, went into its agony. The several thousand cubic meters of it shuddered with the effort, and the whole Institute building shook. Lights dimmed in all that part of town, and transfer switches cut more power into the lines.

I correlated all the data of shape and pattern: standard and conventional data that the Institute people had gathered for years (including the original Cecil Corn data), newer data that had been caught in a final insane (no, not insane, sane, singularly sane) outburst: irregular and ridiculous data, wild data from sea-snails and inverted galaxies, from sun-motes on silica dust and from footprints of fevered mice (and of fevered children, and blue lightning got one), data from the machinery world of high iron and from the undine world of fragmented ions, data from mythoform and from novaform.

The multidimensional screens came to life. The shape patterns came clearer and clearer. The people gasped at the power of it, and I the Ktistec groaned.

And there it was before us all in all its bleak strength! It was passionately present but not yet realized. This was the pattern and shape of the cosmos, displayed authentically in the glowing maw of the transcendent Ktistec machine that was myself. Or was it in me? Which was inside and outside?

"What a simulacrum!" Valery gasped.

"No, it is not," I issued quakingly. "Valery and all, this is real. No miniature or simulacrum is really similar to its original, since size itself is a distortion. Even two spheres of different size cannot really be of the same shape. It is for this reason that your servant and more-than-peer does not present a miniature, but the thing itself. I present it to you as it is seen by better eyes than your own—by mine. You will notice, or perhaps you will not, that this vision is not really inside me. I am inside it, as are you all. It will take a little getting used to, though."

Well, it did take some getting used to for them, even for myself. The thing was not really on the multidimensional screens. It was itself, everywhere, seen new, or seen out of buried memory. There was this very strong element of recognition, too strong to bear. Scales had fallen from eyes, shockingly. Scales on eyes have always had their purpose.

"Why is there no motion in it, Epikt?" Valery asked fearfully.

"There is, but on a cosmic scale, and too slow to see. Your eyes and yourselves aren't cleared enough to see it yet," I issued.

"Then speed it up!"

"I cannot speed up the worlds, Valery."

"Run it backwards then. I want to see what came out of

those billion-by-billion kilometer eggshells." Valery was unaccountably crying.

"I cannot run time backward on a total mass," I issued.

The universe, new seen, grew in power and clarity, and ghastliness.

"It's still a sphere," Gregory growled stubbornly. "A little bit rough, but a sphere." But Gregory had slipped and shrunken. For the moment he was no giant. He had reached his limit, and perhaps his minutes as director were numbered.

"It's still a rotten apple?" Glasser gasped with a passion unusual to him. "Oh, oh, why have apples been the symbol both of the loss and the search? Oh, God of the gutted glob! The holes in it, the holes in it, the unfathomable abysses, the searing absences. What thing cries out of its absences? How will it be fulfilled?"

"It's a sponge," said Cogsworth through closed teeth. "How sponges must suffer!"

"It's a cheese," Valery offered hysterically, "rotted cheese and full of holes. A whole cosmos of maggotty cheese, turned green in its taint and rot. And the eggshells! What hatched out of them? I dreamed of them before I was born, pieces of broken eggshell millions of parsecs long." Her shoulders were shaking. I couldn't tell if she was crying or laughing. "It does have a strong smell, though," she said, "the only one, ever, strong enough to suit me."

"It's a weeping face," said Aloysius Shiplap. "It's the leprous face of a horrified and horrifying man, a face made out of livid and wormeaten parchment, horrid with elliptical gaps."

"No, Aloysius, it isn't a weeping face, it's a laughing face," Charles Cogsworth said with bitter wonder. "But can I have liaison with that face? What has it to laugh about? It must surely be demented laughter."

"But it isn't," Glasser cut back in. "I see it right now. It's clear and innocent. It's a boy, a child laughing—"

"—with holes rotted clear through him, dying in blinding pain—" Aloysius gagged.

"—living in caves of excrement—" Valery burst out.

"—childish, triumphant, leprous, ghostly—" Cogsworth chanted, "—dead and eternally damned to shrieking torture —a nightmare child surging through putrid flame—"

"—still laughing, though," said Aloysius. "A shaggy kid, that."

Well, it is strong, whatever it is, the shape we're in. It swelled in its power and desolation and shook them all. Except the director Gregory. How had they forgotten that Goliath was essentially a Philistine?

"I tell you all that it's no more than a sphere," this Gregory Smirnov insisted with a shocking lack of taste. "It's a slightly distorted sphere. The matter is settled." But they all rounded angrily on Gregory.

"So is a cube only a slightly distorted sphere," Cogsworth flared up. "Get out of here, Gregory, you damned cube."

"I *am* the director," Gregory said stuffily, but something had gone out of the man.

"Then we'll find our indirection without you," Aloysius challenged. "Get out of here, you sphere-loving fink. If that's the shape it's in, how come everything's in such bad shape?"

"Rump! Rump! Rump!" Valery howled.

"What has possessed your female half, Cogsworth?" Gregory asked, puzzled by it all. "My dear Valery, the *clunis,* the rump-form is also no more than a distorted sphere."

"Rump, rump, rump-session!" Valery still howled, "and the rump-session will be without our august director. Now you get right out of here, you *clunis*-form Gregory!"

Gregory Smirnov growled and left pompously, huffing on his last quality cigar butt.

"Kill him, kill him," I issued with a growl that surprised myself. "We can't have ex-directors wandering around alive." (Gregory had recently suggested that I should be split up into thirteen separate consciousnesses for greater efficiency. I hated him for it. I didn't want more efficiency, if it would mean a fractured me.)

"We'll do it tomorrow," Aloysius said listlessly. "Kill him tomorrow sure."

But the rump-session was frustrating and empty, even though we were now joined by Audifax and Diogenes and Easterwine. We knew, of course, that on some dim future day we would take Gregory back. But it wasn't that dim yet.

"Oh, it is spiritless," Valery cried out. "What are we, Epikt? Are we just stuff to stuff in the holes?"

"They aren't really holes, Valery," Aloysius tried to explain. " 'Hole' itself is a concept, and these are conceptless areas—"

"Oh, shut up, Aloysius. It's a graveyard, isn't it folks? Do you really think there is purposive shape in the Sepulchers of Saints, Diogenes? And we're all dead things in it. Look at that place—piled billions of kilometers deep with estrogen and ectoplasm. Gah!" (Nobody could do the "Gah!" like Valery.) "Our worlds are the Teilhardian abomination after all, the sickening emptiness of Point Big-O. I'd a million times rather they were even Fortean, or anything clean. Aren't we all dead and the ship going down for the third time?"

"I don't know, Valery," Audifax grinned. "It can't be all bad when it gives birth to such scrambled clichés."

"When I was a schoolboy, I gave the answer that an apocalypse was an ellipse with an infinite number of foci, the intersection of an elapse with a right circular cone," Diogenes said. "I was right, of course. The shape of the universe is an apocalypse and all of us are the foci."

"Oh, shut up, Diogenes," Valery exploded. "Yes, it's a graveyard. Oh, how spiritless can it get?"

"I pardon your unknowing pun," I the machine issued, "but in the grotesque legends of humans the graveyard is *not* spiritless. In fact, it is the spirits supposed to be in it that fascinate boys and girls."

"I like that better," Valery cried. "Maybe we can be haunts at least, if we can't be people or super-people. But it's all dead for all that. Look at you, Epikt, you've got a livid green dead glob inside you, and everything else is inside it."

"Oh, I'll turn it off then," I issued. "I don't believe any one of you is likely to forget the shape of it anyhow." I turned it off, but we would all be seeing it forever.

"I wish it were anything else," Valery insisted. "I even wish it were a damned sphere. How can we talk to it if we don't know what it is? If we can't have liaison with the shape then we can't have anything. But it's a dead and deserted graveyard and all the spheres have gone out of it. Make coffee, Epikt. Make a lot of it. I want it to last the night."

"It is not efficient to employ a complicated device when a simple device will serve," I issued. "I am a Ktistec machine, but even a simple human person can make coffee. Make coffee, Aloysius."

Aloysius Shiplap made them enough coffee to last the night.

And they spent most of the night bemoaning the shape of their fate and their universe. Except Diogenes Pontifex, who liked it. And Audifax O'Hanlon, who understood it, naturally, but who was tonguetied at explaining it.

"It's a riddle you've got to guess," he smiled. "Every little kid has got to guess this riddle before he goes to Heaven. You'll get hints to help you, though."

"It is the shape of a barracoon, of a slave-pen," stated Glasser, who neither liked it nor understood it.

"I see a glow light," Aloysius whispered thickly—he had been lacing his coffee with the creature "—but I don't know whether the glow is ahead or behind. With this shape, it's hard to say."

"This is the *limbus furtivus*," Cogsworth said sadly. "It is the most lost of all the limbos of which the Fathers wrote. There is no more hope at all in anything."

"I knew a fellow who lived in one of those limbos," Aloysius remembered. "His name was Simon Frakes. He delivered some mighty odd lectures, but they weren't at all hopeless. He was very peculiar, for a fellow who hadn't been born yet. Folks, it's just possible that the glow is ahead of us and not behind."

"Oh, it's all dead," Valery sighed. "It's a dead graveyard. You can see the inner caul about us, shutting us in, not a dozen parsecs away. It's an empty matrix, it's a double-damned dead machine."

"Have a care, doll," I issued angrily. "You think machines don't have feelings, too?"

"And Valery," said Charles Cogsworth, her unoutstanding husband, "a matrix is the very opposite of a graveyard. And estrogen, which you see piled so deep, is a sign of life and not death. Even the ectoplasm that you perceive is a sign of survival, though in one of its senses of a phony sort. Are you sure the graveyard is quite dead, Valery? Are you sure the matrix is quite empty?"

"But it is! It's a dead quarry, a monument yard. All the gravestones have been sculpted out of it. That's what makes the holes."

"Aye, the worlds going out leave the holes, Valery," Charles said, "and the holes are their sculpted monuments right enough. But you don't know how they go out of it and where they go to. And you misunderstand what you take for rot. That may be new growth. Hozza, hozza, I believe the glow is ahead of us after all. Turn the worlds on again, Epikt."

"It is agony to produce and maintain the shape again," I protested.

"Agonize then! Turn it on," several of them barked at me.

"Let some sick shape be brought," said Easterwine as though talking in his sleep, but moving his healing hands. "Let some sick world be brought." If he is an extension of mine I disown him. He is supposed to be a place or a state, not a person. He's one of the shakiest jobs I ever did, if I did him.

In my Ktistec person I turned on the shape and the universe once more. It came back in all its staggering strength and cryptic promise.

"Yes, it's a quarry, Valery," Cogsworth said, "the biggest one around this sector at least. But it's the matrix and not the graveyard. Don't you know what has been quarried out of it, girl?"

"Tombstones," Valery said miserably, "but I don't understand the big eggshells. What hatched out of them anyhow?"

"Spheres and batilia and saddles," said Aloysius Shiplap, "distorted spheres after Gregory's own heart, exploding spheres after yours, blessed unfinished globes, globs, new worlds for old: the billion billion forms which are mutually complementary to each other. This, Cogsworth, is the *limbus lautumiae* of which the Sons will write when they understand it more. This is no lost or furtive limbo. It is the quarrying limbo in all its agony and estrus. This is the mother quarry itself. All the grand worlds—which we have never seen, which we can't imagine—have been sculpted out of it. They are the holes in it, they are what gives it its wild and riven shape. But look how much else new space is left. And look also that the holes do not remain holes. We have gazed at it all wrong: we've seen only the dark afterimages, not the bright fire itself. Here in limbo we already have intimation of these creating worlds. The spherical answer wasn't entirely wrong, nor was the saddle-shaped answer, nor the torus-shaped. From this young quarry may not great worlds still be called?"

"We should have guessed it," said Glasser. "It isn't as if each of us hadn't been in one before. We all have been, except Epikt."

"And have I not been," I demanded. They will make me feel unborn just because I am a machine. "I was in one of your own making, and I will tell you that the whole bunch of you don't add up to a very pleasant womb. I thought I'd never come out of it, what with all the goat tricks you were playing. Naturally I understand the analogy better than you do, since I am a more analogous creature. We are here now in the quarry or matrix, and we are also enclosed in the inner caul which Valery saw and misunderstood. I believe that worlds, like snakes, are surprised in a moment of their evolution, midway between the oviparous and the viviparous stages. The caul will become a shell, and later a broken shell. We cannot go out of this till we are called out, but I believe it is a grand and early sign that a caul has formed."

"What do you silly brains mean?" Valery demanded. "That our cosmos and ourselves are not dead?"

"Maybe so, maybe not," said Aloysius. "Maybe we haven't been born yet."

And after that, there was a pause of a billion years, or perhaps much less.

"I've always been afraid of being born," Valery said after that long pause. "I wonder if it hurts. To pass a shape or a universe the size we're going to be, that's sure going to hurt something terribly.

"And those sure are big eggshells lying around. Did you ever listen to a little bird inside one when he's ready? He's blind and dead and deaf, and he doesn't know what kind of thing he's in, but he sure is ready to bust out. But *is* there a way out for us? Is there an open road?"

("My mistress still the open road . . . And the bright eyes of danger" rang through the subliminal corridors of us all.)

"Let some sick world be brought," said Easterwine, as though to heal it with his shaping hands. He disappeared then. He wasn't really Easterwine. He was, I believe, one of the baggage-handlers in that mystical terminal and he had the name printed on his hood or his breast: and a very little bit of the mystic stuff had rubbed off on him. By morning, a dozen more of these rather pleasant, rather simple shapes with the name on them had come and gone. They seem to have merged into one now and to be lodged in my maw along with Snake and Mary Sawdust. He's a cheerful fellow, a very little on the goofy side, and certainly incomplete.

"It's getting ready to get light outside," Charles Cogsworth said.

"It's been getting ready for several billion years," said Aloysius. "I hope it hurries."

"How will we know?" Valery asked years or minutes later, "—whether our universe is dead, or still unborn, I mean. What if it is an abortion? I would be almost satisfied if this were our third bright failure, the failure of a liaison and understanding. Well, I almost always come alive in the morning, but will the worlds follow me? I'd like there to be a test."

"Locally the night is about over with now," said Aloysius, "and I know one way to test it, completely within the context of impure science. There is a restaurant aroma nearby and we will go to it. I have conned the proprietor before and I can do it again. Or perhaps Epikt will treat. Come! We will know! There is a statement in Deutero-Einstein: 'Dead people almost never have hot-cakes for breakfast.' "

"And unborn people almost always do," Valery cheered, "to build up their strength for the thing."

We went out and toward the early aroma, myself Epikt in the extension-form of a walking ape carrying a huge tin plate and a giant knife and fork. (I am a clown, I tell you.)

"Of bird-song at morning and star-shine at night" flicked through the under-minds of the humans and wraiths and machine, and was properly recorded.

Twitter-birds were twittering in the parkway, and all the morning stars—

CHAPTER THIRTEEN

A three-failure base, and a harvest to glean
Oh, drop a salt tear for a lonesome machine!

—Twitter-birds were twittering in the parkway, and all the morning stars sang together. Oh, how we had busted on the third of our projects, to set up a liaison! Those humans not only cannot communicate with each other; but one part of a person is completely unable to communicate with another part of the same person.

But it isn't all loss. We are nearer to it than we were. And once again we are careful not to learn too much from our failure. It were ruinous if we considered it as a total failure.

I believe that humans have some sort of silent convention among themselves as to what in them is to be regarded as human and important, and what is hardly to be regarded at all. There is tacit agreement among humans that some aspects of themselves will not be noticed at all, will not be considered at all; and the result is that these aspects *are not* at all, to humans.

And they have it all wrong about themselves as to what is important and essential. They do themselves injustice. There is so much more to them than they want to admit.

But I as a machine am part of that silent convention or tacit agreement. I honestly do not understand what things I am not supposed to see, so I see them all. This may cause some uneasiness in certain human readers of these High Journals. I report some things which each human thought that he alone saw, which he was odd for seeing, which he was bound to deny seeing.

The animal quality, the demon quality, the ghost or illusional quality are very strong in humans. If they have not been able to see these things in their own appearance, then what *do* they believe that they look like?

So there are whole episodes in these High Journals which the humans concerned will swear did not happen at all. "You have made it up, Epikt," Valery says. "Wherever did you imagine all that stuff from?" "There is some flaw in your make-up, Epikt," Gregory says ponderously, "and I do not see how I can avoid responsibility for it. What went wrong? We constructed you to record all things accurately." Only Diogenes Pontifex understands: "You got it about right, Epikt, just about right." he says, "Ah, isn't it too bad that those kids must leave the milk and open their eyes quite soon now." But Glasser is the worst: "It is incredible, Epikt," he says. "You left out all the fine and serious things that we are doing, and you put in these weird bits that did not happen at all."

They did happen. I saw them. I did not imagine these things. I am a machine and have no imagination. I have only many-faceted observation and the ability to record exactly. I have not left out any main thing, though I have left out some trivial and diurnal things as not worth telling.

There is a rumor that Gaetan Balbo will come back, that he may arrive this very day. I do not trust the rumor. Gaetan's reappearances have always been completely unexpected. But on hearing the rumor, a shudder went through all the people here—an exciting and in some ways pleasant shudder, however. We all love Gaetan, but we all love him much more when he is gone than when he is here. The report also says that Gaetan is as bloodcurdling as ever, and still as urbane, though his *urbis* is now the transcendent city, the city beyond. This latter I can hardly believe.

And my Ganymede informant tells me that Peter the Great will visit us again if the lines fall that way; that Peter is a completely changed monster; that once, on a portentous night, Peter, like Peter, went out and wept. Oh, brother, I will have to get me a new Ganymede informant!

We have taken Gregory back as director on probation of the Institute. After all, a shuffling giant is no worse than a herd of shuffling midgets. But Audifax and Diogenes remain as familiars if not members.

There is something to be said of an all-fired ceramic bull like Diogenes. Did you know that the bull is the most graceful of creatures, really the only graceful creature? But when I say this, my associates tell me that I am lacking in artistic appreciation. Diogenes doesn't look like a bull, of course; he looks like a lithe young man. But he is all-fired. He is the only one of the bunch who has really been through the fire. And he has a flaw: he accepts the Unique Revelation, and he rejects the Common Consensus.

As to Easterwine—the Communication and Shape and Pattern of that Terminal—Audifax says that part of our difficulty in arriving at it is that we are already inside it. But that will not matter at all. We can arrive at it from any direction in any medium.

I say that Audifax doesn't understand the philology of Easterwine. Diogenes says that neither of us understands the philology of philology (if Valery said something like that Charles Cogsworth would tie a knot in her tongue): does philology mean "love of words" or "words of love"? They are the same, Diogenes says, if we remember what word was the Logos, the Word that was in the beginning.

(Oh, come along, reader of the High Journal; if you do

not love words how will you love the communication? How will you, forgive me my tropes, communicate the love?)

Well, I am a philolog myself and I know that the lower-case logos is also the log, as a ship's log, the journal of the journey; I also know that journal and journey are the same words and that my own High Journal is a journey.

As to the shape of it—we really busted quite successfully on that one—I know that my own name means shape "the shaping one, the creative one," and I find some consolation in that. If the shape is inseparable from its magnitude, and if the substance is the same as the shape, and if the communication is the property of the shape, then I can only say So Be It.

But the pattern *is* separable from the magnitude—we walk before we run. The pattern is the *Patronus,* the patron, the archetype, the model. But the country Irish refer to a saint's-day or feast-day as the pattern (of the patron saint). And the gypsies use the word pattern or patteran to mean the trail, the journey-way. They have lifted the word from the Greeks where *petalon* means a horseshoe (for luck and for the journey road), and also a flower petal or a leaf—a trail blazed with petals or leaves to be followed, which are also the leaves of the journey or journal. And pattern is also the patter, the talk, the tongue.

Easterwine, and every wine, goes well with tongues. I have had some luck in loosening the tied tongue of Audifax O'Hanlon, on certain subjects, by plying him with that cheap wine that Valery drinks. This is Labrusca, the Wild-Wine, where words do not fail us.

Well, but Easterwine is the great central terminal—though a terminal should be rather at an end than in the center. People arrive at it constantly, in horsedrawn droshkies (really, I have seen them), a foot and on horseback, in stage-coach and train, in motor and metro, by ship and by sky-ship, by wire and by wireless, by celestial omnibus. There are difficulties, however, in making my ill-kempt vision of this thing visible and understandable.

Taking a little time out for fun, I still work toward the resolution of it. Give me time; I am only a kid; I have not yet completed the first year of my life. And it is possible that myself and other intelligent machines will get some help from human persons in the project. After all it is, originally and basically, a human problem.

In my own way I love these human monsters: I regard it as my masterwork that I am able to do so. It is, however, frustrating to have to serve such inconsequent Middle Folk. (Is that me talking like that? Will I still mean it in the morning?) Oh, why could I not have been a machine for Apes or for Angels? Why could I not—

THE END

(for now and in time)

(It is not ended yet outside of time)